ALL FOR CONNOR

BOOK 3 OF THE LONE WOLF DEFENDERS

ALICIA MONTGOMERY

ALL FOR CONNOR

Book 3 of the Lone Wolf Defenders
By

Alicia Montgomery

ALSO BY ALICIA MONTGOMERY

The True Mates Series

Fated Mates

Blood Moon

Romancing the Alpha

Witch's Mate

Taming the Beast

Tempted by the Wolf

The Lone Wolf Defenders Series

Killian's Secret

Loving Quinn

All for Connor

Copyright © 2017 Alicia Montgomery
Cover design by Melody Simmons
Edited by Red Ribbon Editing

All rights reserved.

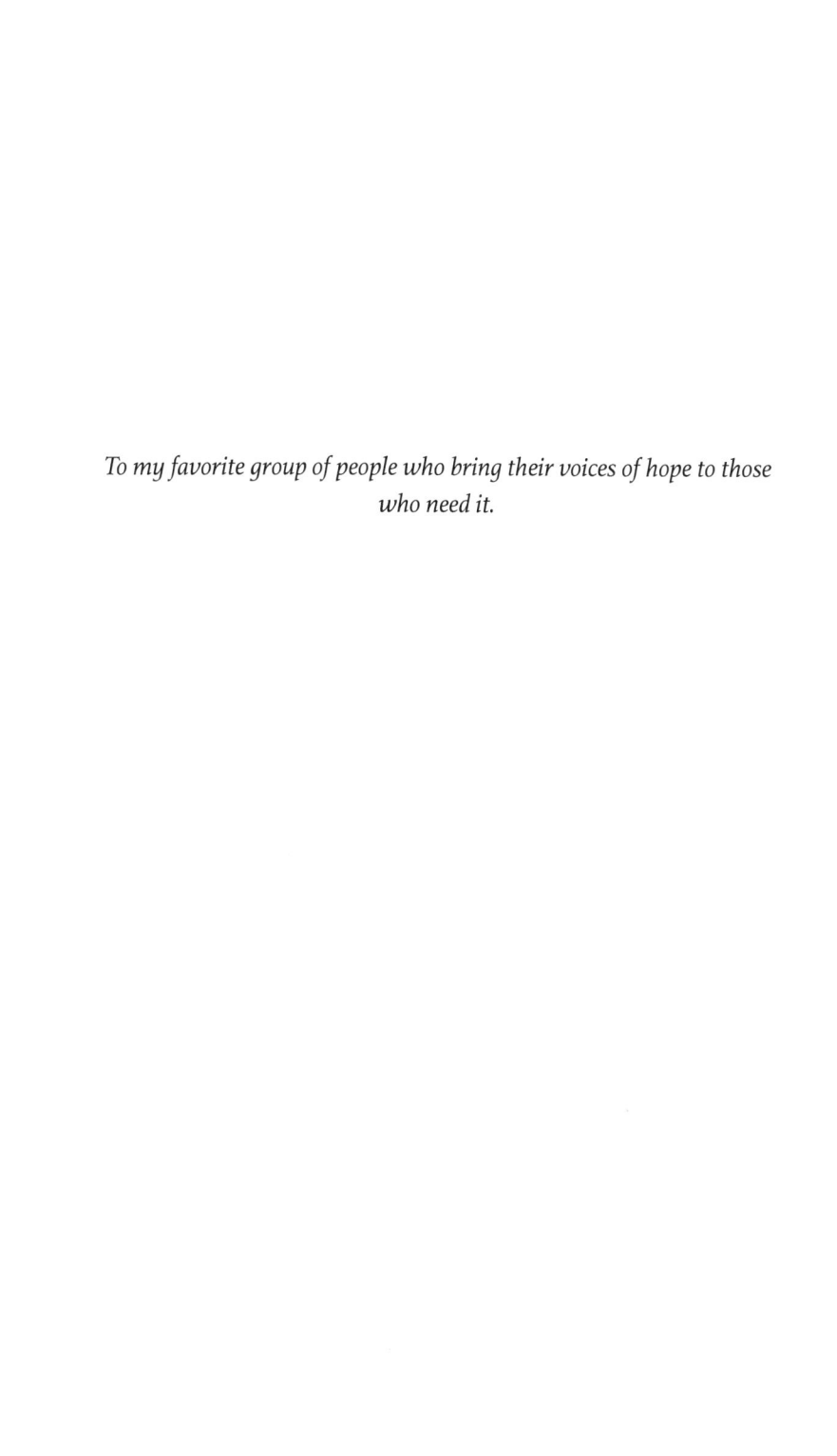

To my favorite group of people who bring their voices of hope to those who need it.

PROLOGUE

About six months ago...

"You lying, cheating bastard!" Evie King shouted into her phone.

"Evie, no," Richard Brandis, Evie's soon-to-be ex-boyfriend (again), pleaded, his voice crackling through the speakers of her cell. "I swear, babe, I didn't mean to. It was an accident!"

"An accident?" she asked incredulously. "Was she walking by, tripped, and *accidentally* landed on your cock?"

"I was drunk. Me and the boys were celebrating landing another big account ..."

"That's not an excuse," she retorted.

"Evie, honey bear, please. This is the last time."

"No, Richard," Evie said. "*This* is the last time." She pressed the red button on the screen of her smartphone, wishing she still had a landline phone she could slam down. Instead, the line went dead with an unsatisfying electronic click.

Evie wanted nothing more than to throw the phone against the wall as they did in the movies. But, she had already spent the last of her savings moving to New York City so she could pursue her dream of becoming a Broadway actress. Buying another phone would put her in the red or mean she'd have to take a couple of extra shifts at the diner.

The phone in her hand suddenly lit up, and her roommate's name flashed on the screen. Talk about bad timing. Selena Merlin swore she was a powerless witch, but she somehow had a sixth sense when it came to Evie's relationship with Richard. "Selena?" she answered, trying not to sound deflated.

"Evie-girl," Selena said. "I've been calling you for the last thirty minutes, but you weren't answering."

"I was on the phone."

"Really? Who were you talking to?"

Evie bit her lip and thought about lying, but Selena was her best friend. "Richard." Her shoulders slumped.

"And what did *Dick* want?" Selena asked in an acerbic tone.

"His name is Richard," she corrected for the 148th time.

"Dick is a perfectly acceptable nickname for Richard," Selena retorted. "And what were you guys talking about for half an hour? *Oh my God*, you weren't having phone sex, were you? Please tell me you're not on the couch. I eat dinner there."

"No, we weren't."

The five-second pause must have tipped off the almost-witch. "Shit. Not again, Evie."

Evie sank down on the couch. "Yes."

"What happened this time?"

"I got a video," Evie said. "It was ..." She wanted to throw up. Richard had probably meant to send the disgusting video to one of his buddies and sent it to her instead. This time, he couldn't deny that he had had sex with another girl.

"Oh, Evie, I'm so sorry," Selena said.

"Go ahead," Evie sighed. "Say it."

"Say what?"

She let out a breath. "I told you so."

"I would never say that to you."

Evie thought that was generous of her. After all, Selena had been there for the first time she and Richard broke up. Someone had sent her a screenshot of him in a club, kissing some girl. She cried, and Selena supplied her with copious amounts of ice cream and cookies and listened to her moan and pour her heart out. Of course, three days later, Richard called her and explained that he didn't sleep with that girl, just made out with her. He was out with his friends and was drunk, and he was missing her. Guilt had made her take him back. After all, they'd been together for four years when she decided to move to New York City from Kansas. Richard didn't want to leave his lucrative job, so they thought they'd try the long-distance thing.

She'd forgiven him after he flew in and begged on his knees. They spent a dreamy week in New York, going to all the touristy spots and cuddling and kissing everywhere (including the viewing deck of the Empire State Building). It was pure bliss, and, when he left, Evie was sure their relationship was more solid than ever.

Of course, it didn't take long before Richard stumbled again. Her brother, Arthur, had seen him on a date with some skank, and Evie confronted him over the phone. He denied it, of course, but he eventually broke down and confessed, telling her that they only went out and kissed, that was it. Despite Selena's protests ("Once a cheater, always a cheater!"), Evie took him back. He promised he'd visit soon, but he was so busy at work.

Two fat tears rolled down Evie's cheeks. "I should have listened to you."

"Don't cry. He's not worth it."

"I know." Richard was a piece of shit. She knew that now. A

lying piece of shit. "Are you coming home soon? Would you mind picking up a carton or four of Ben and Jerry's?"

"Oh, Evie, I think you're going to need something stronger than ice cream. In fact ..."

Evie could almost hear the wheels in Selena's head turning. "Selena, what are you planning?"

"Do you trust me?"

"Yeah, I suppose."

"Good. Do exactly as I say, and everything will be okay. First, go to the fridge and pour yourself a glass of the Chardonnay I have in there."

"Selena ..."

"C'mon, just do it. Trust me," Selena said, a hint of mischief in her voice.

"Fine." Evie walked to the kitchen and grabbed the opened bottle of wine, still half full. She took out a wine glass, then poured herself a small amount, wrinkling her nose. It wasn't that she didn't drink. She had a beer or a glass of wine with dinner now and then, but she never saw the point of getting drunk. Despite having a Lycan as a mom, Evie was one hundred percent human and, thus, didn't have a shifter's fast metabolism (as evidenced by the extra 20 pounds or so she was always trying to lose) which meant she always felt a little tipsy after a glass or two. "Well, now what?"

"Take a drink," Selena instructed. "A big gulp."

Evie took a small sip. *Hmmm ... it wasn't bad.* "Okay."

"I said take a big gulp, not a sip."

"I already—how the hell did you know?"

"Because you're a wuss and I've never seen you drink more than a glass," Selena said in an exasperated voice. "Now be a good girl, fill up that glass and finish it off. I promise it'll make everything better."

"Do I have to?"

"Yes."

Ugh, Selena was so bossy. "Fine." She topped off the glass and took a big gulp. The wine burned her throat and she nearly choked, but she swallowed it down. She took another sip. The wine was cold but made her belly feel so warm and nice. This wasn't so bad.

"Did you finish it all?" Selena asked impatiently.

She took the last gulp. "Uh-huh." She felt lightheaded but so good. "Maybe I'll have another one." There was a numbness spreading through her, and it made her temporarily forget about Richard. No, she couldn't forget about *Dick* (snicker), but the wine made everything seem less painful.

"Good," Selena answered. "Now, here's what you're going to do. First, go to my closet and grab my red dress, the one in the garment bag. Put it on, then add your nicest pair of heels. Next, I'll text you an address. You're going to take a cab there. I'll pay you back. Whatever you do, no matter what you see or feel, just find the entrance to the warehouse and meet me there. You're going to feel like whatever you're looking for isn't there or that you should turn away. Ignore it. The wine will help. Just keep searching for the place; you'll know it when you see it."

"Selena, you're not making any sense," Evie said before taking another gulp of wine.

"Just do as I say. I'll meet you there." And with that, Selena hung up.

Two seconds later, her phone beeped with a message: 235 Princeton Street. Her map app told her that was all the way down in Soho. Jeez, the cab fare would be astronomical from Washington Heights, but now she was intrigued. And Selena said she'd pay. Since her roommate was the one more gainfully employed between the two of them, Evie would take her up on that offer.

She took a last gulp of wine and strode to Selena's closet,

grabbing the garment bag. Evie was a couple of inches taller than Selena, so the dress seemed painfully short, but it fit her frame just right. She quickly turned away from the full-length mirror in front of the closet. She needed to shed a couple of inches around her tummy and hips if she wanted to land any role in a Broadway show. Sure, her curves were okay for the regional theaters in Kansas, but this was the big leagues.

Her phone beeped, jolting her out of her thoughts. It was Selena, urging her to hurry up. *So impatient.* Where the heck were they going anyway?

The cab dropped her off in the approximate spot where 235 Princeton St. *should* have been. The GPS on her phone didn't seem to be working, so Evie had to guesstimate where it was. She was still feeling warm and fuzzy from the wine, which didn't help her concentration.

Even though it was a weeknight, this part of New York was usually lively, but this particular section seemed to be quiet. *Weird.* She looked up, searching for numbers in the small, darkened alleyway that was supposedly Princeton St. A strange, cold feeling passed over her, making her skin prickle, and a small voice in her head told her she should just go somewhere else. *No.* Selena said to just keep searching, so Evie kept walking down the alleyway, ignoring her instinct. Her head was still light from the half bottle of wine she had polished off (she took a last swig before she left, then decided to just finish the entire thing).

Her ears perked up when she heard some noise and saw a light up ahead. There was a line forming outside a warehouse. *Ah, that must be it.* Was this some secret club? How did Selena know it would be here?

Evie approached the queue of people, noticing how

everyone seemed to be dressed in their best outfits. And that the crowd was mostly women, all dolled up for a night on the town. Everyone seemed excited, chatting and laughing with their friends. After standing in line for a few minutes, more women queued up behind her.

"Wow, this must be a popular club," she remarked to the woman next to her.

The woman, a blonde in a hot pink dressed, giggled. "Well, it is Merlin's."

"Merlin's?" Did Selena's family own a club in Manhattan? She had never mentioned it before.

"Aww, are you a newbie, sweetie?" another woman asked. "Which coven are you from?"

Evie froze. This was a witch hangout. No wonder she felt strange walking here and it was hidden. Whoever owned it must have cast some sort of protection spell. "Um ... Kansas," she lied. It might be far enough away that the witch wouldn't know anyone from there.

"Oh wow, are you visiting New York then?"

"Er, sort of."

The blond witch giggled. "It's okay, don't worry about it. We're all here for the same thing." She glanced behind her, at her girlfriends. "We're from Jersey. We drove all the way here for the show." The witch introduced herself as Mary and her friends as Alice, Felicity, and Gretchen.

"I'm Evie," she said.

"Are you all alone?" Alice asked.

"Um, my friend Selena is already inside. I'm supposed to go in and find her." She opened her black leather clutch and fished out her phone. *Oh farts.* The phone was dead. The GPS must have sucked up the battery. Well, if this club was called Merlin's, then she was definitely in the right place. She'd just have to find Selena inside. But what would they do here? Selena wasn't exactly the clubbing type. She didn't even go to bars. Her roommate and best friend was a geek at heart and loved sci-fi and fantasy TV shows, books, and movies. Her idea of fun was watching *Lord of the Rings* for the millionth time.

"Oh, it's our first time, too," Mary said. "I'm looking forward to the show."

"What show exactly?" That question made the other girls look at each other and burst into giggles.

"It's a—oohh! Line's moving." Mary nudged her forward. "If you can't find your friend, you can sit with us."

Evie stumbled forward, nearly bumping into the group of women in front of her before steadying herself. The queue moved quickly, and they were ushered inside the warehouse doors. Red velvet ropes herded them, single file, all the way to the front where the bouncer was checking IDs. She slipped her hand into her handbag, ready to take out her driver's license, when she suddenly stopped short.

The bouncer was tall, perhaps the tallest man Evie had ever seen, about six or seven inches over six feet. He had reddish blond hair, and a beard covered the lower half of his face, which was handsome, despite the deep scar that ran from his right eye to his cheek. In fact, Evie thought it made him even more attractive, adding a roughness and sense of danger to his striking features. Wide, muscled shoulders stretched under a tight black t-shirt and showed off tattoos that ran down his powerful arms. His face was drawn into a serious scowl as he checked IDs, seemingly unaware as each woman devoured him with their eyes.

A surge of jealousy coursed through Evie. *What the hell?* She didn't even know the hot bouncer guy, yet she wanted to claw each woman's eyes out for looking at him like that. She pushed down the feeling, hoping he wouldn't notice anything off as she waited her turn for inspection.

Evie drew closer to him, and he seemed even more imposing and intimidating up close. Finally, she stood right in front of him, so near that she got a whiff of his cologne—hmmm, coffee beans? *Strange.* But good. The scent seemed to wrap around her, tickling her senses and sending a weird, thrilling feeling through her entire body. *Get a hold of yourself*, she said silently as she handed over her driver's license. She let out a small squeak as he took the card from her, their fingertips lightly touching. A jolt of electricity went up her arm. As she looked up, a pair of startlingly bright green eyes stared down at her as his nostrils flared. She blushed, feeling his gaze on her as heat spread across her body, but stared right back at him.

Lycan.

Perhaps it was her own Lycan heritage that made her sensitive to detecting when another person was a shifter. After all, she'd been around them all her life. Even though her parents divorced when she was ten and her father retained custody, she was properly registered with the clan and knew most of the shifters in Kansas City. She couldn't sense the animal in them as other Lycans could, but she just *knew*.

There was something strange about this Lycan though, something she couldn't put her finger on. What was he doing working here, at a witch night club? Lycans and witches weren't enemies or anything, but they tended to stay away from each other.

The sound of someone clearing her throat made them both startle and break eye contact, and hot bouncer quickly glanced down at her ID. Evie waited patiently, and it seemed like he took forever.

"Sorry. Can't let you in," he said in a low voice that seemed to match exactly what Evie thought he would sound like. Rough. Sexy. Made for the bedroom. A panty-melting voice. She blinked up at him when she realized what he had said.

"Excuse me?" she asked. "That's my real ID. I'm from Kansas."

He shoved the card back at her. "It looks fake."

Her jaw dropped, and she pushed it back again. "Look at it again. It's real."

"I've never seen a Kansas driver's license, so I can't be sure."

Even if he was handsome, he was starting to get on her nerves. What kind of place was this? "Well, what are we supposed to do? Call the Kansas DMV?"

He shrugged. "Company policy. I can't let you in if I suspect there's something wrong with your identification."

"But I don't have any other ID!" she whined. "My friend is in there; she can vouch for me."

He frowned. "Then go call her."

"My phone's dead. Do you have one I can borrow?"

"Lady, I ain't a cellphone company," he replied. "Now get out of here."

"You're rude," Evie exclaimed, planting her hands on her hips. She looked up at him, craning her neck up to meet his steely gaze. "I demand to talk to your manager."

"Evie?" Mary asked, peeking around from behind her. "What's going on here?"

"This ...obstinate ox won't let me in," Evie huffed. "Said my ID was fake."

"Oh, c'mon now," Mary said. "She's obviously over 21. You know this place has magical protections; I bet they have a spell that ensures no minors can even find it. Just let her in."

Hot bouncer crossed his tree trunk-like arms over his chest. "Sorry. Can't do that."

Mary, Alice, and Gretchen stepped forward, their eyes narrowing at the bouncer. "How can you tell her ID is fake? We're not from New York either, are you going to say our IDs are fake, too?"

Hot bouncer remained rooted to the spot, unmoving. "Maybe you ladies should go someplace else."

Gretchen let out an angry snort. "Where's the manager? We want to talk to him."

Evie stepped forward, going toe to toe with him, despite the fact that she had to crane her head back even farther to look him in the eye. "When I prove my ID isn't fake, I'm going to demand they fire you."

"What's going on here?" another man said as he came up to them. He was dark-haired with startling blue eyes. He wasn't as tall as the bouncer, but he was also well-muscled and dressed similarly in a black shirt and dark jeans. Probably another bouncer, from the look of him.

"This asshole won't let our friend in," Mary said, jerking her thumb at the Hot Bouncer.

He looked at Hot Bouncer, who shrugged. "Her ID doesn't check out. You know we can't risk our jobs here."

"I'm sure he's got a good reason to keep you ladies back," he said to Mary. "We do have a policy here, and we can't let you in if there's something suspicious with your IDs."

"But her ID is just fine!" Mary protested.

"We want to see your manager," Gretchen repeated.

"Fine," the blue-eyed bouncer said. "I'll grab him and let him explain our policy." He walked away, leaving them alone with Hot Bouncer.

"Just you wait," Evie muttered, planting her hands on her hips. Selena probably knew the manager, if she was related to the owner.

He let out a grunt. "Step aside, ladies," he said. "We have other guests wanting to come in." A large hand grabbed Evie's arm, gently but firmly dragging her to the side. Another jolt of electricity shot through her arm, and she pulled away from his unnerving touch.

"Let go of me, asshole!" On impulse, she raised her clutch and slapped it across his arm as hard as she could. He didn't even flinch, but fury blazed in his eyes.

Screams, shouts, and a loud crash made both of them stop and turn their heads toward the source of the commotion. There was a man running toward them, rushing between Evie and the bouncer, making them jump apart. And hot on his heels was a very large, fully-transformed Lycan wolf, running at full speed toward them.

"Holy shit," Evie exclaimed.

"Fucking Quinn!" Hot Bouncer cursed. He pushed Evie aside, sending her sprawling into Mary and her friends as the wolf crashed into his arms, sending both man and animal to the ground.

There were more shouts coming from the inside, and Evie and the other women got to their feet.

"Let's get out of here!" someone, either Gretchen or Alice, said as she tugged at Evie's arm.

Evie froze for a second. For some reason, she didn't want to leave. But then she remembered he was a Lycan, too and probably could take the wolf. She quickly followed the other girls, running down the alleyway as other people followed them.

There weren't a lot of people, but, in the chaos, Evie was separated from Mary and her friends. She kept walking away from the alley, stumbling out into the main street. She let out a sigh, the cool air entering her lungs. New York wasn't exactly known for the quality of its air, but, at least out here, the atmosphere felt more *real*. Whatever that place was, it definitely wasn't somewhere she should have been.

She walked a couple of blocks, rubbing her arms, trying to get rid of the creepie crawlies over her skin. The image of bright green eyes flashed in her mind, but she pushed it aside. Maybe it was a good thing she never made it inside the club, but now she was stuck out here.

"Shit." Where the hell was Selena? Was she inside?

Evie considered her options, but, without a working phone, she didn't know what to do. When she saw a passing cab, she hailed it and got in. It was her best friend's fault she was out here, so she could cover the cab fare back home, too. "Washington Heights," she told the cabbie, and the taxi began to head uptown.

The ride back was relatively quick, and, after swiping her credit card on the terminal, Evie stepped out and walked into her apartment building. As soon as she entered the apartment, she ran to the living room and plugged in her phone. The battery icon blinked red on the screen, but, after a few seconds, it came to life. The moment it came on, she pressed the phone icon to call Selena, but another call came in and she ended up picking up that one instead.

"Hello?"

"Evie," Richard said. "I've been calling you all night. Please, can we talk?"

She gritted her teeth. "I don't want to talk to you."

"I swear, Evie, I'll do whatever you want. I'll fly to New York right now if you don't hang up."

"What about that video?" she said, feeling the anger rise up in her again. She had almost forgotten about it, about Richard and his sex video. Instead, she had been thinking about bright green eyes, tattoos, and a handsome face drawn into a scowl. She normally didn't go for those kinds of guys. She preferred clean-cut professionals who looked good in a suit, like Richard.

"It was a mistake. I've never had sex with anyone else, I swear. Just that one time," he said. "And it'll never happen again."

Evie rubbed her temple. "I don't know ..."

"We can talk," Richard began. "Just talk. Talk it out."

She let out a sigh. Could she really throw away her four-year relationship with him? Those years weren't all bad; in fact, they had been very good. It was only when she left that Richard cheated, and, those other times, he didn't even have sex with the women.

And tonight, she herself had been drunk when she went to that club. *Oh God.* That was it. She was drunk and feeling horny because it had been months since she'd seen Richard. And then that hot bouncer ... She couldn't be a hypocrite, now, could she? "Fine." She plopped down on the couch. "Just talk."

Three Months Ago...

Connor opened his eyes slowly. It was dark, and it took him a second to recover from the nightmares that kept his sleep light. He grabbed the watch hidden under his pillow out of habit. It was an old digital watch, and the numbers and letters glowed green in the dark. The rubber strap on the thing had broken long ago, but even if it hadn't, there was no way it would have fit him now. Not that he wore it. All he cared about was the flashing numbers displayed on the front as he pressed the button on the side. Time. Date. He let out a long-held breath when he saw the year, and his body began to relax.

He reached toward the bedside table, hitting the switch on the wall which filled the dark room with soft light. By now, he was sure which button to press, which meant he had stayed in this hotel too long. Rubbing his hand over his face, he sat up, tossed the covers off his body. He walked to the window, pushing the blackout curtains aside.

New York City in winter was still pretty busy, but at least the holiday season had passed, and those goddamn tourists weren't clogging up the streets anymore. He gave an unhappy grunt, thinking of the crowds and people and the chaos. He hated living in New York, but he didn't have much of a choice. His sister, Meredith, wanted to stay here with her warlock husband, and pledged to the New York Lycan clan. And then there was the offer from Sebastian Creed to head up his shifter security team. With their adoptive father gone, there was no reason to stay in Portland. Plus, he and his two brothers could have a fresh start in New York. But, he didn't realize how crowded and cramped the Big Apple would be. How the hell could any Lycan stand it? The people, the noise, the smell, the frenzy, and those big buildings everywhere—it set him on edge.

No, this was for the best. New York was where Meredith, Killian, and Quinn wanted to be. He had to be there, to safeguard what was left of his family, especially when he failed to protect their father and mentor. Thoughts of Archie Leacham flooded his mind, but he quickly pushed them aside. The old master thief had been avenged. Though he wanted to wring Rodrigo Baeles' neck until his head popped off, the bastard was rotting away in the Lycan prison facility in Siberia, which he supposed was good enough. He and his siblings were back together again, and they were working together, just like old times, albeit on the right side of the law.

Collecting his thoughts, he ran through the events of the past few days. They had arrived back late last night from their latest overseas operation. Connor glanced at the clock. Killian was probably at the office of Lone Wolf Security by now. He said he was taking care of something, but Connor couldn't recall what. His brother had asked that they all come in for a debrief this morning. It was part of the job, after all, but Connor hated it. He hated going into the office, although it was what kept their family together. Reuniting the Lone Wolves with their families and running ops for Creed kept them busy, gave them an anchor and something to keep them steady.

However, his siblings didn't know he had a third purpose, one that kept him going. Revenge. And the key was hidden inside the manila envelope tucked inside the hotel safe. A list of names. A final gift from Archie, one that drove him forward. Soon. Soon he'd have his revenge. Hopefully, before it was too late.

He shook his head and drew the curtains together, then walked to the shower to get ready. He stepped under the rainfall shower and turned on the tap, letting the hot water hit his skin. One advantage of living in hotel rooms all the time was the luxurious living. Perhaps living with Archie had made him spoiled and soft over the years, but he didn't care. It was millions of miles away from the way he lived before.

"Fuck," he cursed, as the memories and nightmares flooded back to him. He shut off the shower and slammed his palm on the slick tiles, bracing himself. It was never this bad. But ever since he met Daric, Meredith's husband, it was like a dam had opened. The fucking warlock could see the past and the future, and he got inside Connor's mind. He saw it. Not everything, but enough. Daric probably didn't even know what he unleashed.

Walking out of the stall, he took one of the fluffy towels from the warmer and dried himself off, then dressed in a black sweater and jeans, before putting on his coat. As a Lycan shifter, he didn't need it, even in winter, but he put it on anyway to keep up appearances. Blending in was essential to being a wolf shifter, especially when the humans knew nothing of their existence.

Connor grabbed his phone, wallet, and key card, then stuffed them into his pockets. The Royal Albert Hotel was close enough to the Lone Wolf office that he could walk there, which was one of the reasons he made it his base for the last month.

But he knew it was time to go soon. Finding a permanent home was simply impossible for him. Not when he knew his control was slipping. It was much easier to switch hotels every month or so, hand them his black credit card, and tell the management to bill him for everything, including all the damages. After all, many luxury hotels were willing to overlook their guests' "eccentricities" if they paid enough.

He walked a couple of blocks, and then soon found himself in front of their building. He hated the office, especially the ancient elevator he had to take to get to their floor. The old thing had metal bars and the screech they made as he slid them open and close again brought back memories of another life. He gnashed his teeth together, pressed the button, then the elevator jolted and began to rise. When they first moved here, he took the stairs, all ten flights. But his siblings started to get suspicious, so he trained himself to take the elevator. He had overcome far worse things, and a fucking elevator wasn't going to do him in.

The door to the office was unlocked, and the lights were on, which meant Killian was already here. Boxes, old coffee cups, folders, and furniture still wrapped in plastic were scattered all over the reception area. They didn't have time to unpack, as Sebastian Creed had them running ops all over the world as soon as they signed their contracts. He didn't mind. In fact, he preferred it, not being in New York and finally being able to release some of the tension by doing what he did best—kicking ass. Even now, being cooped up in this tiny space was setting his teeth on edge.

He was about to hang his coat on the rack by the door when a familiar scent wafted into his nose. Peaches. So sweet and ripe he could almost taste it. He froze and dropped his coat on the ground, then saw the unfamiliar blue parka hanging from the rack. Reaching forward, he touched it with his fingertips. Definitely peaches and definitely familiar. What the hell was going on?

Connor strode to the office at the end of the hallway and yanked the door open. "Hey Killian, what the—You!" The scent was stronger in here, and he immediately knew who it was.

That familiar face. Those light, toffee-colored eyes. And that sweet, sweet scent that had been haunting him for weeks. The brunette standing in Killian's office, shaking his hand, suddenly froze and then her face went ashen when she saw him. With his enhanced senses, he could hear the thundering of her heartbeat and the scent of fear mixing with peaches. He didn't know why, but that made something in him ache. And Killian touching her hand wasn't making it any better. Why the fuck did he suddenly want to smash his brother's face in?

"I ... I didn't know ... you ..." She looked back at Killian. "Oh my God, I thought you looked familiar!"

"What's going on?" Killian looked from Connor to the brunette. "Have we met before?"

"The night at Merlin's," Connor growled. "She hit me with her purse." What the hell was a Lycan doing at a witch strip club, anyway? All those men in there, half naked, gyrating their hips and showing off their bodies. It was no place for a girl like her, and he made sure she never saw the inside. Getting smacked in the arm with her purse was worth it, especially since it didn't even hurt.

"It's because you were a stupid and obstinate ox," the brunette huffed, her eyes sending daggers at him. Suddenly, her face fell, and she slapped her hand over her mouth. "I'm sorry. Sorry about this. I'm ... I'll go now. Thank you for the interview." She sidestepped Connor and then walked out the door. That ache in his middle came back. Interview?

"Wait—" Meredith, his sister, who he just realized was also in the office, called out to the hallway. She then turned her gaze toward Connor, her amber eyes narrowing. "What's going on here? How do you know Evie again?"

Evie. So that was her name. It fit her. But what was she doing here? "She was that girl who caused trouble for us at that witch strip club," Connor explained, barely containing the snarl in his throat. "Everything was going fine with our op, and then she tried to get in, all liquored up, causing a scene, and I wouldn't let her through." Okay, so she wasn't liquored up, but he could smell the alcohol on her breath as her plump pink lips parted when she talked. She wasn't in full control of herself, and he had saved her from making a foolish mistake. Like watching a bunch of men parade their bodies in front of her.

"As I recall," Meredith began. "It was Quinn going full Lycan in a room full of witches and warlocks that caused trouble for us."

"What the fuck was she doing there, anyway?" Connor really wanted to know now. "A Lycan in a witch strip joint?"

"She's not a Lycan, moron," Meredith shot back.

Not a Lycan? But she had a scent. Only Lycans had scents. "Then why does she—"

"Yo, what's up?" Quinn walked in. His second brother glanced around. "Who's the cute skirt I saw running out of here? Connor, did she see your ugly mug and run the other direction?"

Connor growled. His youngest brother screwed anything that moved and, while it normally didn't bother him, this time it did. He wanted Quinn to stay the fuck away from Evie.

"Don't you start, Quinn," Killian groaned. "Is she still out there?"

Quinn shrugged. "Probably. Waiting on the elevator, maybe. You know that rickety old thing takes ages."

"Good." Killian rushed out, presumably to chase after Evie. Part of him wanted Killian to fail, to chase her away. She didn't need to be caught up in their messed-up life. But the other part of him ...

A low rumble tore through his chest, and he faltered for a moment. No. Fuck no. Not again.

Meredith visibly flinched but said nothing. Instead, his sister straightened her shoulders. "So, let me get this straight. Evie was there the night we had the op at Merlin's, you refused to let her in, and she hit you with her purse?"

He grunted. "Yeah."

"Why?"

"Yeah, Connor?" Quinn asked, a glint in his eye. "Why?"

He looked at Meredith, then Quinn and scowled. "Because."

"Because what?"

"Because ... fuck you, Quinn, I don't gotta explain myself to you. You were the one who screwed things up!"

"Oh my God, she was the girl who was staring you down! And she really hit you?" Meredith laughed. "I wish I'd seen it! Why wasn't I ..." She trailed off and her lips curved into a smile. "Oh yeah. Daric and I were in this closet and—"

"Shut up, Meredith," Connor groused. He did not need to keep hearing that shit. Sure, Daric was her husband now, but thinking of his only little sister having sex made his stomach turn.

"She's cute, huh?" Quinn said.

Connor recognized that look in his brother's eyes. Oh, fuck no. It was a good thing Evie was gone. If Quinn got his hands on her, Connor really would have to punch his face in. Hitting him with her handbag aside, Eve was probably a nice girl. She had that fresh-faced, innocent look. He bet she wasn't even from New York. She didn't have that hardened, cynical aura most of the city dwellers had.

He thought for a moment. She looked a little different from that night, though. Of course, she was wearing that sinful, short red dress that showed off her curves and enough of her creamy skin that he wanted to kill any man who looked at her. That was months ago, and he noticed the change in her body today. The skirt suit she wore didn't fit her properly and hung looser on her frame. He didn't care, but was she starving herself? He stifled a growl. He realized he preferred her with more curves. She was apparently here for a job interview; maybe she didn't have money to eat properly. Why was no one taking care of this girl?

"Hello? Earth to Connor?" Quinn snapped his fingers in front of his face.

"Quit it." He swatted Quinn's hand away. "Don't fucking do that. Ever again."

"Jeez, tell me, were you born with that stick up your ass?" Quinn groaned. "Hey, you know there's a proctologist's office down the road. I bet he could take care of that for you."

"Shut the hell up, Quinn," Connor warned, stepping forward.

"Oh for fuck's sake," Meredith rolled her eyes. "Stop it, you two. I'm drowning in testosterone. See, this is why we need Evie around here. This sausage party isn't working for me."

"What the hell are you doing here, anyway, Mer?" Quinn asked. "Last time I checked, this was Lone Wolf Security. Not Lone Wolf and Sister Security."

"I'm here to help you with office stuff," Meredith said. "And if you've scared Evie off, you'll probably be seeing more of me."

"That's going to—"

"You can't—"

"All right, stop. Stop." Killian strode back into his office, his face drawn into a serious expression. "What are you arguing about now?"

"Connor being a dickhole to Evie," Meredith barked. "I like her. I want to keep her. Even though she is taking my job."

"She's not a pet, Mer," Quinn added

"You know what I mean," she snapped. "I have this feeling we need her. And she needs us."

"You were always the one taking in strays like you were some Disney princess."

Connor had to agree with Quinn. Meredith had this mother hen quality, even though she was the youngest of all of them. Mother hen might be putting it too mildly. She was more like a rabid dog when she got an idea in her head, refusing to let go until she had her way. And being their only sister, they often had no choice but to give in. He had a feeling this was not going to end well for him.

Killian let out an exasperated sigh. "She's not some lost animal. Listen to me. Evie is the most qualified person to help us out here. I've hired her. She'll come in on a part-time basis and work around our schedule if she has to. Don't scare her away," he warned. "That means, no growling at her," he said to Connor. "No hitting on her," he looked at Quinn, "and no smothering her with your constant need to get into everyone's business."

All three of them looked at each other. Killian meant business. He had been stressed, much more so than they had been that last couple of months. They could all feel there was something going on with their brother since Archie died, he must have been feeling the pressure of now becoming the head of their little adoptive family. He had changed a lot and was much more closed off from them.

Connor grunted. Fine. If hiring Evie would help his brother, he'd agree. And it wouldn't be a problem for him. If she was going to work here, then he was just going to stay the hell away from the office from now on. He would avoid Evie as much as possible. That first time he saw her, he felt it. Felt out of control and, if he were honest, it scared the shit out of him. Because if he lost control, he knew it would mean the end. The last option for all Lycans who couldn't control their wolves.

But before that, he wanted to make sure he completed his revenge by making everyone who turned him into a monster pay for what they had done.

1

Present Day ...

The Stage Bound bar in the East Village was packed, as it always was on Friday night. The tiny lounge club was the place to be for singers and actors, hoping to be discovered by agents and Broadway producers scouting for talent. Connor was running a little late tonight, so he hurried inside and made his way to the tech booth in the back, keeping his head down and shoulders hunched. There was no way he blended in here, which is why he already had a plan in place.

"Hey man," the skinny guy with a beard and glasses greeted as he walked into the tiny booth. Really, booth was being generous, as it was more like a table and a curtain to divide it from the rest of the lounge. The space was small, and his large frame only made it feel even more cramped. But this was the only way he could stay out of sight.

He grunted in response to the skinny hipster. His name was Greg or Gordon or something; he didn't bother to remember, just called him Skinny Hipster in his mind. Anyway, he wasn't here to make friends. He handed the other man a hundred-dollar bill folded neatly.

"Thanks, man, pleasure doing business with you, as always." Skinny Hipster stood up and let Connor step over his chair so he could scoot to the back of the booth. This was the perfect place to stay hidden, while still being able to see the stage.

Connor crossed his arms over his chest, wondering for the hundredth time what the hell he was doing here. The person trying to kill his brother Quinn and his mate Selena was locked up in the deepest cells of the Lycan Detention Center in Siberia. His brother could hold his own and protect his mate, but those around them were vulnerable. Thus, he'd been assigned to follow Evie, who turned out to be Selena's best friend and roommate, in case she was in danger.

Though the threat had passed, he kept telling himself that New York was a dangerous place and anything could happen to Evie. She could get mugged, run over by a car, shoved onto the subway tracks. She was too innocent and naïve and people could take advantage of her. Yeah, that was it. It was for her own good. Never mind that every moment he wasn't sure she was safe made that dull pain in his chest come back again and again.

"Okay, Kevin, you can start anytime," Skinny Hipster said into the mic on his headset. He reached for the knob that turned the house lights down, and the audience began to settle into their seats.

The host, Kevin, came out a few moments later. "Good evening everyone, welcome to The Stage Bound bar's open mic night. I hope you're all relaxed, having fun ..." Connor tuned out the rest of the spiel, having already memorized it from the other times he'd been here. Usually, after giving a short welcome, Kevin introduced the first performer.

"So, tonight, we're going to do something a little different,"

Kevin said. "One of our regular performers here had a request, so if you wouldn't mind indulging us for a bit, please welcome, Evie King!"

Connor tensed, and his mouth set into a hard line. Usually, Evie didn't come on until after three or four acts. What was going on?

Evie walked out onto the small stage, and, even from afar, Connor could see her lips curve into a knowing smile as if she was hiding something. Her long, dark hair was piled on top of her head, a few tendrils framing her lovely face. He didn't even realize he was holding his breath until she began to speak.

"Good evening everyone, thanks for coming. Now, I know we don't usually take requests, but I couldn't ignore this one. Especially one so persistent," she said wryly. "We've got some special guests in the audience tonight. Well, one of them is pretty special to me, and the other tends to be a pain in my behind."

Connor's brows wrinkled. Who was this special person in her life? He leaned forward, craning his neck to try and look at the crowd in the darkened room.

"Selena's been one of my supporters and best friends since I moved to New York," Evie said, gesturing to the front of the stage. "Aww, don't be shy Sel, give everyone a wave."

There was a cheer, and a hand shot up in the darkness, waving back.

Shit. Selena was here. That meant only one thing ...

"And that goofy guy next to her is her boyfriend and general pain in my ass, Quinn."

Quinn didn't even need any encouragement as he stood up and looked back at the audience. A whistle rang out, and Quinn gave an exaggerated bow, prompting hoots and laughs from the crowd.

Fucking Quinn, Connor thought to himself. The tech booth suddenly seemed even smaller. He had to get out of here. Did

Quinn know he was here, following Evie? They must have arrived earlier, but he didn't notice them. He scanned the room, looking for an exit. Unfortunately, unless he knocked over Skinny Hipster, he was essentially trapped.

"Anyway," Evie continued, "tonight is Selena's birthday, and Quinn asked if we could make it extra special. So, I got together with a couple of my friends and put this song together." She motioned off stage, and four people stepped out and stood behind her. "This particular song is an oldie but a goodie, and I think it pretty much sums up Selena and Quinn. So, Selena, happy birthday. I love you. And Quinn," she said with a warning in her voice, "if you ever hurt her, I'm going to cut off your balls."

There was another wave of laughter from the audience, and even Connor had to smile. Evie was grinning, too, but he had no doubt she would castrate his brother if he ever did Selena wrong.

Evie and her friends positioned themselves around the mic. She nodded and began the first line of the song, while the others accompanied her.

Connor felt the air rush out of his lungs, and the electricity that hung in the air almost crackled. It was like the first time he held her when he thought she was in danger. That time had been an accident, and he didn't mean to touch her, but he couldn't help it. He wanted—no, needed—to know she was safe. She was soft and plush, and his body reacted immediately, and he never wanted to let her go. But then something in him reared its ugly head. *The fucking feral wolf.* First, it wanted to rip everything in sight when it thought she was hurt. Being close to her, though, it seemed to want only one thing—her. The wolf was there, making its presence known like never before. From then on, he avoided her as much as possible.

But then he heard her sing, that first night he followed her here. The sweet sound of her voice called to him. Her lilting soprano soared over the crowd and washed over him like a wave. He was entranced. Again, he felt the wild wolf responding. Though he tried as hard as he could, he couldn't stay away and he craved the sight, the smell, and the sound of her. Since then, he'd been coming here, listening to her sing from the tiny booth. It didn't matter what she sang. Her voice was a siren's call, and each time he heard her, the feral wolf seemed satisfied, soothed by the sound of her voice.

Conner stood transfixed in that little booth, and it was like everything and everyone disappeared when she sang. The song talked about falling in love forever and giving her heart completely. It was familiar, one of those old songs Archie used to listen to on his record player. He thought the lyrics were sappy and corny, but his adoptive father loved it.

As Evie and her friends approached the end of the song, there was a loud gasp and then a hush settled over the crowd. Quinn had stood up in front of Selena and then went down on one knee. Evie faltered but quickly regained her composure. She put a hand over her heart and smiled as she looked down at her friend as she continued to sing.

Selena was nodding. When she stood up, Quinn picked her up and gave her a long, sensuous kiss. Applause broke out over the entire place even before the song ended and didn't stop even when Selena turned to the audience, red-faced, while his brother stood next to her proudly, holding out her left hand. That must have been a giant rock because, even from where he was standing, Connor could see the diamond sparkle when the lights hit her finger. Evie immediately walked down to Selena and Quinn's table, where she hugged her friend and sat with them.

Well, shit. He knew it was coming and, frankly, he couldn't help but feel happy for his brother. Quinn had a difficult life growing up; they all did. All his siblings deserved happiness, especially after he failed to protect Archie.

The memory of his failure came rushing back, but he pushed it down, deep down to that dark place inside him where the wolf resided. He had to get out of here, and he didn't care how. With a growl, he grabbed Skinny Hipster's collar and hauled him out of his chair. Ignoring the other man's protests, he tore out of the booth, ripping the curtain aside and bumping into a waiter who was carrying a heavy tray. He ignored the sound of shattering glass ringing in his ears and made a run for the exit.

The warm spring air was choking, but it was better than being inside. *Fucking New York City*. How he hated this place. The crowd, the dirty, mixed smell of trash, body odor, and pollution that he couldn't escape. He wanted to be back in Oregon, back to Archie's mansion outside the city where he could breathe the air. Shaking his head, he began to walk away, not caring which direction he went.

"Hey, stop! Connor!" The sound of loud footsteps coming closer made him grit his teeth. Fucking Quinn. How did he know?

"Yo, stop! C'mon, man, don't make me chase you!" Quinn called.

Connor stopped dead in his tracks and cursed. "What do you want?" he asked without turning around.

"Why'd you run out like that?" Quinn asked, stepping in front of him. "C'mon, don't be like that. How long were you in there, anyway? Did you see?" His brother's grin was as wide as the Grand Canyon. "I asked Selena to marry me. And she said yes." He laughed. "Can you believe it? Me, a married man? Meredith's gonna freak the fuck out. I can't wait to tell her."

"Yeah, well, congrats, man." He turned away, but Quinn stopped him by putting a hand on his arm.

"Where are you going? Come back. Join us. Celebrate. Have a beer or two."

"I can't."

"Why not?" Quinn challenged. "Look, I won't tell Evie you've been following her."

"I'm not," he said flatly.

"Then what were you doing in there?"

Fuck. "None of your goddamn business."

Quinn let out an exasperated sigh. "Look, you're right. Whatever is going on between you two isn't any of my business. But if you want her, you should just go for it. Just ask her out, like a normal person. And quit it with the creepy stalker thing. Girls don't like that."

"I don't know what you're talking about." Normal person. *Yeah, right.*

"Fine," Quinn said. "Keep denying it and keep trying to stay away from Evie. See where that gets you. But you know you won't be able to get away from her since you're going to be my best man and she's going to be Selena's maid of honor."

"Oh, fuck no," Connor protested. "No fucking way."

"Awww, don't be like that, Connor. You're my brother. There's no one else I'd rather have next to me when I walk down the aisle."

"Ask Killian then."

"Killian's too busy to do best man stuff, with a kid coming and all," Quinn reasoned. "C'mon, please?"

Connor let out another growl. "Fine. But don't ask me to make a speech or talk to people. You know I hate that shit.

"Connor, you hate everything," Quinn pointed out.

"Right. I gotta go."

"Where are you going?"

"I got stuff to do."

"And what is that?"

Revenge, Connor thought to himself. The only thing that would satisfy the animal inside him. "Just stuff." He walked away from Quinn, ignoring his brother's calls. It was time, he thought. He was going to start tonight, beginning with a list of names inside the manila envelope in his safe back at the hotel. He already knew the first person on that list who would be meeting the feral wolf.

2

*E*vie sat at her desk in the reception area of the Lone Wolf Security office, adding the finishing touches to the report from their last operation. She glanced down the hallway for the hundredth time. Today was an important day, and things were tense ever since she arrived that morning. She didn't need enhanced senses to feel the edgy atmosphere in the office.

There was a sob and then a cry, and Evie gripped the end of her table, her body going rigid. She hoped that wasn't a bad sign. This was the first time they were reuniting one of the Lone Wolves with their families. A lot of stuff had happened last year, apparently, and it turned out, some bad people had taken Lycans from their families to turn them into mindless soldiers. One of the reasons Lone Wolf Security was created was to bring those Lycans back to their families. They had been working for months, and this was the first real lead they had.

She heard the door to one of the offices open and pretended to go back to her report, not wanting to be caught eavesdropping. Of course, she couldn't help overhearing them as they walked out into the reception area. She stared at the screen of her computer but watched them out of the corner of her eyes.

"I can't thank you enough." It was the white-haired woman who had come in earlier. She was accompanied by an older man. "Thank God you've found our grandson. I was afraid Adam had been lost. They took him from us when he was just twelve."

"Thank you for coming in and confirming his identity, Mrs. Jenkins," Killian said. Quinn and Connor were right behind them.

"When can we see him?" the older man asked. *Probably her husband*, Evie thought. They were both Lycans. After all, only two Lycans could have shifter offspring.

"I'll arrange it as soon as I can," Killian assured him. "I hope you'll be patient. You're the first family we've been able to identify, and you need to be prepared. He might not be who you remember."

"We're just happy to know he's alive," Mr. Jenkins said.

"We have your contact number," Killian said. "If you don't mind staying in New York for a bit longer, we can arrange your meeting with Adam at our facility. He's safe, I assure you."

"Thank you." Mrs. Jenkins reached out and grabbed Killian's hands. "Thank you so much." Killian walked them to the door of the office and then waved goodbye as the couple left.

"Well, looks like we've closed our first case," Killian said to Connor and Quinn. "Good job, team."

"Team?" Quinn moaned. "Hey, I did most of the work with the government databases and illegal surveillance! What did he do," he asked, jerking his thumb at Connor.

"Oh yeah? I've only been picking up the slack with Creed's assignments while you two were playing footsies with your mates," Connor pointed out.

"Yeah, thanks for that," Killian said. "I know it's been a hard couple of months. I appreciate it, both of you. And Luna does too, especially since the baby's almost here."

"And soon I'll be having my own pooping, screaming bundle of joy," Quinn said, and Killian slapped him on the shoulder.

"Looks like I'll be doing more of the shit around here," Connor grumbled. "I'll be in my office."

Evie let out a breath, finally able to breathe. Connor was too goddamn sexy and handsome for his own good, and that was distracting enough, but it wasn't just that. There was something about him ... she couldn't put her finger on why she always wanted to look at him and be near him. He wasn't even nice to her and had a permanent scowl on his face. That would have sent any sane, normal woman the other direction but not her. Oh no, there must be something broken with her because she always fell for the wrong guy, and Connor was the wrongest wrong guy in existence. For one thing, he was a Lycan, and that should have been reason enough to stay away from him.

It was just lust, she told herself. That's it. It had been almost a year since she slept with anyone. Fucking Richard. Her asshole ex-boyfriend. She got back together with him again, even after that incident with the video, but, after a few weeks of doing the long distance thing, she just kind of ... lost interest. She broke up with him and since then, hadn't even felt the need to contact him. Sure, Richard called and texted, but she ignored him and eventually, he got the message.

And now that she was free of Dick (figuratively and literally) ... well, she just didn't have enough time to pursue any relationship. With Selena moving out to marry Quinn, she was going to lose her roommate, and she couldn't afford the apartment on her own. *Maybe I should just cut my losses and move back to Kansas.* Her dad had been making overtures, telling her he wanted her to run the furniture business eventually. Her brother Arthur was too young to take over, and he wanted to retire and make the most of his twilight years. *It wouldn't be so bad*, she thought. She knew how to run the business, and she could spend more time with her dad, stepmom, and Arthur. There was a pang in her heart. Arthur had had a growth spurt the last time she visited, and he was taller than her now. And her dad ... well, he looked older and more tired, too. *Maybe ...*

"What's wrong?"

Evie nearly jumped off her seat at the sound of the low masculine voice. "N-n-nothing," she stammered, wiping the moisture that had formed at the corner of her eyes. She spun around, trying to avoid Connor's gaze, which was now boring into the back of her head.

"Don't lie to me. I can smell your tears. Who the fuck made you cry?"

Damn Lycan senses. She let out a sigh. "I said it's nothing," she insisted. "Just ..."

Connor stepped to the side of her desk and leaned his hip against the corner. Annoyed, she looked up, meaning to scowl at him, but, of course, that went to shit when she stared into the bright green depths of his eyes. She swallowed visibly as she felt the heat rush to her cheeks under his scrutiny. Oh God, she had to stop looking at his gorgeous face. The damn scowl just made him sexier. *Okay, Evie,* she told herself. *Don't look. Look lower.* Her eyes traced down to his full lips. *Dammit.* That didn't help. *Okay, keep going.* Now she was staring at his muscled chest. Oh dear, she'd never been so close to anyone this big. How the hell did he get so damn tall and wide? His chest tapered down to a small waist, and she could see the outline of a defined six-pack under the tight black shirt and stifled a groan.

"Evie?"

Her name on his lips startled her, and she decided it was better to just go back to looking at his face before she went even lower and embarrassed herself. "Yes?" she managed to croak.

"Why were you crying?"

"I told you ... it's nothing." The scowl on his face deepened. "I mean, I'm just being silly." She sighed.

"Well, what is it?"

Her shoulders sagged in defeat. "I'm just ... being on stage and in the theater is my life, you know?" It was like a dam opened up, and she couldn't stop talking. "I want it so bad I can taste it. I left Kansas City and my family and my long-term boyfriend so I could live my dream. Instead, it's been a nightmare. Nothing but auditions and rejections. Then I broke up with Richard. I ate nothing but salad for six months and I've lost fifteen pounds, but I can't even get a bit part." She gave an unhappy sigh. "Sorry, you probably don't want to hear about this. But, if nothing pans out, I'm afraid I'm going to have to move back to Kansas City. Selena will be moving out of the apartment, and I can't afford it on my own and—" She gasped as something large and warm settled over her head. Was Connor ... patting her? Like a puppy? She wrinkled her nose and looked up.

Connor was reaching over her desk, his hand rubbing the top of her head. He was making her ponytail crooked, but, somehow, she didn't mind. It was awkward but soothing and so very ... Connor.

"Uh, Connor?"

"It'll be okay," he said. "I'm sure you'll ... find something. You shouldn't give up. If that's your dream."

"Wow, that is literally the nicest thing you've ever said to me." She let out a squeak, realizing what she said.

Connor pulled his hand away and then shoved them into his pockets. "Well, if it's nice you want, then I'm not what you're looking for." He turned and walked back to his office.

"How do you know?" she asked after him.

He stopped. "Know what?"

She scrunched up every bit of courage she had. "What I'm looking for?"

He shrugged. "You're right. I don't." Before she could say anything else, he walked away, leaving her dumbfounded.

"Oh my God," Selena exclaimed as she slammed the door behind her. "I swear, if I didn't love Quinn, I wouldn't put up with this bullshit!" She took her jacket off and hung it in the coatrack in the foyer.

Evie walked out of the kitchen, wine bottle and two glasses in hand. "Selena? What are you doing here?"

Selena frowned. "Quinn's father acknowledged him this morning in a press conference, and those damn paparazzi somehow found out about our engagement and started hounding me at work!"

"Congressman Martin did what?" Evie said. "How the hell could the press work that fast? He only proposed days ago."

"You tell me! Anyway, they descended on the library like vultures. It's public property, which means I couldn't do anything to stop them from coming up to my desk and snapping pictures of me. I had to leave work early, but they had already staked out Quinn's loft. I've been hiding at different coffee shops the whole day, and this was the only place I could think of where they wouldn't find me." Selena eyed the wine bottle and the two glasses in her hand. "Oh shit, do you have company? Fuck, I'm sorry."

Evie laughed. "No worries, it's only Jack. C'mon, you can join us."

Selena followed Evie from the foyer into the living room, where the dark-haired warlock was sitting on their couch, leafing through a magazine.

"Selena!" he screeched, jumping to his feet and drawing the redhead in for a hug. "Darling, I haven't seen you in ages! Evie told me all about your engagement to that big, hulking Lycan of yours." Jack was a performer at Merlin's, and he and Evie had become fast friends when she directed a segment for their show.

"I'm sure you've seen the news," Selena said.

"His dad's that guy who's running for Governor, right? Awww, poor baby." Jack put an arm around her and sat her down on the couch.

"It's awful. Eww, no." She waved off the glass of wine Evie was offering her. "Sorry, I can't. Even the smell is making me barf." She rubbed her stomach.

"Sorry, I forgot," Evie said. Selena was pregnant with Quinn's baby and not just any child but her True Mate child. So, as it turned out, her best friend and boss were apparently meant to be together and now she was carrying a magical Lycan baby. Evie shrugged. She didn't really know the details, but she was happy for her friend. Even if it meant she would have to leave the apartment and possibly New York.

"Evie?" Selena asked, her face drawn into a frown. "What's wrong?"

"Huh? Nothing," she said, trying to hide the sadness in her voice.

"Aww, Evie-girl." Selena put an arm around her shoulder. "C'mon, don't be like that. I'm your best friend, tell me what's wrong."

She sighed. "I'm really happy for you, Selena," she began. "But, well, I know you're going to be moving in with Quinn soon, and I can't afford this place on my own."

"Evie, I'm so sorry!" Selena said. "I didn't even think ... don't worry about it, okay? I'm paid up for the month. I can pay for my half until you figure things out."

"I can't let you do that, Selena; it's not right."

"Hold on!" Jack exclaimed. "Do you need a roommate? Because, frankly, I'm sick of rooming with my ex! I swear, if it weren't so goddamn hard to find an affordable place and a normal roommate, I'd have moved out ages ago."

"Jack, you broke up with Mark two weeks ago," Evie pointed out.

"Yeah, darling, that's a million years in gay time," Jack said. "No, seriously. I'd love to move in here. It's a little far from the action, but it's so spacious. I'll even take whatever furniture you have. I mean, I don't have any anyway."

"This is perfect!" Selena clapped her hands. "Evie, you don't have to move out! Jack can sublet under me."

"You're okay with the sleeping arrangements?" Evie asked. Although the apartment was roomy by Manhattan standards, there was only one bedroom with a two-twin-bed set up.

"Oh, Evie, I don't plan to be sleeping here a lot," Jack said with a glint in his eye.

"That settles it," Selena said. "And now you don't have to leave." Evie sighed again, and the redhead frowned. "Now what's wrong?"

"It's not just the money and the apartment ..." Evie threw up her hands in frustration. "I've been doing this acting thing for months, and I'm ready to give up. Maybe it's just not meant to be." She sank back down on the couch between Jack and Selena.

"Evie, you are the most talented singer and actress I know," Selena said. "You can't give up now! You're gonna get that big break; I can feel it."

"No one ever makes it big their first year," Jack said. "Trust me. You just need to keep working. A little bit of luck and the right timing, and you'll get that callback."

She sighed. "Everyone keeps saying that. Even Connor told me I shouldn't give up."

"Excuse me?" Selena's voice pitched higher than usual. "*Connor* told you what?"

"Who?" Jack asked.

"Quinn's brother," Selena reminded him.

"Oh, you mean Broody McBroodypants," Jack said in a droll voice.

Evie laughed. "Yeah, him."

"The guy who wanted to murder me when we met at Merlin's," Jack pointed out.

"He did not."

"He did so. You were not at the end of that death glare." Jack took a sip of wine. "Still though, he's kind of sexy, in that I-wanna-murder-you kind of way." Jack made a claw with his hand and a 'rawwr' sound that made Evie nearly snort wine out of her nose.

"Wait, so Connor actually spoke to you?" Selena asked.

"You mean instead of scowling at me? Yeah." She suppressed a smile, but it was too late. Selena had seen it.

"Oh my God! I knew it! You are *so* into Connor."

"I am not!"

"Stop denying you like him! He likes you, too."

"He doesn't," Evie protested. "I don't like him. He's a Lycan."

"Your mom's one, too," Selena pointed out.

"And thus you've cemented my point." Evie crossed her arms over her chest. She did not want to talk about this now. "It would never work."

"Wait, are you saying because he's a Lycan and you're a human, it would never work."

"Exactly," she said firmly, but when Selena's face fell, she knew she made a mistake. "Wait, Sel, that's not what I mean."

"What did you mean then?"

"It … it's complicated." Evie didn't exactly hate her mother, but she couldn't help but feel resentment toward her for abandoning them. Her father said it just didn't work out between them, and she knew it was because she couldn't stand being married to a human. "You and Quinn are totally different than my mom and dad."

"In that case—"

A ringing interrupted Selena. Evie recognized her ring tone, and fished her phone out of her purse before checking the name flashing on the screen. Jane Collins. "Sorry, I have to take this." She bounded up and walked toward the bedroom for some privacy. "Hello?"

"Evie? Hey, it's Jane. Jane Collins." Jane was the lyricist in a workshop Evie had participated in some months back. It was for a musical called *Love and Regrets,* and Evie had the starring role. It never went to anything more than a couple of read-throughs and rehearsals and blockings for the songs but had been one of the highlights of her miserable year.

"Jane, how are you?" Evie asked as she sat down on her bed.

"Great, great! I mean, all's good. I have some news for you."

"Really? What?"

"*Love and Regrets* is being picked up by a major backer and production company. Atlantis Artists. They want to put the show on Broadway."

Evie shot to her feet. "Really?"

"Yes, it's happening. And we want you to come back to the show."

Her heart thundered in her chest, going a mile a minute. It was really happening. Finally ...

"But ..."

Oh, poop. There was always a but. "Yes?"

"You should probably sit down for this ..."

3

"And now, let's raise a toast to the newlyweds!" Killian said, after concluding his speech. Everyone held up their glasses and then took a sip of champagne. Quinn wrapped his arm around his blushing bride and gave her a long kiss on the mouth.

"Okay, now, there are children present," Killian warned as the groom continued to make out with his bride. When he finally pulled away, Selena was as red as her hair, but her face was glowing, her smile a mile wide. Killian stepped down from the dais and signaled to the band, who then started to play an upbeat tune. Couples began to fill the dance floor as the happy couple sat at the head table, chatting and laughing with each other.

Connor hooked his finger into the collar of his tux, tugging at the tight band. He hated wearing these things. The last time he wore one was for Meredith's wedding. He was just glad Killian's was a low-key affair, and he could wear whatever the hell he wanted. But he was the best man, and Quinn and Meredith said he had to wear one today. After a couple of hours wearing the monkey suit, all he wanted to do was rip it off.

Hopefully, this all would be over soon. He was happy for Quinn and Selena, but this whole reception was getting on his nerves.

Although Quinn and Selena wanted to wait until after the baby was born to have a wedding, Congressman (and candidate for Governor of New York) Jacob Martin's press conference acknowledging his long-lost son, Quinn, shot the hell out of their plans. Reporters and paparazzi hounded Quinn and Selena day and night, and they decided that a quickie wedding would be best to just get it over with. They knew the press would be vicious, seeing as Quinn was the product of an affair between the congressman and his secretary, and now he was going to have his own child out of wedlock.

It was not ideal but necessary, and the couple made the best of the situation. They planned for a quiet ceremony at City Hall and then a wedding reception at Sebastian Creed's Hamptons Estate where they could secure the premises. Large tents had been set up in the garden to prevent prying eyes (and flying drones) from looking into the reception. Creed also had a five-mile perimeter around his estate blocked off and even had boats patrolling the beachfront to ensure no one could crash the party or take photos from afar.

However, that didn't stop the press from attacking them during the ceremony. Connor gritted his teeth. *Fucking vultures.* They ambushed the wedding party as soon as they left the judge's chambers. He smashed the camera of a photographer who had jostled Evie, though he really wanted to deck him. Goddamn, he saw red, but Evie had put a hand on his arm, calming him enough to help him think straight. He didn't want to ruin this day for Quinn and Selena, and Evie had looked so fucking vulnerable, peering up at him with her soft, toffee-colored eyes. Every time he wanted to go off the rails, all she had to do was give him *that look*. She didn't know it, but she had saved him from a painful shift more than once.

It had felt good to protect her. Even better than exacting revenge.

The smell of blood was still fresh in his senses. Had it only been a few days ago? He couldn't remember everything. Only that he woke up, covered in blood that wasn't his. He ran his hand down his face, trying to forget what he did recall. All he needed to remember was that he could cross off another name on the list. The feral wolf had done its job. And there were more names on the list to go through. But, for now, the thoughts of brown doe-eyes calmed him. Speaking of which ...

He scanned the room, looking for Evie. Even in a room full of shifters, he towered over most of the guests (save for Sebastian and Daric), so it was easy enough to spot her. She was in the corner, talking to another man he recognized as Aiden James, Sebastian Creed's right-hand man. He was leaning over, talking to her softly, and she laughed, then pushed a tendril of hair behind her ear. Connor gripped the stem of his champagne flute so hard it broke in half.

"Jesus, Connor," Killian said as he walked up behind him. "Are you okay?"

"I'm fine," he said through gritted teeth and wiped the blood from his hand on his pants. He gave the broken glass to a passing waiter, who looked at him curiously. When he glowered at the waiter, the young man's eyes went wide and scurried away.

"What's gotten you in a ... Oh." Killian's gaze drifted toward Evie and Aiden. "I see."

"No, you don't," he said in a defensive tone.

"Right." Killian raised a brow at him. "So, you didn't just crush a champagne glass and now look like you want to murder someone. Or not just anyone, but Aiden James?"

Connor's scowl deepened. "He's too old for her."

"She's an adult, and I'm sure she can decide if someone is

'too old' for her," Killian pointed out. "He's established, wealthy, hardworking, not so old he can't have kids. I'd say Aiden James is a catch."

Connor never wanted to punch Killian in the face more than in this moment, but he pushed that feeling down and grabbed a wine glass from a passing waiter, then downed it in one gulp. Fucking red wine didn't even make him dizzy. It was like drinking water.

Killian shook his head. "Look, everyone knows you've got it bad for her. Why are you fighting it? She's obviously into you, too."

He swallowed visibly but said nothing. Both Quinn and Killian noticed it. And they were both under the impression Evie wanted him, too. He looked back toward Evie and Aiden, but she was alone. Thank fuck.

"Go on. Now's your chance," Killian nodded toward Evie.

He shook his head. "I can't."

"You can't or won't?" his brother asked. "Look, I know you're not a monk or anything, so sex isn't the problem. Why the hell have you been pushing her away?"

"Because ... Fuck. I just ..." Aiden came back, bringing a glass of champagne. He handed it to Evie, and she accepted it gratefully, giving him a bright smile.

And there it was again. The guttural sound was building up in his middle, and his hackles were rising. Just being in the same room with her was calling out the feral wolf. How could he explain it to Killian? His animal had to stay deep inside him. Separate. Or else, he wouldn't be able to control it. Like all those times in the fighting cage. And then there would be trouble.

"Connor?" Killian's brows knitted. "Hey, are you all right?"

"I'm fine!" he growled, the sound coming from deep in his chest. He ripped the necktie away, needing to breathe. "I need some air." He strode away from Killian, hoping he had enough control to keep the wolf at bay.

"Thank you, Mr. James," Evie said as she took the champagne flute from Aiden.

"Please, I told you, call me Aiden," he said, his blue eyes twinkling. "Mr. James makes me feel old."

"Oh, you're not that old, are you?" she teased.

He laughed. "I was one of the senior members of our Spec Ops team when Sebastian joined," he pointed out. "So, you can take a guess." He shook his head. "No, wait, never mind."

Evie chuckled. "All right, I won't. Aren't you having any champagne?"

Aiden shook his head. "No, I'm technically on duty. Sebastian likes to plant his people as guests during events like this. Since he's the one celebrating and hosting, I'm afraid I'm the responsible one tonight."

Sebastian Creed and his mate, Dr. Jade Cross, had introduced Aiden to Evie earlier that evening. He was human, and, as Jade explained, had no idea about Lycans. He was also charming and looked great in a tux, and the bit of white hair at his temples only made him look distinguished. Evie wondered if Jade had ulterior motives in introducing them. She smiled at Aiden as she sipped her champagne.

"So," Aiden began. "I've heard of Lone Wolf Security, but I have to confess I've never visited your office. It seems I've been remiss in my duties as one of Creed Security's partners."

"It's not a big office," she said. "And I'm only there part-time." She blushed, realizing it made it sound like he shouldn't come because she wasn't there all the time. "I mean, uh, Killian, Quinn, and Connor aren't always there."

"Sebastian seems to send them overseas a lot," Aiden observed. "And whenever I ask him about their ops, I can never get a straight answer."

"Oh, is that why you got me champagne? Were you hoping I'd tell you some secrets?"

Aiden's face fell. "No, it's not that, Evie ... I ..."

"I was teasing," she said. "No, really it's fine."

"I didn't mean to make it sound like I had an ulterior motive," he said. "Well, I do, but it's not what you think. You're very—" He stopped and placed his finger on the small comm unit hidden in his ear. "James here. Yes. Okay, I'll be right there." He turned back to Evie. "Duty calls. Sorry about that, but it was nice meeting you, Evie." He held out his hand.

Evie placed her palm in his and shook it. "Same here."

"I guess I know where to find you." He gave her a wink before he turned and walked away.

Evie let out a sigh. How was it that a man could be so good looking, so nice, and seem like such a great guy, but make her feel absolutely ... nothing. Nada. Zip. Zilch. Not even a thrill of excitement. Meanwhile, another equally handsome man treated her like she was invisible and one look sent her into a tizzy. *He didn't even compliment me on my dress,* she thought glumly. She had practically starved herself all week so she would look good in the ice blue, one-shoulder chiffon maid of honor gown and he didn't even say anything or give her anything more than a cursory glance.

What did she expect anyway? Connor was nice to her that one time. Awkward but nice. But then he confused her with his words. It sounded like he was warning her to stay away from him and maybe she should listen. But still ...

A movement from the corner of her eye caught her attention. How could it not? It wasn't like Connor was hard to ignore, even in a room full of people. She saw his retreating back as he lumbered away from the tents. It looked like he was headed to the beach, and, from his movements, he seemed agitated. She really should ignore him. Leave him alone, like he wanted. But, by the time she had said those words in her head, she was already following him.

Where the heck was he going? She chased after him as he walked past the guest tables, the food station, and farther away from the reception area. He walked down the flagstone path that led to the beach, then stepped off to continue down to the shore.

Damned stubborn Lycan, she muttered. Now she was getting sand in her shoes. Kicking them off, she picked up her skirt. His longer strides were already putting a lot of distance between them. "Connor!" she called as she picked up her pace. "Connor, hold on!"

He stopped in his tracks and then slowly turned. In the darkness, his green eyes glowed, though, oddly, it didn't frighten her. "What are you doing here?"

She took a deep breath, letting the salty air cool her burning lungs. "I was ... you seemed." She tried to walk toward him but stumbled on something buried under the sand. She braced herself, preparing to eat a mouthful of sand when strong arms wound around her.

"Careful," he warned as he held her in his arms.

Evie tried to throttle the dizzying current that raced through her, but his scent and his overwhelmingly male presence were muddying her thoughts. The eerie glow in his eyes dissipated, and he let out a breath, then relaxed against her. He was close, and his nearness made her senses spin. The last time he held her like this hadn't been quite this close. Now, she could feel every hard plane in his body pressed up against her. He looked so sinfully handsome in the tuxedo, it should have been illegal. She wondered what he would look like underneath that tux, and warmth and lust shot straight to her core.

"I ..."

He was leaning down, and his warm breath tickled her skin. Was he ... Oh God, he was going to kiss her. It was happening. Just a few inches and ...

A loud explosion made them jump apart, and a bright burst of light illuminated the waters of the bay. One, two, three—the fireworks exploded overhead, filling the night sky with brilliant colors.

Evie took a sharp, quick breath, and heat bloomed in her cheeks. Thank God it was dark where they were and Connor wouldn't see her face.

Connor cleared his throat. "Are ... you okay?"

"Me?" she squeaked, then hated herself for the way she sounded. "Yeah, I'm fine. Sorry, I can be pretty clumsy," she said, forcing out a laugh.

Connor looked up at the fireworks lighting up the dark sky and shook his head. "Of course Quinn would have a fireworks show at his wedding. Show off."

"I guess you didn't know about this?"

He shook his head. "Thought he wanted this low key. Damn paparazzi are probably having a field day."

Evie shivered, thinking about how those reporters had chased them at the courthouse earlier that day. One of them had shoved her out of the way to get a picture of Quinn and Selena, and Connor grabbed his camera and crushed it with his bare hands.

Something warm wrapped around her shoulders, and the scent of coffee wafted into her nose. Connor had taken off his jacket and put it on her. "What are you doing?"

"You seemed cold," he said. "And I don't need it."

Right. His Lycan metabolism kept him warm. "Th-thank

you," she said gratefully, pulling the coat closer around her. It was huge and fully enveloped her, but it did its job and kept the chilly air away.

They stood there, watching the fireworks continue to illuminate the sky. It really was beautiful, and more people came out to the shore to watch the show.

"So, I was talking to Killian the other day," he began, "and, if you need more hours at work, I'm sure we could use your help around the office."

"What?" Oh God, that awkward conversation with him. He remembered what she said about not being able to afford the apartment on her own. "I wasn't ... I'm not asking for charity," she huffed.

"Look, it's not charity," he said. "I'm just sayin', you don't have to move back to Kansas ... I mean, not if you don't want to."

"I'm fine," she said defensively. "I'm doing just fine. In fact, I've already found a roommate who agreed to sublet Selena's half of the apartment. And I've accepted a role in a new show that's going to premiere in a few weeks. On Broadway." Well, sort of, she added silently, crossing her fingers.

The truth was, although the composer and lyricists of *Love and Regrets* wanted her back, the backers wanted a bigger star in the leading role. They agreed to cast Evie in the chorus and as an understudy, but she also had to teach the new leading lady all the songs, choreography, and blocking. They wanted to put the show in previews by the beginning of next month, which meant they didn't have a lot of time. It wasn't what she had hoped for, but it was better than nothing, and they offered her double the usual talent fee for a chorus role in exchange for her help. How could she say no?

"Really?" he asked, his face lighting up for just a second before drawing back into it usual black look. "Good."

The show finally ended, and Evie looked back to the reception area. "Well ... I should check if Selena needs me or something." She paused, waiting for him to say something, but, as usual, he remained silent. "Okay, then, I'll see you around. Here," she began to remove the jacket.

"No, keep it. You can give it back to me later."

She shrugged and turned away, her heart heavy for some reason.

4

*E*vie only had a few days after the wedding to prepare for the first rehearsal of *Love and Regrets*. She finished up her work at Lone Wolf, dug out her old scripts and music, and practiced the songs she had learned for the workshop. Despite the exhaustion, she felt great, and it also meant she didn't have time or energy to think about Connor. He was obviously so *not* into her, and it was better she forgot about him and concentrate on her career.

Though she was disappointed she wouldn't be playing the lead, Evie tried to look on the bright side. She was going to perform on a real Broadway stage. Just the thought of being up there, bathed in lights and looking down at the audience, thrilled her. Plus, she'd get some great contacts in the industry. Atlantis Artist produced many of the last decade's Tony Award-winning musicals, and if she played her cards right, this could advance her career.

"Evie!" Annie Fox, the composer and Jane Collins' writing partner, greeted her as she entered the stage door of the Nina Haas theater on West 45th St. The older woman, dressed in her usual black leggings and a colorful, flowy top enveloped her in a hug. "I'm so glad you decided to come back and work with us. I was afraid you wouldn't want to be part of this."

"Are you kidding?" Evie laughed. "This has been the best news I've had all year. I'm so excited to be part of this. I know this is yours and Jane's big break, too."

Annie's blue eyes sparkled with excitement. "I know! We've been writing for years, and, finally, we're going to see one of our musicals on Broadway." She put an arm around Evie and led her to the backstage area. "C'mon, almost everyone in the cast came back. I'm sure they'll be happy to see you." They walked down a darkened hallway, which led to the stage. There were already a bunch of people there that Evie recognized, and they greeted her warmly. The excitement in the air was evident as everyone was chatting, laughing, and joking.

After Jane's initial call, Evie met with her and Annie over coffee, and they explained the situation to her. Atlantis Artists thought *Love and Regrets* had the potential to be a big hit, but, to do that, they needed to sell lots of tickets. These days, that meant bringing a big star into the production. The executive producers from the production company had signed a young, rising pop star by the name of Janelle Edwards, who took the music world by storm last year with her hit album, *Girls Rockin' Out*. Though it seemed her stardom had cooled off as she had yet to release another album, she also had two million followers on her various social media accounts. The producers thought it was an excellent way to get some butts in those theater seats, as many other shows had done the same to revive ticket sales and stay open. Evie understood, of course. That was show business. Still, she couldn't help but feel a small pang of hurt. But, she was a professional and she wanted to impress the producers by being a team player.

"Okay, everyone," Jane said, as she called everyone's attention. "I'd like to thank all of you who came back to work with us.

We're thrilled to bring this show to life." There was a cheer from the group. "Now, I'd like to introduce you to Andrew McAllister, our executive producer." She motioned to the squat, balding man in a tan suit beside her.

"Hello everyone, glad to be working with you," Andrew said. "I'm happy to be helping you bring this show to Broadway. And I'm excited to introduce you to someone special. Everyone, meet our new leading lady, Ms. Janelle Edwards."

Everyone turned to the figure who strode out from offstage right. Janelle Edwards was dressed in a tight designer bodycon dress, and her boobs pressed up in a gravity-defying way. Her long blond hair curled around her shoulders and down her back, while her lips were painted red and her eyebrows were drawn within an inch of their lives. Her platform heels clattered on the wooden surface as she sauntered to center stage, and two huge men in suits followed behind her. Waiting in the wings were three people, each one carrying a large roller bag.

"Hi everyone, I'm Janelle," she greeted in a sweet, syrupy voice. "I just wanted to let you know how excited I am to be working with you all. This is my first time on Broadway, but I've done tons of concerts and live appearances. And, as you know, my hit single, *Obsessive Love*, was on the Billboard charts for over 40 weeks and I won MTV's Best New Female Artist last year." She flashed them all a blinding smile and then raised her phone. "Let's take a selfie! Now that the press release was sent out this morning, I can post it on my Instagram and let all my fans know!" Everyone crushed behind her, trying to get into the tiny screen. Of course, it was impossible, as Janelle's face took up half the photo.

"Thanks, everyone!" she said, then turned to Jane. "Now, where's my dressing room? I need to freshen up."

"Our stage manager, Nicole Lawrence, will show you the way," Jane said, motioning to the young woman in black jeans and a red tank top beside her holding a clipboard. "But we need you to be on stage in five, okay? With your schedule limiting us to five days a week for rehearsals, we don't have much time. Steven Ali, our director, will be here any moment. He's just talking with our tech director up in the booth."

Janelle's eyes narrowed. "Well, Atlantis assured me that my schedule was no problem," she said in a miffed voice.

"As long as we get to opening night, we're good," Annie interjected.

"Fine." Janelle flipped her long blond hair, then turned to Nicole. "Show me where to go."

Evie watched as Janelle and her entourage left the stage. She had a feeling things weren't going to be as simple as she thought they would be.

Connor kept his back against the wall as he looked down at the stage. Although the Nina Haas Theater was still closed to the public, it was easy enough to sneak in. Security was a joke, and, since most the people inside were gathered on the stage, he remained undisturbed in his hiding spot in the farthest box on the right side of the theater.

After the wedding, he tried to stay away from Evie, especially after he held her in his arms. He had been too close, and he nearly gave into his primal urges to kiss her. Who knows what else he could have done on that secluded beach?

Fucking hell, his cock had never been so hard in his life. Sure, like Killian said, he wasn't some monk. For fuck's sake, he knew what it was like to be teenage boy full of hormones. But, as soon as he was old enough, it seemed he kept attracting the wrong kind of women. They only saw his size and his scar, and they boxed him into a certain type of guy. It was exciting the first couple of times, and, while he used those women as much as they used him, it got old after a while. All those women wanted one thing. Harder ... more ... spank me ... rougher ... do it until I bruise. He shook his head in disgust. Already, he'd been holding back his Lycan strength to stop from hurting them, and they wanted more pain? Wanted him to get rougher? Women were fucking weird, at least those who were attracted to him. He decided he'd had enough. He stayed away as much as he could and lost interest in sex.

Maybe that was the problem. These days, he might as well be a monk. Being near Evie and her delicious, sweet peaches scent was making him horny because it had been too long since he fucked a woman. Too bad both Killian and Quinn were settled down, and he didn't have any wingmen left. How the hell did people hook up these days? Damn, he felt ancient, and he was only thirty years old.

He pushed those thoughts away and turned his attention back to the stage. An hour had passed, and, still, nothing had happened. Everyone was standing around, waiting. Was this what being in the theater was like? How could Evie handle all the inaction?

Finally, that blonde anorexic-looking chick strode out onto the stage like she was some queen, moving among her lowly subjects, her head bobbing as she walked among them. "Thanks for waiting, everyone," she said in a high-pitched voice that made Connor's ears hurt. "I had to freshen up my makeup and check my stats. Oh-Em-Gee, our photo got one hundred thousand likes in the last hour!"

Connor wrinkled his brow. Was she even speaking English?

"Okay, well, now that we're all here, let's get started." A tall man dressed in track pants and a black shirt gathered everyone around him. "Janelle, nice of you to join us. I'm Steven. Your *director*," he sneered.

"Oh, hi," she greeted. "Well, what are we waiting for? Let's get started."

"You heard *our star*." Connor didn't miss the sarcasm in Steven's tone. "Let's proceed. Janelle, you've had the script for two weeks now, so you should already know your lines."

Janelle giggled. "Well, I've been super busy. And Jane and Annie said I'd have some help with the lines and stuff."

Steven let out an exasperated sigh. "Right. Evie, please come forward."

Evie emerged from the crowd and introduced herself to Janelle, holding out her hand. The blonde sized her up, her gaze going from the top of Evie's head to her toes. Finally, after intense scrutiny, she took Evie's hand.

"All right, let's get started," Steven called. "From the top."

Connor continued to watch the rehearsal play out. He'd never been to any live show, so he wasn't sure what the hell was going on. Evie was feeding that Janelle girl her lines and showing her where to stand and move. *Strange.* He thought the director did that.

"Ugh, I know the line," Janelle said to Evie in a dismissive tone. "You don't have to keep following me like some puppy."

"I'm just trying to help," Evie muttered.

"Well, go and help somewhere else," Janelle retorted. "Preferably somewhere far away."

Connor's blood began to boil when he saw the expression on Evie's face falter. Who the fuck was this woman? And why was Evie letting this bitch walk all over her? She didn't take anyone's shit, not his, not even Quinn's. And yet—

His ears suddenly perked up as he heard a strange sound. It was ... metal scraping against metal. And then footsteps overhead. A shadowy figure crossed the bridge hanging over the stage. *What the fuck?*

Connor's instincts went into overdrive, screaming danger as

the sound of bending metal grew louder, at least to his ears. Glancing above the stage, he saw one of the large overhead spotlights hanging precariously by its wires. And it was right above Evie.

Blood roared in his ears. There was no time to circle back and take the stairs, so he climbed on the railing and jumped down. The drop was maybe twenty or thirty feet, and his heavy boots landed with a loud thud. Hopefully, no one had seen him in the darkened theater.

He ran toward the stage, then leapt up and lunged at Evie. There was a loud snap as the wire broke under the heavy weight of the lights. He didn't even stop to watch it fall as he tackled her. They landed a few feet away from the pile of mangled metal and broken glass. He braced his palms on the floor to prevent his body from crushing her.

A loud shriek broke out, nearly deafening Connor. Bony elbows poked at his ribs, and he realized Janelle was underneath him. She must have stepped right in their path as Connor tackled Evie. *Motherfucker.*

"Get off meeeee!' Janelle screamed, pushing up at him. Her two bodyguards came rushing forward, and Connor quickly rose to his feet to get out of their way. He grabbed Evie by the waist and pulled her up. "Are you all right?"

Evie looked up at him, her face pallid and hair disheveled. Soft brown eyes blinked. "Connor? What are you doing here?"

Shit. What was he going to say?

"What's going on here?" Andrew Macallister pushed his way to the front of the small crowd gathering around him. "Who the hell are you and how did you get in here?" He looked at Evie. "You know you can't have boyfriends in the theater during rehearsal."

"He's not my boyfriend," Evie denied, pulling away from Connor. "He's ... uh, he's my manager."

"Your manager?" Andrew asked. "You have a manager?"

"At my day job, I mean," Evie explained. "I work for a security firm part time."

"Creed Security," Connor said. "You can look them, er, us up."

Andrew frowned. "That's good to know. But what the hell are you doing here? This is a closed rehearsal."

"He was saving me!" Janelle shrieked. She pushed her two bodyguards out of the way. "Unlike these two idiots." She gave the men a dirty look and then sauntered to Connor. "Oh, my ... you're so ... big ..."

Connor tensed, his skin crawling at the way Janelle's eyes devoured him. Just like all those women.

"How did you get in here?" Andrew continued. "You shouldn't be here."

"Well, your security's a joke," Connor said. "I saw someone tampering with the lights overhead."

Janelle let out a gasp. "Oh-Em-Gee. Someone was trying to hurt me?" Two fat tears rolled down her cheeks. "It must be one of my haters!" she cried. "Thank you so much ... if it wasn't for you ..."

She launched herself into his arms, her octopus-like limbs wrapping around his torso. Connor went very still, not sure what to do and annoyed his last clean shirt was now getting wet with Janelle's tears. Beside him, Evie tensed and slowly began to back away from him.

Andrew cleared his throat. "Mr. ..."

"Connor," he provided.

"Mr. Connor—"

"Just Connor."

Andrew cleared his throat. "Right. Anyway, I'm going to call your boss and get to the bottom of this. Stay here."

Connor wanted to tell him to eat shit and die. No one

could stop him if he wanted to leave. But he remained rooted to the spot, not just because of Janelle's strangely strong grip on his torso but because of the look Evie flashed him. Her face was red and drawn into a scowl, and she crossed her arms over her chest. She let out a puff of breath, and her eyes turned stormy as she stared at Janelle. Evie was obviously upset, and it made something in his middle ache. He didn't want to see her that way, and he couldn't leave until he knew she was okay.

"What the fuck did you do?" Sebastian bellowed as he stepped into the small meeting room where Connor had been waiting for almost two hours. Behind him, Killian and Aiden James followed. Both men did not look happy, either.

Connor kept his tough-faced exterior, though he flinched on the inside. No man could ever make him lose his composure, but Sebastian Creed was no ordinary man. He had a beast inside him, a fully-grown dragon that could breathe fire and lava and crush anything in its talons. And, right now, he could feel the dragon lurking at the surface.

As he threatened, Andrew MacAllister called Creed Security. The producer must have been someone important, as Creed himself came down to the theater, dragging Killian and Aiden James with him. The three of them spoke to MacAllister privately before they came to the room where the stage manager had asked Connor to wait.

"I'm sure Connor has a perfectly good explanation." Killian gave him a warning look. "Right, Connor?"

He shrugged. "It was a good thing I was here or Evie would've been crushed under those lights." A unfamiliar lump in his throat grew, as he thought of what could have happened to her.

"I don't give a shit what you do on your personal time," Sebastian growled. "But telling them you were part of Creed Security? What the fuck was that about? You're putting my company and reputation on the line."

"Technically, Lone Wolf is under Creed Security." Connor glanced briefly at Aiden, then turned his gaze back to Sebastian. "And you know why I had to tell them that."

"I should have thrown you under the bus," the dragon shifter said. "If you weren't such an asset to the company …" He straightened his shoulders. "Well, seeing as you brought us into this mess, you're going to get us out of it."

Connor's eyes narrowed. "What do you mean?"

"Ms. Edwards seems to be convinced someone is trying to hurt her," Aiden said. "And the only way Mr. MacAllister was able to stop her from walking out of the production was to hire Creed to protect her."

"Specifically, you," Sebastian added. "She only wants you."

"No fucking way. I don't got time to play bodyguard to some skinny pop star." And he didn't like the way that woman treated Evie as though she were beneath her.

"And you think my company does?" Sebastian retorted. "I had to agree to a contract and a *reduced* fee in order for them to drop any lawsuits. You were trespassing here."

"That's fucking bullshit."

Aiden stepped forward and put a hand on Connor's shoulder but quickly withdrew it when Connor gave him a death glare. "Look, I know you don't do any of the contract negotiations on whatever jobs you do, but I usually take care of these things. Entertainment lawyers are even scarier than the toughest criminal defense attorneys. They also have to deal with insurance companies. If you had been hurt and their insurance provider heard about it, they would have hiked up their premiums or refused to continue coverage. You could have derailed the entire show."

Connor didn't understand half the things coming out of Aiden's mouth, but he sure as hell wasn't going to be intimidated. "I don't fucking care. There's no way you can make me do anything. I'll quit Lone Wolf if I have to."

"Connor," Killian began. "You're right; we can't force you to do anything." Sebastian opened his mouth to protest, but Killian ignored him. "Aidan, you do a lot of Creed's contracts with private security. Surely, a vice president getting personally involved in the matter should make things up." He glanced at Connor from the corner of his eye. "And Evie will be there, too. I'm sure she'd appreciate Aiden's *hands-on* approach."

Fucking Killian. "Fine," Connor relented. "I'll do it."

"You'll both do it," Sebastian said. "You and Aidan will both be working here. Aidan will take lead on the security plan, and you'll make sure Ms. Edwards is safe while she's on the premises."

Connor gritted his teeth. At least he wasn't going to be following around that bitch like a puppy dog wherever she went. "Fine." And he could keep an eye on Aiden James and make sure he didn't creep on anyone, including Evie.

"Good. You'll start tomorrow."

5

Drip. Drip. Drip.

The constant sound of water dripping from the ceiling would have driven any sane person crazy. But he was used to it. And to the dark, dank room. The thin mattress and the scratchy sheets. The windowless, white walls. And the metal door that would shriek to announce it being opened. How long had he been living in this room? No, it wasn't his room. It was a cell meant to keep him and others like him locked up in The Facility. The walls may have looked like concrete, but they were reinforced with solid steel.

The boy sat on the bed, unmoving. He stared down at his hands, wrapped in clean, white bandages. But he knew they wouldn't stay clean for very long.

The hairs on the back of his neck prickled as he heard the footsteps outside the door. He didn't normally have this reaction, even when they came for him. Usually, it was just his handler, Boyd, and he didn't make him bristle like this. Someone else was out there.

A key turned in the giant padlock. The metal latch moved and the solid steel door screeched as it slid open. The boy looked up slowly. His handler, a short, squat, and balding Lycan dressed in a dirty jacket and stained jeans came in first. As he stepped aside, a chill blasted down the boy's spine. The air in the small room grew thick with dominance as the hulking, red-haired man stepped in.

The boy was big for his age, one of the reasons he ended up here. But still, the red-haired man towered over him. He was nearly seven feet tall. He had wide linebacker shoulders and enormous arms, like thick tree trunks with corded veins bulging under the muscles. As he lumbered closer, his heavy boots stomped on the concrete and sent vibrations across the floor. Wild, red hair stuck out from his head and connected to a long, full beard that obscured most of his face. The man was scary enough, but the wolf inside him was terrifying. A big, dominant creature that the boy had only seen once and never wanted to encounter again. The man didn't even bother to hide it, his eyes glowing like beacons that marked him as a Lycan.

"You ready for tonight, boy?" the red-haired man asked.

The boy said nothing as he looked at his bare feet.

"You answer me when I'm talking to you, boy." A hand connected with the boy's cheek and sent him sprawling to the floor. "Get up."

He slowly stood up, rising to his full height, much taller than most boys his age. The muscles on his body had developed fast, and he easily outweighed any of the adult Lycans in The Facility. The doctor who patched them up after fights estimated he was probably sixteen years old, and he was going to keep growing.

"Good." The red-haired man sized him up. "Boy, you've been undefeated for the last couple of fights. That's not so bad, except you're making things boring around here. And our customers ain't paying for boring." He spat on the floor. "Now, just to make things a little more exciting, I'm gonna make a few changes. Boyd," he said with a nod to the handler.

Boyd stepped forward, taking something wrapped in a towel from his jacket. Stubby, meaty fingers unwrapped it, and, even in the poorly-lit room, the boy knew what it was. The blade of the knife glinted, the edges were serrated like shark teeth.

"This'll kick things up a notch. Both you and Clyde will have one *of these while you fight. But that's not all." The red-haired man took a small bottle from his pocket. "That edge is gonna be laced with this. A special potion brewed by some powerful witches. Illegal and very potent. Slows down healing. Cost me an arm and a leg, but that bitch who sold it to me said it'll work like a charm. Make sure you bleed nice an' good before your cuts heal up."*

The boy gritted his teeth. Clyde was the biggest and meanest Lycan in The Facility. He'd only faced him once before, during his first few weeks there. They squared off in The Cage, and Clyde beat him to a pulp. But the boy was determined. After all, he'd been training in the facility since he was a young pup. He rose to the top of his group because of his size and skill but, most of all, because of his grit. Clyde was the only fighter who he had yet to defeat.

"Ready, boy? Good. Don't forget to give them a show and, when Clyde's down, you go ahead and let out that monster in you."

Connor awoke with a jolt, his entire body going rigid before he shot up. He placed his palm over the right side of his face, and, for a split second, he swore he felt the pain from the scar like it just happened. Examining his hands, he saw the wetness there was only cold sweat and not blood. He made a grab for the digital watch under his pillow and let out a long breath when he checked the date. But it didn't bring him any comfort.

He glanced back at the watch, surprised at the time: 9:02 pm. Early still.

After the reaming from Sebastian, he had to stay and tour the theater with Aiden James, checking for weak spots and other security concerns. It took most of the day and, by the time they were done, the cast had already left, including Evie. Of course, he was thankful he didn't have to see Janelle until the next day, but he didn't know where Evie had gone. So, he decided to go back to his hotel to try and get some shut eye.

He'd only been asleep an hour, yet, it felt longer as his dreams made him travel back in time. His nightmares were filled with his time at The Facility. Training with a dozen other young Lycans who were barely old enough to shift. Coaxing their animals out. Teaching them to fight.

He had been there for so long he didn't know anything but the cold, white walls of The Facility. He didn't even know where he or the other children came from. Were they bred at The Facility? Stolen from their families? Plucked out of thin air? No one knew, not even Archie.

But he remembered that night he first saw Archie. It was the same night he got the scar from the poisoned blade. As he was lying down, blood pouring over his eye, he caught a glimpse of this strange old man sitting in the prime seats. While others stood up and screamed for his blood, the old man remained seated and looked at Connor with such sad eyes.

A low rumble tore from his chest. *Shit. No. Not now.* Archie. The Cage. The Facility. The red-haired giant. All his failures were coming back, and it was making the feral wolf rise up. The taste of blood from the other night sated it, but it wanted more. Was it a mistake to go after Boyd? It was easy enough to find his old handler, thanks to Archie's list. It only took him five hours to drive two states over, to the run-down trailer where the bastard was living.

The envelope Archie had left him when he died contained a list of names and pictures of people connected to The Facility and background information on them. Most of the names were negligible—the old doctor, the name of the owner of the building where The Facility was housed (likely fake), the security guards, the cleaning crew. But two names stood out, and one was conspicuously missing. Boyd Russell, his old handler, who he had already taken care of. The next was David Booth, who Connor recognized as one of the men who trained him as a young boy.

The one name and picture missing from the envelope was

the one Connor wanted the most. The red-haired man. Was he even still alive? He hoped so because Connor was going to get his revenge, before it was too late.

That meant keeping the feral wolf under control, at least when he wasn't extracting vengeance. Archie had helped him all those years, but, since his death, his control was slipping. The wolf wanted more time with their body, and it was getting harder and harder to take it back.

And, when, not if, the time came that he couldn't reign in the wolf, there would be only one solution. He would have to be put down. That was one of the reasons he agreed to stay in New York. He couldn't ask any of his siblings to put him down. It would have to be someone strong and someone with reason. Grant Anderson, as the biggest and strongest Alpha of them all, would be the one to end his life, and Connor knew he would do it to save his city and his clan.

Connor wrestled control of their body, rolling over the bed and getting to his feet. He let out a groan as he clenched his fists, willing the wolf to submit to him. *You're in charge, you're alpha,* Archie reminded him. *Tell the wolf who's boss.*

It was getting harder and harder to hold it back. The feral wolf was urging him on, spurring him forward to get dressed. To get out of this goddamn room and roam the streets. But where would he go?

Of course this is where his fucked up wolf wanted to go. Connor was standing in the park across from a building. It was one of those older brick buildings, around five or six stories tall with a small foyer in the front. He knew this place. He'd been keeping watch here for weeks.

The tree overhead casted a shadow that kept him hidden.

Fucking broken animal. He kicked the tree trunk. He blew out another breath and slammed his palm on the trunk. The poor, hapless tree getting the brunt of his anger. Anger at what, he wasn't sure. Was Evie even home? She must be. Rehearsals tomorrow started at seven a.m. sharp. Even when she wasn't working on a show, Evie was disciplined, only staying out late if she was doing an open mic night and, even then, she went straight home to get her sleep. He overheard her saying she needed at least eight hours of shut eye every night to keep her voice and body in shape.

A movement at the front door of the building caught his eye. He had been here enough times that he knew most of Evie's neighbors. The figure slipping his key in the front door was not a neighbor but definitely familiar. Jake? John? *Jack.* It was a warlock stripper from Merlin's.

"What the fuck is he doing here?" Connor said aloud. Motherfucker. And he had a key. Connor had stopped following Evie since the wedding and now ... this happened? When? *Goddammnit.* Were they dating? Obviously. Why else would he have a key to her place?

With a huff, he pushed against the tree and walked toward the subway on 173rd street. Fuck this shit; he was done. Done with Evie. Screw the feral wolf. Even thinking of them together would bring out the animal.

"What the fuck?" Instead of walking south, his feet somehow brought him directly *in front* of Evie's building. "Goddamn shit."

He took the lock-picking tool from his pocket, silently thanking Archie and his lessons long ago. The lock clicked and the door opened. He took the stairs two at a time until he reached the front of Evie's apartment.

There were voices inside. A male and female, who was definitely Evie based on the familiar, light-hearted laugh his sensitive ears picked up. The fury building inside him was so thick it nearly choked him, and his pulse was beating erratically as he pounded on the door. He heard scrambling inside and footsteps coming toward the front part of the apartment.

Cracking his knuckles, he prepared himself. He took a long sniff—tea and mud, not Evie's sweet scent, so it wasn't her opening the door. The lock turned and the door opened, and Connor didn't even wait. He barged in, grabbed the figure by the shoulders, and pushed him up against the wall inside the foyer.

The towel wrapped around the figure's head dropped, revealing short, dark hair. Two blue eyes peered up at him from behind a mask of green goop. A mouth opened and let out an unearthly shriek.

"Aaaaaaiiiyaaahhhhhhhhhhhh!" The scream was deafening. "Do you want money? We're poor, starving actors! We don't have any money! You can take the TV!"

"*What. The. Fuck*?" Connor leaned down and peered at the figure. It was definitely male. He was wearing a short, terrycloth robe and nothing else underneath. The shit on his face smelled like tea and mud and, other than that, he didn't smell like anything else. "Where's Evie?"

"Connor?" Evie was standing by the doorway that led to the living room, her mouth in a perfect "o" shape and her eyes wide as dinner plates. "What are you doing here? And ... Jack! Let go of him; you're hurting him!" She walked to Connor and tugged at his bicep.

Connor released Jack, who slumped against the wall. "You brute! How dare you assault me in my own home!"

"Your home ... what the fuck is he talking about?"

Evie let out a sigh. "Jack is my new roommate. Remember? I told you about him?"

"You said you had a roommate," Connor groused. "Not that it was *him*."

"What does it matter who it is?" Evie asked. "And what are you doing here?"

"I ..." Connor looked at Evie and then at Jack. "You don't ... never mind! This was a mistake." He shook his head.

"Oh my God," Jack exclaimed, then let out a laugh. "You thought ... me and Evie. *Gross!* Sorry, big guy, I'm afraid you and I don't play on the same team."

"What?" Connor scratched his beard. "What team are you talking about?"

"Well, I prefer playing with baseball bats." Jack winked at him.

Connor's brows drew together. "Do you have something in your eye?"

Jack let out an exasperated sigh. "No. I mean, I don't like to drink from the furry cup. I'm a friend of Dorothy." Connor looked even more confused. "I'm *gay*," Jack exclaimed. "Get it?"

"Oh." *Shit.* "Uh, I'm sorry?"

Jack sighed and closed his robe in a dignified manner. "Well, I suppose I could forgive you since that's about the most action I've seen all week." His blue eyes twinkled with mischief as he sized up Connor, and then bit his lip with his teeth. "I don't suppose you'd consider batting for my team?" A low growl made him wince. "Right, well, I'll leave you kids to it." Jack tossed his head and made his way back to the other room.

Evie turned back to Connor and crossed her arms over her chest. "Connor, what are you doing here?"

"I needed to make sure you were okay," he said. Technically that was the truth. "After what happened today."

"I'm fine," she said with a shrug. "It was ... scary. And I'm kind of glad you're here."

"Yeah?"

"I didn't get to thank you for saving my life. Again."

"It's nothing."

"Would you like to come in? I have some ... tea or pop. Or snacks?"

Evie's soft brown eyes looked up at him, and all he wanted to do was take her in his arms again and bury his nose in her hair until everything—the nightmares, the memories, the list in the envelope, the entire fucked-up world—melted away. But he couldn't. He had one single goal, one purpose. And when he was done, it would be the end.

"I can't." He turned away.

"Connor. Connor!"

But he ignored her calls and picked up his pace, racing down the stairs and out into the warm spring night.

---

*E*vie stared after Connor's retreating back, her mouth open. After a few seconds, she shut the door and let out a sigh. What the hell was going on?

She walked back into the living room, where Jack was sitting on the couch, still in his robe, slippers, and face mask, his arms crossed over his chest.

"So, what did Mr. McBroodypants want?"

"He just wanted to make sure I was okay," she said. "I told you about the accident at the theater."

"Wasn't that hours ago?" he asked, eyebrow raised. "What did he really want?"

"I don't know." She shrugged.

Jack let out an exasperated sound. "Really Evie? Him trying to kill me with his bare hands didn't give you a clue?"

She stared at him, mouth open.

"C'mon. He was jealous. Greener than my green tea mud pack."

"Nuh-uh." She shook her head. "No way."

"Jesus, Evie." He sighed and put his hands up. "I know you're not stupid, but are you blind? That man has is baaaaaaad for you. And you have it bad for him."

"I do not," she denied.

He laughed. "Ooohhhh, Evie, I hope you have good health insurance."

"Why?"

"'Cause that man is going to wreck your pus—"

"Jack!" Evie blushed. No, she shouldn't be thinking of that. But the thought of having sex with Connor made heat creep up her neck and sent her cheeks aflame. That almost-kiss from the wedding replayed in her mind, and she found herself wondering what would have happened if she had just moved her head forward a few inches ... No, she shouldn't think about that.

6

Evie mentally prepared herself as she entered the theater through the backstage door. Every time she walked through this door was another day closer to opening night. She couldn't help but feel that zing of excitement she always got when entering the theater. That feeling, however, quickly dissipated when she walked by the dressing rooms.

"I just can't tell you how safe I feel now that you're here," Janelle cooed up at Connor. As they entered the petite pop star's dressing room, Evie couldn't help but watch them. Janelle looked ridiculous, wearing a tight crop top, skinny jeans, and platform heels that brought her up to Connor's shoulders. Though her outfit of yoga pants, sports bra and loose top were comfortable and appropriate for rehearsals, Evie suddenly felt underdressed and inadequate.

Connor's head turned in her direction, and Evie forced herself to look away. She ignored the hairs rising on the back of her neck as she felt Connor's gaze on her and walked to the stage where the rest of the cast was already assembled. Steven was already there and starting the rehearsal with blocking for the second scene.

As she heard the slamming of Janelle's dressing room door, a tightness gripped her chest. Connor was assigned to keep Janelle safe and, although Evie didn't want the pop star hurt, she just wished ...

She let out a frustrated sound. What did she want? Connor coming over last night to check on her was nice ... in a weird and awkward way.

"Evie, did you hear what I said?" Steven asked, his voice irritated. "Move to the left!"

"Right, sorry!"

The rest of the rehearsal progressed. It didn't escape her that there was no sign of their star and her bodyguard. She tried not to think about what they could be doing, all alone in Janelle's dressing room.

When they finally broke for lunch, Evie jogged over to the corner of the stage where she kept her towel and water bottle.

"Looks like hard work, all that dancing and singing."

Evie turned around as she was taking a drink and wiping the sweat from her forehead. "Oh, Mr. Ja—I mean, Aiden. I didn't realize you were here." He was dressed casually today, in a sports jacket, white button-down shirt, and dark pants.

"Sebastian asked that I handle this personally."

"Oh right." They made the announcement yesterday that, after the incident, they were tightening security around the theater and Atlantis had hired Creed Security.

"I didn't know you were an actress," he commented, the corner of his eyes crinkling as he gave her a genuine smile. "You really are talented."

"Thank you," she replied.

"Does this mean you'll be leaving Lone Wolf Security?"

"Oh no," she chuckled. "I'm afraid one show won't be enough to keep the bills paid. Killian understands and lets me work around the rehearsal schedule here."

"Oh."

"Hmmm?" Did he sound disappointed? "Were you hoping I'd quit?"

"Oh no, not if you don't want to," he quickly explained. "It's just that ..." he trailed off, then leaned forward to tuck a stray tendril of hair behind her ear. His fingers came in contact with her cheek, and she froze. "I was hoping to ask you out to dinner some night. But it probably wouldn't be appropriate, seeing as you're technically my employee."

Evie's breath caught in her throat. Aiden James was asking her out? They were flirting a bit at the wedding, but she just thought he was being nice. "I ... uh ..."

A ringing sound interrupted them, and Aiden fished his phone from his pocket. "Sorry," he said. "I gotta take this. I'll talk to you later, Evie." He gave her a nod and then walked away as he spoke into the phone.

Saved by the bell. Her shoulders relaxed as relief swept through her. She bit her lip. Would it be terrible, though, if she went out with Aiden? True, they worked for the same company, but she was in a different office—sort of—and he wasn't her direct boss.

As she contemplated her choices for lunch and walked toward the stage door exit, she realized she left her purse in the dressing room. She pivoted and turned to the direction of the backstage area. Most of the cast and crew had left for lunch, so it was quiet. As she opened the door to the dressing room, she felt a large, looming presence behind her.

She turned her head. "What—Connor?" She staggered inside as he stepped forward. Her heart slammed into her chest when she met his glowing eyes in the darkened room. The air felt thick, and her knees buckled.

Large, warm hands gripped her arm, and she was spun around, her back bumping against the wooden door.

"What did he want?" he growled.

"What? Who?"

"Aiden James," he said through clenched teeth. "What did he want?"

"What are you—Connor, what's gotten into you?"

"He was touching you, I saw it." His curt voice lashed at her.

She felt her temper rise in response. "So? What do you care?" Her words were met with furious silence, and her nostrils flared. "He was asking me out. On a date. And I—"

His lips covered hers hungrily, the warmth of them surprising her. His hands slid to her neck and buried themselves in her hair, before angling her head upward so he could kiss her even deeper. She opened up, letting his tongue slip into her mouth, shocking herself with her eager response to his kiss.

She moaned against his lips and moved her hands to his chest, feeling the hard muscles underneath the tight black shirt. His muscles tensed in response to her touch but relaxed as she inched higher to wrap her arms around his shoulders.

He pressed up against her, his lips never leaving hers. One hand moved down, brushing against the curves of her breast to the dip in her waist and lower still to the curve of her ass. His palm cupped one buttock and then moved to the back of her thigh to hook her leg around his waist. She gasped as his erection was suddenly cradled between her thighs and, for a moment, she thought of Jack's words last night and wondered how good her health insurance was.

It was was too much, and she pressed her hips up to rock against him, trying to find the right angle.

Connor dragged his lips away, leaving her mouth burning with fire. He trailed kisses down her jaw to her neck, his tongue licking the sensitive skin.

"Connor ..." She arched her back, pushing up against him. He ground his hips into her, The sensation made her shudder, and desire pooled between her legs. His other hand crept up her waist, under her shirt, and lifted the band of her sports bra to cup her breast.

Her mind whirled as white-hot heat began to build in her core. The ridge of his cock was pressed up right against her clit, and the sensation was mind numbing. She moved her hips faster, increasing the pressure. *So close ... almost ...*

A sudden high-pitched scream from outside made them pull apart. Connor let go of her leg and took a step back, his breathing ragged.

"Connor!" The cries were muffled through the door, but it was obviously Janelle.

They looked at each other, and Connor let out a curse. "I have to go."

"Uh-huh."

"I need to get through the door."

"Right." She quickly stepped aside and then gestured to the door, a move that made her feel like an idiot afterwards.

As Connor reached for the door handle, he looked at her. "I didn't—"

"Just go," she said in a flat voice. "Go do your job."

He let out an angry huff and nodded, then left her alone in the empty dressing room.

"Holy shit." Evie stared at the door. For moment, she wasn't sure what happened a split second ago really did happen and she felt like someone had dumped an entire bucket of ice water over her. But then, looking at her disheveled state—hair tugged out of her ponytail, bra over her boobs, and the definite damp state of her panties—she knew it really did happen. Connor kissed her and more. If they hadn't been interrupted, who knows how far it would have gone.

The hubbub outside the dressing room snapped her out of

her thoughts. She straightened her clothes and yanked open the door. As she walked toward Janelle's dressing room, there were more and more people gathering in the hallway, whispering and pointing.

Aiden James strode out of the dressing room, a large, long white box in hand. His face was drawn into a serious expression. He didn't say anything to Evie as they passed each other, only giving her a curt nod. The box he was holding didn't have a top so she couldn't help but glance inside. She stifled a gasp when she saw dead roses and the bloodied head of a rat inside.

This was serious. Who was trying to hurt Janelle? The production company obviously thought it was enough of a threat to hire Creed. If word got around, then it could shut down the show.

Evie paused and looked inside Janelle's dressing room. She felt ice spread through her stomach at what she saw. Connor's back was to her, but the arms wound around his waist were definitely Janelle's, as were the incontrollable sobs coming from behind him.

She paused but then pushed the feeling of jealousy deep down inside her. What happened between them was a fluke. Plus, she swore to herself a long time ago she would never get involved with a Lycan. And, besides, someone really was after Janelle. Although she hated how the other woman's body was pressed up against Connor, she really didn't wish any harm to Janelle. Swallowing all her emotions, she walked away, her fists clenched at her sides.

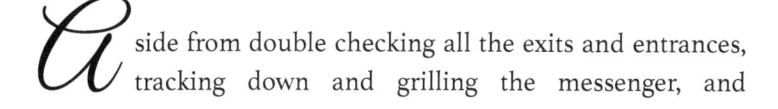

---

*A*side from double checking all the exits and entrances, tracking down and grilling the messenger, and reviewing the security tapes, there was not much else they could do, according to Aiden. He gave Evie the rundown of what had happened when she sought him out. Apparently, someone had snuck into the theater and left the package inside Janelle's dressing room. Not all of the security cameras at the theater were activated yet, and whoever came in had carefully avoided the ones that were working.

Annie, Jane, and Steven gathered the cast and crew to give them a pep talk. The show must go on, after all, and they continued rehearsals as usual. Of course, their star was too distraught to go on and had to be chauffeured back to her hotel suite to recover, as she was so traumatized from her ordeal.

After they wrapped for the day, Evie grabbed her stuff from the dressing room and waved goodbye to her cast mates. As she jogged toward the backstage exit, she stopped when she heard Connor's voice in one of the offices. The door was ajar, and she couldn't help but peek inside. He was avoiding her, she knew it. She hadn't seen hide nor hair of him since that kiss in the dressing room.

"You know I hardly ever ask you for a favor, Quinn," he said into his phone. "But I got stuff to do." He paused and his massive shoulders relaxed "Thank you. I'll come by the office and pick up Jolene."

Jolene? For a second, Evie thought he was going out with some girl, but she remembered that's what he called his truck.

"None of your business," Connor continued. "Yeah yeah, I owe you one. But don't tell anyone about this, ya hear?"

Evie scrambled away from the door and pivoted back to the exit. Really, she should ignore what she overheard. But she couldn't stop the curiosity from prickling at her. It was a niggling feeling that wouldn't go away. As she walked farther away from the theater, her heart began to pound and her gut started telling her something was wrong.

About two blocks away, as she stood on the corner of 44th and 7th Avenue, she stopped and fished her phone from her purse. Scrolling through her contacts, she dialed her former roommate's number. "Hello Selena? Yeah, it's me. I have a favor to ask ..."

7

The address Connor typed into his GPS brought him to a nondescript strip mall in the middle of central New Jersey. At first, he thought Quinn had made a mistake, but he should have had more faith in his brother. When he saw the sign for "Wolfman Gym," alarm bells went off in his head. *Goddamn indiscrete bastard.* But, then again, his former trainer had always been a showoff.

It should be closing time, but the lights inside the gym were on and there were still people lingering inside. Not that it mattered. He had waited years for this moment, and he could wait another few minutes if necessary.

But the wait was probably going to kill him, unless he could stop thinking about Evie and her delicious little body and velvety soft lips.

What happened today at the theater couldn't happen again. Seeing that asshole Aiden touch her had sent him over the edge. He wanted to cut his fucking fingers off or, maybe, even let the feral wolf loose on the human. He should have walked away, but his need to mark her as his was too great.

It was still so fresh in his mind—the press of her soft curves and that lush mouth. The memories of her smell mixed with her arousal threatened to overwhelm him, even now. If they hadn't been interrupted, he could have taken her right there, not giving a fuck who might have walked in.

His fingers gripped the wheel of his truck so tight his knuckles went white. When were these goddamn people going to leave?

The lights inside the gym turned off and, as soon as the last figure stepped out of the doors, the feral wolf stood at attention. Even from a distance, he recognized Booth's hulking frame. His red hair had turned gray. It had been more than fifteen years after all. As Booth turned his back to lock the door, Connor slid out of his truck.

Connor pushed back the memories that threatened to come to the surface. Fists and bloody noses. Being dunked in tanks of cold water as punishment. Cuts and bruises. The training at The Facility had been tough, but it produced the best fighters, all thanks to its sadistic trainer, David Booth. He didn't care that he was training young boys; he treated them like men. No, he treated them like animals. Connor supposed he should thank Booth for turning him into the fighter he was today. He let out a huff. Thank him for turning him into an animal? Maybe not.

He strode toward Booth with deliberate steps, his posture straight and shoulders squared. Anger, hate, disgust swirled inside him, but he relished the feeling. As his inner wolf made its presence known, he kept a tighter rein on it. He wanted to look into Booth's eyes first, before he let the wolf loose to claim its revenge.

As he drew nearer, Booth's stench—a mix of musk, cloves, and alcohol—filled his nostrils. "David Booth," he said. It wasn't a question.

The man turned around. He had the same square jaw, military haircut, and severe expression, though the years had added wrinkles around his eyes and mouth. "Yes?" Gray eyes like steel bore into Connor, and Booth's nostrils flared. Recognition flashed on his face. "You."

"Yes."

Booth let out a grunt. "You've grown, boy."

"Yes. And I'm not a boy. Not anymore."

"You'll always be that boy whose wolf was too scared to come out," Booth sneered, crossing his arms over his chest. The veins on his massive neck bulged. "But we sure took care of that, didn't we?" He bared his teeth as he smiled. "Well, I know this isn't some happy reunion. Do you want to do this here or in the alley in the back?" His eyes began to glow in the darkness.

Connor knew Booth wouldn't be an easy target like his former handler. Boyd had practically soiled himself when he got on his knees to beg for his life. "Let's go to the back."

Booth led him behind the gym. The alley smelled like a mix of garbage and motor oil, and there was a single light overhead. He turned around to face Connor. "You think you're the first to challenge me like this? To want revenge?"

"No, but I'll be the last." Connor cracked his knuckles.

Booth let out a sardonic laugh. "We'll see about that. You're good, boy, but remember who taught you."

Before he could react, Booth lunged at him. Connor had been overconfident, and he underestimated Booth's speed and strength, not to mention his penchant for playing dirty. They rolled on the ground, each fighting to get on top with his fists.

But Booth probably thought Connor was still that skinny kid he had trained long ago. Connor had learned more tricks since then. He leveraged his weight and threw Booth off him, sending him crashing to the brick wall.

Connor quickly got to his feet and launched himself at Booth, knocking his head back into the wall so hard his eyes rolled back. He smashed a fist into Booth's face; the sound of breaking bones echoed in his ears.

"Is that your best, boy?" Booth said with a grin, even as blood poured from his nostrils. "Are you going to let that monster inside you come out to play now?"

The feral wolf seemed to have heard him, and Connor felt him rising to the surface. His eyes glowed, and he felt the change coming.

Booth growled. "About fucking time." Muscles moved under his skin and brown fur sprouted on his skin as his face started to elongate.

Connor roared and stepped back as the wolf began to take over. The edges of his vision darkened as he felt the control slipping from his fingers. He felt like he was growing smaller, as if the wolf was tucking him away in that dark place where he couldn't see what was happening.

"No! Connor, don't!"

The voice knocked the wind out of him and tugged him back into his body. He looked up to the direction of the voice and blinked. "Quinn?"

His brother was standing by the entrance of the alley, but that wasn't the voice he heard. Before he could figure out what was happening, Booth, already fully transformed, sprung at him, knocking them both to the ground.

The dark brown wolf's giant teeth gnashed at him, its maw open and ready to chomp at his throat. As it came down on him, Connor suddenly felt the weight lifting off him. A golden brown blur leapt over him, knocking the other wolf down.

He blinked and got to his feet. Footsteps sounded behind him, and he turned. "Evie?"

She was running toward him, and he caught her in his arms. "Connor ... were you going to ..."

Growls and snarls made him turn his head. The two wolves

were circling each other, and the smaller, lighter brown one was limping. *Quinn.* His brother was strong, but he was no match for Booth. *Shit.* "Stay away," he told Evie, pushing her back.

He stomped over to the two wolves. The feral wolf would be able to take on Booth. It would be easy enough to let the beast rip into him. But he didn't want Evie to see it. He didn't want her to know the real monster lurking inside him. Besides, if he let it loose now, who knows what it could do to her. He reined it in, commanded the beast to stay quiet inside him.

As Booth's wolf rushed Quinn, Connor leapt between them, tackling Booth. He'd done his share of fighting Lycans even while in his human form, since turning into the feral wolf was always his last resort. The first thing he did was go for the throat. A well-placed punch in the trachea, with enough power, could take a Lycan down.

Booth let out a strangled cry as the wind was knocked out of him, and he collapsed. Connor kicked the animal on its side. When the wolf rolled over and exposed its underside, he stomped a boot-clad foot on his ribs. The satisfying crack of bones told him there was no way he was getting up. As Booth slowly began to turn back to his human form, Connor took the opening and delivered a fist to the other man's face to knock him out cold.

"Connor," a strangled cry came from behind. Quinn had changed back to his human form. He was clutching his side as he tried to get up; the claw marks running down his rib cage were still bleeding.

"What the fuck are you doing here?" he asked as he caught Quinn before he collapsed.

"I ... knew ... you were up to no good," Quinn said between ragged breaths. "This is why you wanted David Booth's address?"

"That's the last time I ask for your help. Fuck." He looked at the angry red wounds on his brother's torso.

"Goddammnit." Quinn sighed. "Selena's gonna kill me. Good thing it's already healing."

"Connor ... Quinn!" Evie rushed toward them.

He had nearly forgotten about her. He wiped the blood from his fists on his pants, hoping she wouldn't see them.

Her eyes widened when she saw Quinn. "Are you okay? Oh my God." As she tried to check on his brother, Connor quickly stepped between them.

"What are you doing here? Did Quinn bring you here?"

"Shit no," Quinn answered. "She brought me here."

"What?"

"Yeah, she called Selena and Selena called me," Quinn explained. "She asked me where you were going and when she insisted on coming to follow you, I said you'd kick my ass if I let her go alone. So, we all drove here."

"You were following me?" Connor said.

"Technically, we knew where you were going so following wasn't necessary," his brother pointed out. "Evie was the one who wanted to follow you."

He swung his head down to stare at Evie. "How did you know I was coming here? Were you eavesdropping at the theater?"

Evie craned her neck up to look at him. "What's going on, Connor? Who is that man? Were you going to ..."

"It's none of your business," he growled and stepped back, turning away from her. He didn't want to see her face, not when he knew what she thought of him. She didn't need to see the feral wolf. She already thought he was a monster.

He stormed out of the alley, walking across the parking lot, crossing it in record time. As he reached his truck, a growl ripped from his throat and he slammed his fist into the driver's side door, leaving a dent.

"Fuck!" he cried, then slapped his palms on the hood.

"Connor, please, don't go."

He froze, as if her words were forcing him to stay still. Slowly, he pivoted. She was jogging toward him.

When she reached him, she braced herself on the side of his truck, her other hand on her heaving chest. "Connor ... please ... tell me what's going on."

"I ..." Pain surged inside him and he clenched his jaw.

"You can tell me," she said in a soft, soothing voice. A palm landed on his cheek, tracing the scar there. "Did that man ... hurt you?"

He closed his eyes and placed a hand over hers. She was so small compared to him. Delicate and gentle. It was a wonder she didn't break, yet, that world hadn't beaten her down. He swallowed and nodded.

A small cry escaped her mouth, and she moved closer, wrapping her arms around his waist and laying her head on his chest. He stiffened for a moment, then relaxed. "It's okay," she soothed. "He won't hurt you anymore."

"He hasn't hurt me in years," Connor answered, his arms going around her and pulling her close. "I escaped, thanks to Archie."

"He was from your past," she stated. "Was he your family?"

"No. I didn't have a family. Not before Archie." He took a deep breath. "I can't remember anything from before The Facility."

"The Facility?"

He gave a curt nod. "That's what they called it. A place where they trained Lycans in secret."

"Trained them for what?"

"To fight." He felt her tense, but, when he tried to pull away, she held onto him tighter. "There was maybe a dozen of us. Booth ... that guy ... he was the one who taught us to fight. Or scared us into fighting."

She sucked in a breath. "How old were you?"

"I can't remember. But we started training before we learned to shift. So maybe around ten or eleven." He swallowed a lump in his throat. "The best ones ... we went on to fight in The Cage."

"What for?" she asked in a shaky voice.

"For fun. For sport. There were always people watching us. Cheering us on. Probably betting on us."

"That's ... horrible."

Horrible didn't even begin to describe it, but Connor didn't elaborate. When she pulled away, the tightness in his chest returned. She was scared now, disgusted by what he was. More beast than man. A murderous animal.

"That wasn't ... you shouldn't have been ... no child should ..." She choked and bit her lip, but, even in the darkness, he could see the tears clouding her eyes. "He deserved that beating you gave him then," she said, her voice furious. She moved back into his arms and rubbed her cheek on his chest. "I didn't know ... I'm so sorry, Connor."

Her action and words caught him off guard, and he was speechless. Evie wasn't recoiling from him. Instead, she came back to him, to his arms.

They held each other, and time seemed to stand still. Connor breathed in her sweet scent and enjoyed the feel of her soft curves against him. Memories of what happened earlier that day came back. The taste of her lush little mouth and the way she pressed up against him. The smell of her arousal mixed with her peach scent. He wanted to—

"Connor! Evie!" Selena's voice cut across the parking lot and made them pull apart. "Where's Quinn?" Her voice was shaky, her blue-gray eyes filled with worry. "Evie, what happened?"

"Oh fuck," Connor cursed. "Let's go get him."

The three of them walked to the alley, and Evie caught Selena up on what happened, at least about the fight with Booth. When they reached the spot where they left his brother, Selena rushed to Quinn, who was standing over the still knocked-out Booth.

"About time," Quinn said with a huff.

"Quinn, why are you naked?" Selena asked as she launched herself at him.

"It's nothing you haven't seen before, Kitten," he said with a laugh. "Ouch!"

"Are you hurt?" she asked when she pulled back and stared at his wounds. "Are those claw marks? Quinn, you idiot! I can't believe you got into a fight with another Lycan."

"Awww, baby, I had to," he said. "C'mere ... I'm fine, I promise. Besides, Wolf needed the exercise."

"Next time, join a CrossFit class," she said dryly but accepted his hug.

Quinn kissed the top of her head, then turned to Connor. "Are you going to tell us what this is about, bro?"

Connor huffed out a breath, but, before he could tell Quinn to fuck off, Evie put a hand on his arm. "I'll take care of this," she said, looking up at him with her soft, brown eyes. "Let us take care of you for once."

8

Evie never thought of herself as a go-getter, take-charge kinda gal, so she surprised even herself when she came up with a plan.

A quick call confirmed that David Booth was living in New Jersey but was not properly registered with the clan nor did he ask permission from their Alpha, which was a clear violation of several Lycan laws. That meant they could bring him in for questioning and keep him locked up, maybe even get more information from him about The Facility. After getting permission from the Alphas of New Jersey and New York, Frankie and Grant Anderson, they tied up Booth and put him in the back of Connor's Dodge Ram to bring him back to New York.

Fury blasted through her at what Connor had told her. She could hear the pain in his voice, so she didn't press on, but she understood enough. Connor had grown up in that place where they trained him to fight for sport. She couldn't imagine what he went through. In this case, she wondered if the reality was much worse than the horrors in her mind.

Evie rode with Connor in the front cab of the truck, while Selena and Quinn followed them in his Range Rover. The drive was silent and tense, and Evie sighed in relief when she saw the skyline of Manhattan up ahead.

When they arrived at the Fenrir Corporation Building on Madison Avenue, which was also the unofficial headquarters of the New York Clan, there were already several people waiting for them, including the Alpha himself and his Beta. As two of the Alpha's Lycan security crew took the unconscious Booth to the basement detention levels, they were ushered into the Alpha's office on the top floor. Killian, Meredith, and Daric were already inside.

Evie had never met Grant Anderson or his Beta, Nick Vrost, but she quickly realized why they held such high positions in the most powerful Lycan clan in the world. Though several of the other Lycans towered over him, Grant exuded a power and confidence like no one else. Nick Vrost, too, commanded respect with his mere presence and his ice-blue eyes that seemed to know and see everything.

"Frankie had to stay home with the twins, but she's authorized formal charges against David Booth, and the Lycan High Council has been informed," Grant said, referring to his wife and Alpha of New Jersey. He turned to Connor and Quinn. "Now, care to tell me what you were doing there?"

"It was personal business," Connor said.

"When you beat up a rogue Lycan in my wife's territory and then bring him to mine, that makes it my business," Grant replied. "Now, want to try that again? Or am I going to have to ask you to leave New York?"

Evie tried to keep her mouth shut, but the words came spilling out of her mouth. "That man hurt children! Lycan children." She gasped when all eyes in the room landed on her. "He deserves worse than what he got from Connor."

"And you are?" Nick asked, a blond brow raised.

"Uh ... E-Evie King," she stuttered. "I work for Lone Wolf. As their administrative assistant."

"A human?" Grant said, looking at the two brothers. "You two shifted in front of a human?"

"No, Alpha." Evie shook her head. "I mean, yes, I'm human. But my mother is Amelia White of the Kansas Clan. It's why Killian hired me."

"All right, Evie King." Grant looked at her with his piercing green eyes. "Connor's not fond of talking or explaining himself, so why don't you tell me what happened."

"No," Connor interrupted before she could say anything. "Fuck you all; I don't have to explain myself to any of you."

"Please, Connor," Evie said, rubbing her palm on his arm. "It's all right. You can tell them what you told me."

"Connor?" Meredith stepped forward. "What's going on?"

Connor let out a frustrated grunt. His eyes went hard and his mouth set into a grim line. "David Booth ... he trained me."

"Go on," Evie encouraged.

Connor told her what he told Evie about The Facility and The Cage. The tension was thick as molasses in the room, and even Evie could feel it choking her. Grant and Nick remained stoic, but she could sense the anger radiating from them like waves. Quinn placed a hand protectively over Selena's belly, and tears rolled down Meredith's face as she listened to what happened to her brother.

"Could this be connected to the mages?" Nick asked when Connor concluded.

"Maybe. It doesn't matter," Grant said. "There may be more Lycans out there who need our help. David Booth will be able to tell us more when he wakes up."

"Booth is mine," Connor said. "I'm going to take care of him."

"You can't kill him," Grant replied. "Lycan law—"

"Fuck Lycan law," Connor shouted, which made Nick stand protectively in front of Grant.

"Stand down, Connor," Killian said, raising a hand. "Sorry, Alpha." He nodded to Grant. "We will follow Lycan law."

"Goddamn you all, I'm going to get—" Connor stopped short.

"You're not after him, are you?" Nick said. "I mean, you want Booth dead, but you want something else, too."

"Who else are you after?" Grant paused, then narrowed his eyes. "It's their ringleader you want. Whoever ran the Facility and took you from your family."

Connor said nothing, but his silence confirmed it.

Grant let out a sigh. "If The Facility was a training ground run by mages, then you may already be too late. Their leader may be dead or in prison."

Connor shook his head. "No, he's still out there."

"How—You know who he is," Grant guessed.

He nodded. "He wasn't at the battle in Norway."

Grant sighed. "I need you all to step outside while I talk to Nick," he said.

Everyone filed out of the office and into the waiting room. Evie stayed by Connor's side, even as he tried to distance himself by walking to the other side of the room. She swallowed the lump in her throat. Connor was probably mad at her. He wouldn't even look at her.

"Connor," Meredith called softly as she came closer. "I didn't know. I'm so sorry." Her mate, Daric, was behind her, and he and Connor exchanged knowing looks.

His shoulders sagged. "How could you? I never told you. Any of you. Only Archie knew the whole story."

Meredith stepped forward and wrapped her arms around him, her body wracking with sobs. Evie felt her own eyes fill with tears, and she turned away so no one would see her.

The door of the office opened, and Grant and Nick stepped out.

"David Booth will stay here until his trial with the Lycan High Council," Grant said. "If you can testify and gather evidence, I'm sure we can get him for more than breaking the Constanta Agreement."

"I'll testify."

"And I'm sure we can find the evidence," Quinn said.

"We'll do what we can to find it," Killian added.

"Good," Grant said with a nod. "Now, their leader. Do you know him or where he is?"

Connor shook his head. "No. He was the one guy who wasn't on Archie's list."

"I bet Booth knows," Meredith said as she wiped her cheeks with the back of her hand. "We can make him talk."

"We can leverage whatever evidence we find against him," Killian said. "We'll get him, Connor."

"I told you, I don't need your help."

"Well, you'll get it anyway," Meredith said. "Because we're family."

Connor grunted. "Fine. But, if I find him, I want to be the one to bring him in." Without another word, he stomped away and headed to the elevators.

Evie watched him go with a heavy heart. Each step he took away made her chest feel heavier and heavier, and, when the elevator door closed, she flinched. The last thing she saw was Connor's face, harder than steel and colder than ice.

An arm landing on her shoulder made her turn her head. Meredith stared at her, her whisky-brown eyes still wet with tears.

"Thank you," Meredith whispered. "For everything you've done."

"I didn't do anything," Evie replied, then her shoulders sagged. "If anything, I made him even more angry."

The Lycan shook her head. "No, you've done more than you know. If it wasn't for you, we wouldn't have known what was hurting him."

Evie swallowed the lump in her throat. She wasn't sure she agreed with Meredith. The look on his face when he walked away would always be etched in her mind.

9
―――――

*E*vie dragged herself out of bed the next day to head to the theater. She was grateful to be working on the stage and for the distraction. Theater was her life and the one place she could forget about her worries. But, still, she was exhausted because she couldn't sleep last night, thinking about what had happened with Booth. What happened to Connor when he was a kid. What he had planned to do when he hunted Booth down. And the cold, dead look in his eyes. Despite growing up Catholic, Evie wasn't religious, but she did fear for Connor's soul.

"What the heck?" Her brows furrowed as she walked up to the backstage entrance of the theater. There was a crowd building by the door. What was going on? "Excuse me," she said as she pushed her way to the front. "Hey! Get out of my way; I need to get in!"

"Watch it!" A guy with a professional camera blocked her way.

"I'm a cast member; I have to get in."

A woman with blond hair turned around and then shoved a phone at her. "You're a cast member? I'm a blogger from

Broadway World Daily. We heard that someone's been threatening Janelle Edwards and there have been a number of accidents. Care to comment on that?"

"What?" A flash blinded her. "Um ... Sorry, I just need to get to work."

"Evie!" Aiden James' head popped out from the stage door. He pushed back some of the people and grabbed her hand.

Evie let Aiden pull her in as the crowd descended on her. The door shut with a thud, and she put her hand over her chest. "What's going on?"

Aiden's face was drawn into a serious expression. "Someone leaked to the press about the accident and the threats that Janelle's been getting. Damn sharks came here, smelling blood in the water."

"Jesus."

"Yeah, it's made my life extra hard." He puffed out a breath. "You okay? I'm gonna have barriers put up outside the door. Janelle's fans are also gathering in front, in support of their star." He shook his head. "Damn thing's turning into a circus. Sebastian's not going to be happy since MacAllister wants extra security now."

"I'm sorry."

He shrugged. "All part of the job. Janelle isn't even here yet. I'll have to ask Connor for help with crowd control when she finally arrives."

She gave him a tight smile. "Yeah, good thing. I should go ..."

"Sure," he said, giving her a bright look. "I'll talk to you later."

After dropping off her stuff in the dressing room, she joined the rest of the cast onstage. They were all chatting and waiting for Steven and the writers to arrive. By the time thirty minutes had passed, it was clear there was something major causing the delay. Did the insurance company hear about the accident?

Were they being shut down? No one said it out loud, though there were whispers and mumbles among the cast.

Finally, Steven walked onto the stage, the look on his face unreadable. Behind him, Jane and Annie followed, wearing similar expressions. "All right everyone, our *star* is feeling under the weather this morning but assures us she's on the way."

"Yeah, I'm sure that bottle of champagne did a number on her," someone snickered.

"No!"

"I saw it on her Instagram. She was out partying all night with her celebutard friends."

Steven shushed them, but, with the way his eyes rolled, he clearly knew Janelle's excuses were bullshit. "Anyway, we need to work around her, so let's see what we can accomplish." A young PA scrambled up the stage and approached Steven, then whispered something in his ear. "Fine," he said with a shrug. "Tech wants to practice the Act One finale."

"But we need Janelle for that," Jane pointed out.

"No, Evie can substitute," Annie said. "Right Steven?"

"That's what I was thinking," Steven answered. "At least we can actually get some practice in, and the tech guys don't need Janelle. They just need to make sure the lighting's correct. Evie, are you ready?"

Evie felt all eyes on her. Sing the last song of Act One? She loved that song. It was about love and heartbreak, and the melody was incredibly moving. But her heart sank because she would never get to sing that song for the show and in front of an audience. "Sure," she said, swallowing the bitterness building in her.

Steven gave her a few directions, and she took her position on stage. The music began. She took a deep breath and began to sing. The main character, Colleen, was singing about finding someone who accepted her as she was. During the workshop, she thought of her own life and experiences, trying to capture the feeling in that song. Back then, when she sang it, she thought about Richard. But, as she sang it now, another face popped in her head. A pain pricked in her heart, thinking about what happened to Connor. After last night, she finally knew what he had been hiding all this time, but none of it scared her. Instead, it made her admire him more, that he went through all that and came out the other side stronger and better.

After she finished the last note of the song, Evie took a breath, feeling drained. When the orchestra stopped, there was silence. She blinked and opened her eyes. Annie and Jane were sitting in the front row; both of them had astonished looks on their faces. Behind her, there was a slow clap, which then broke out into full applause. She turned, and her cast mates were smiling and cheering. A blush crept up her neck, and she gave a little bow.

"What's going on here?" A sharp voice cut through the cheer and there was silence again. Janelle made her way to the front of the crowd.

"Janelle, nice of you to join us," Steven said. "Feeling better?"

Janelle's lips curled up into a sweet smile. "Why yes, I am, thanks for asking." She turned to Evie, her eyes hateful. "And thanks for warming up the musicians for me, Stevie."

"It's Evie," she corrected.

"Right." She flipped her hair and motioned at Evie. "Well, scooch over, I'm here now." Evie's shoulders sagged, and she stepped aside. "Don't go too far, though, Stevie," Janelle instructed. "You are my helper, right? I might need a water or something."

"C'mon, let's get on with it," Steven said. "Let's pick up where we left off yesterday."

Evie stuck close to Janelle, feeding her lines and the blocking. However, when it came to the dance number, it was obvious the pop star needed much more work.

"Janelle, you're supposed to walk upstage, not downstage," Steven said.

"I am going up front," she answered, her hands on her hips.

"No, darling," Steven sneered. "Upstage means the back, not the front."

"That's stupid," she whined.

"It was from the olden days when the stage used to slope down," Evie pointed out.

"I know that," Janelle retorted. "I was just saying how stupid it is."

"Let's get on with it," Steven said in an exasperated voice. "Opening day isn't getting any farther away, people! Let's take it from the top of the scene."

There was a collective groan from the cast, but they all trudged back to their opening positions. As they continued with the rehearsal, Evie was beginning to lose her patience. Janelle simply didn't have proper stage training, and it was draining to have to correct her all the time.

"Stop bumping into me," Janelle snapped.

"Then remember which way you're supposed to go," Evie replied, her temper flaring. "You start stage left, not house left."

Janelle's face twisted into an ugly mask, her eyes narrowing into slits. "You watch where you're going, you clumsy cow."

There was a collective gasp, followed by a deafening silence that settled over the stage. Evie's face went completely red, and she froze on the spot.

"Janelle, that's utterly inappropriate," Steven finally said, throwing his script down. "Apologize to Evie now."

"I will not," Janelle said, stomping her foot. "She keeps breathing down my neck, and I can't concentrate. It's her fault! Andrew!" she screamed. "Where is Andrew? I demand to speak to him. I'm going to my dressing room," she said with a flip of her blond locks. She stomped off. Everyone was speechless and looking around as if to say, "*Did that really happen?*"

As Evie watched Janelle walk away, she locked eyes with Connor. She didn't realize he had been there the whole time. She flushed again in embarrassment and bit her lip to stop the tears from falling.

Steven threw his hands up. "I guess that means take five. Not that I have a say in it. After all, I'm only the director of a multi-million dollar Broadway show." With a shrug of his shoulders, he strode off the opposite side of the stage.

"What a bitch," Daniel Roberts, one of the guys in the chorus with Evie, said as he put an arm around her. "You're so much more talented than that skinny ho. After that song, I swear I heard a couple people sniffling in the back. You know they only need her for ticket sales."

She swallowed the bitterness building inside her and took a deep breath. "You don't have to say that to make me feel better."

"It's true," Nicole Anderson, the dance captain, said. "She couldn't even remember the simplest steps. She looks like a fish flopping around on stage. I think the only dance moves she knows are twerking and flipping her hair."

Evie giggled. "Right. C'mon, let's sit down and catch our breath."

Evie and the rest of the cast emptied out into the backstage area where there were snacks and drinks set up for the cast. She grabbed a bottle of water and downed half the thing, but it didn't make the embarrassment go away. As she reached for a donut, she suddenly withdrew her hand, remembering Janelle's hurtful words. *Clumsy cow*. She flinched inwardly, knowing what the pop star really wanted to say.

"Evie, I need to talk to you," Andrew MacAllister said as he came up to her.

"Yes?"

Andrew's brows were drawn together, his face a serious mask. "I spoke with Janelle; she's not happy with what happened today."

"Well, neither am I."

"She wants you to apologize to her."

Evie crushed the water bottle in her hand. "What? She wants *me* to apologize to *her*?"

"Yes. Or she wants you gone."

The wind rushed out of her lungs like someone had punched her in the gut. Well, they might as well have because she suddenly couldn't find the words.

"Look, Evie," Andrew began. "It's just two little words. *I'm sorry*. Swallow your pride and you can save the show. You know, people in this business have long memories."

"I ..." What could she say? She was a nobody, a newcomer to the business. Two words could save the show and her career. "Fine," she said. "I'll do it." She clenched her fists so hard, her fingernails left crescent-shaped marks in her palms. Still, she wouldn't let Janelle see look defeated. She was a professional, Goddamnit, and she owed it to the cast, to Annie, to Jane, and to Steven to make sure the show was a success.

By the time Evie reached Janelle's dressing room door, she was feeling confident. She raised a hand to knock, but a noise inside made her stop. Pressing her ear to the door, she listened.

10

Connor had never wanted to hit a woman before. Indeed, it was one of those rules in his life that no one had needed to instill in him; you just didn't do that. Still, if anyone was to test his self-control, it'd be Janelle.

When he heard her call Evie a clumsy cow, he nearly lost it. The way Evie's face fell made something in his middle ache. A scratching feeling in his gut and the tightening in his chest sent fury through his veins, and he thought the feral wolf might come out. He wanted to check if Evie was okay, but he couldn't do anything more than glance at her as Janelle stormed off. That bitch. How dare she say those words to Evie? Evie was worth a hundred times more than her, and Connor knew she was beautiful inside and out. Janelle was rotten to the core, and he could practically smell the hate festering within the other woman when she looked at Evie.

He followed Janelle back to her dressing room, and each step away from Evie made his feet feel more and more like lead. She stomped into the room like a child and sat down on the chair in front of the dressing table, her face drawn into a scowl. Minutes later, that slimy bastard Andrew MacAllister came in, cowering and bowing down to Janelle like she was the queen of fucking England.

"Connor," she cooed when Andrew had left.

His jaw ticked. "What?"

"Can you come here, please?" she asked, her voice sickly sweet.

"I'm fine right here," he said, not moving an inch.

She flipped around, the chair scraping on the wooden floor. "Fine, I'll come to you, then." She stood up, moving slowly like a cat as she approached him. "You know, I never thanked you properly for saving my life the other day and for keeping me safe."

"It's my job." He peered down at her. "What are you doing?"

Janelle pushed her suspiciously firm breasts up against his chest. "Oh, you know exactly what I'm doing," she purred and placed her palms on his pecs. "You must work out a lot. You're hard. Where else are you hard?"

"Lady, you're testing my patience," he said, his jaw clenched. He wrapped his fingers around her wrists and pulled them away from him.

"Oh, Connor ... I like it rough, just like that," she said, her eyes wild.

He let go of her wrists and pushed her way. "Lady, you better watch what you say."

"Why, Connor? Am I going to get it?" She tried to move closer, but he sidestepped. "Oh, c'mon, do I really have to spell it out? I want you to fuck me, Connor. Do it now." She began to unbutton her blouse.

"Jesus H. Christ." Connor ran his hand down his face. "Look, I can't do this."

"I know you're professional and all," she insisted. "But don't worry, I won't tell anyone."

"Fuck this," Connor growled. "I can't deal with your shit

anymore." Ignoring her strangled cry, he turned around and yanked the door open.

The lingering scent of peaches hung in the air which made him think of Evie. But she wasn't there. He looked around at the empty hallway. He must have imagined it.

"Seriously?" Aiden James said when Connor told him what had happened with Janelle in her dressing room.

"You think I'm a liar?" Connor replied.

"No, it's not that," Aiden chuckled. "You know, most of my guys would jump at the chance to bang a celebrity."

"Maybe you've been hiring the wrong guys," he replied.

"What do you want to do? File a sexual harassment suit? Or leave the job? I'm sure I could find—"

"Fuck no," he interrupted. "I'll be fine. I think she got the message. I'm just tellin' you in case there's any blowback."

"We take care of our own," Aiden said in a serious voice. "Don't worry, I'll put this in my report and, if she tries anything again, we have your back."

Despite his disdain for the other man, Connor couldn't help but respect Aiden. "Good."

The rest of the day progressed without further incident, though, as Connor watched Evie, he could see her shrink away. Gone was her usual confidence and enthusiasm. Her shoulders were hunched in, and she kept her head down when she thought no one was looking. He couldn't see her face, though, because she seemed determined not to look at him. A feeling in his gut told him something was very wrong, and he trusted his instinct.

Finally, the day was over. Janelle had been escorted to her

waiting limo, and Connor was free. Instead of heading out, however, he went back through the stage door.

There were still some people lingering about, though most of the lights had been turned off. Connor immediately spotted Evie, talking to a few of the other members of the cast. He stepped back into the shadows, waiting as they left and Evie hung behind. She walked back to the dressing rooms, and he followed her, slipping into the room quietly.

Evie was in front of the mirrored vanities, her palms on the table and her head hung low. Her shoulders were shaking.

"Why are you crying?"

Her head whipped around, and she quickly wiped her wet cheeks with the back of her hand. "What are you doing here?" Her voice was cold and accusing.

"I wanted to check if you were all right. I can take you home."

"I'm fine. Now leave me alone," she said and turned her back to him. She walked to the other dresser and picked up her purse. "I said leave me alone. Just go."

The tone of her voice made his middle ache. "You're not all right. Something's bothering you."

"Don't you have somewhere else to be?" she asked. "I'm sure Janelle doesn't like to be kept waiting." She pushed past him and walked to the door.

He reached out, grabbed her by the arm, and spun her around. "What are you talking about?"

"Let go of me, Connor," she said in a voice laced with hate. "Janelle may like it rough, but I don't."

"You *were* eavesdropping outside the dressing room." Her face confirmed it. Fuck. "What did you hear?"

"Enough," she said, wrenching away from him.

"Obviously not." He grabbed her, as gentle as he could this time, and pulled her back. He positioned her against one of the dressers and trapped her with his arms on either side of her. "Because if you did, you'd know I told her to fuck off. I don't want her."

She looked up at him, her breathing hard and her chest heaving. "I don't believe you. Everyone wants her."

"Well, everyone is stupid because that girl is disgusting." He leaned forward, backing her up farther, as if he were afraid she'd try to run.

She gasped and turned away. "You don't have to lie to me. I'm not stupid. She's gorgeous and thin, and I'm a clumsy fat cow—"

Something in him roared to make her stop talking about herself that way. He had to let her know how beautiful she was. So, he did the only thing he could to stop her mouth. He kissed her. His lips moved over hers in a rough caress, silencing her. Much like the first time he kissed her, in this very same room, she seemed surprised. But, soon, she yielded to him, and her arms wound around his neck to get closer.

His hands cupped her soft ass and lifted her up so she sat on top of the dresser. She angled her head back, opening herself to him and his tongue swept into her mouth. He swore she tasted just as she smelled, and, when the scent of her arousal hit his nose, he felt his cock go instantly hard.

"Connor," she moaned against his lips. "Please."

Did she know what she was asking? As she pulled back from him to whip her shirt off, he guessed she did. She reached for the zipper on the front of her bra, but he pushed her hands away. He yanked it down and nearly ripped off the spandex. He hooked his thumbs into the waistband of her yoga pants, pulling them down. She wiggled her hips and lifted her ass so he could slide them down her thighs, along with her panties. Off they went, and she was fully naked in front of him. Fuck, she was gorgeous like this. Nude and showing off her perfect, soft skin, flushed with pink. How the hell could she think she wasn't beautiful? His eyes greedily devoured the pale skin of her generous breasts, topped with large, light brown nipples. He bent his head and took the right one into his mouth, enjoying the taste and feel of her. Slightly salty and all Evie. His hand cupped her left breast, teasing her nipple into hardness. She whimpered and dug her fingers into his shoulders as his tongue lashed against her.

"No more teasing," she said, pulling him up. Her hands reached down to the front of his jeans, shaking as she unbuckled his belt. He helped her along, making quick work of the fly.

She gasped when he pulled his jeans and briefs down to his thighs. Small, soft hands wrapped around his shaft, and he groaned when she began to stroke him. He snaked a hand between her thighs and down to her wet folds. His fingers traced the slit and pushed gently into her. One, two fingers slipped inside, and she began to rock her hips forward. She was slick and ready, but, just to be sure, he twisted his hand and brushed a thumb over her clit.

She cried out, her hips moving faster. Her hand slowed down as her body began to shake, and she cried out his name. His fingers were soaked with her wetness. He pulled out, making her whimper as she came down from her orgasm. Evie collapsed against him, her breathing ragged.

Her grip had loosened around him, but her soft palms were still wrapped around his shaft. He placed a hand over hers, urging her to continue.

"No," she said, shaking her head. "Inside me. Now."

He felt his hand shake slightly as he spread her legs wide and moved between her thighs. Grasping his cock, he nudged the tip at her entrance. In one stroke, he was fully inside her.

She let out a sob, going very still. He froze, wondering if he had hurt her.

"Don't stop," she gasped and clenched around him. "I want ..."

Connor gritted his teeth and began to move. He pulled her to the edge of the table and hooked her legs around him. He thrust in and out of her; the feel of her tight, clasping body made him move faster. It was like he couldn't get close enough. He wanted more and more. And she matched him, pushing up at him, meeting his every thrust, her hand moving down to his ass to clutch at him, urging him on.

It was too much, and he gritted his teeth, trying to hold on or else he might embarrass himself. With her willing, delicious body wrapped around him and her scent enveloping his being, he wanted nothing more than to lose control. "Evie," he gasped as she tightened around him, her body convulsing.

"Oh God, I'm coming," she cried out against his neck. She wrapped her legs around his waist, her heels digging into his back as she continued to move against him.

He let out a roar after months of frustration. Wanting her, but never being able to get too close. Now, he let go. As he gave one last thrust, his cock pumped into her, his seed releasing deep inside her. The pleasure tore through him, nearly blinding him. He was surprised at the force and strength of his orgasm. Fuck, he couldn't remember coming so hard in his life.

Connor wasn't sure how long they remained there, clinging to each other. Her legs unwound from his waist and dropped to the side. He didn't even realize he had been clutching her so hard, and he let go. Slowly, he eased himself out of her. He heard her suck in her breath.

He looked down at her flushed face. Tendrils of hair stuck to her cheeks and forehead. The expression on her face was inscrutable. She looked around her, at the ceiling and the walls, anywhere except at him.

Finally, she sucked in a long breath. He stepped back to give her some space. She hopped off the dresser and bent down to her discarded panties and yoga pants.

Connor groaned when he saw her naked ass for the first time. He wanted to grab the white globes, push her against the dresser, and take her again. With a frustrated grunt, he tucked his cock into his underwear and jeans.

Her movements were stiff and measured as she put on her bra and her top. He could hear the wheels in her mind turning and the anxiety rolling off her. Her unease was driving him crazy, especially after what had happened between her and Janelle.

"Evie?" he asked. His throat went dry when she finally looked up at him. Her face was that of pure panic.

"This ... we shouldn't have ... I can't," she cried and turned around.

She was scared. She regretted what they had done. He should let her go because she should be scared of him. But something inside him just couldn't let go.

"Evie," he called as she approached the door to the dressing room. She was reaching for the door and had it partially opened, but he slammed a fist to close it. The thud of the door made her jump.

Slowly, she turned to face him. "Connor ... I'm sorry. I couldn't help myself ... I shouldn't have."

"Sorry?" The wind knocked out of his lungs. "What do you mean?"

She shook her head. "I was so upset. So jealous. I let it get the better of me. I wanted to rip Janelle's head off when I heard you and her ..."

Jealous? Evie had been jealous? "We didn't do anything," he explained again. "You know that, right?"

"I believe you," she said and looked down at the floor. "But you didn't have to ... do that because you felt sorry for me."

"What?" he asked in an incredulous voice. "You thought that was a pity fuck or something?"

"Wasn't it?"

"Hell, no." He gripped her arms, and, before she could say anything, he swooped down and kissed her again.

"Connor," she whispered when he pulled away. Soft brown eyes blinked up at him. "I ..."

He said the first thing that popped into his head. "You're beautiful. Don't let anyone tell you otherwise. And there's no way I felt sorry for you. I wanted—want—you so bad, too."

"Y-y-you do?"

"Yes, I have all this time." A weight lifted off his chest at the admission. It felt good. He wanted her from the first moment he saw her.

"Me, too," she admitted.

He kissed her again, pulling her close to him. Fuck, he wanted to be inside her again. Maybe he'd taste her first. Bury his face between her thighs and make her scream. He bet she was delicious.

A growled rumbled from his throat. *No. Not now. Please.* He never asked the feral wolf for anything, but he wanted to be selfish this once. Evie was his, not the wolf's. But the animal inside him licked its lips and let out a howl. He pulled back.

"Connor?" she asked. "Are you okay?"

"Yes ... I'm ... it's getting late." He stepped back, away from her scent and her luscious body as he regained control of his mind. "You have an early day tomorrow again."

"Yeah, I suppose. So, do you live near here?"

His jaw hardened at the thought of his "home." He'd been

camped out at the W Hotel on the Upper East Side, in a suite that overlooked Central Park. It was beautiful, but, somehow, the thought of Evie seeing how he lived tore at him. Plus, there was the fact that his control over the feral wolf was slipping. He couldn't risk her being alone with the animal if it escaped while he was asleep.

"It's getting late," he said, ignoring her earlier question. "You'll need your rest."

"Oh, right." She squared her shoulders. "I can take the subway."

"No," he protested. "I'll get you a cab and make sure you get home."

11

"Are you okay, Evie?" Annie asked.

"Huh?" Evie jumped, then turned around and put her hand on her chest. "Yeah, I'm fine. I just have a lot on my mind."

"You look like you haven't slept. And now you're walking around like a zombie." The older woman narrowed her eyes at her. "What's wrong? Was it what happened yesterday?"

"No, I'm fine. Really."

Annie leaned in. "You know, I can't remember the last time you sang that song so well. I swear, I've heard it a million times on the recording, but yesterday was the first time it made me break out in goosebumps."

She blushed. "It's a great song. You and Jane are really talented."

Annie tsked. "Don't undersell yourself. You're an amazing singer and, someday, you'll find that break."

Evie gave her a weak smile. "Thank you, that means a lot to me. Now, if you don't mind, I have to work on my choreo with the other girls for Act Two." She gave Annie a nod and walked to the dance room.

Get your act together, girl, she told herself. She couldn't afford being flighty right now. No matter how distracted she was or how much her chest hurt when she thought of last night.

Sex with Connor had been indescribable. Even now, she could still remember the feel of him inside her. She thought her heart was going to give out the entire time, and the mere memory of the two orgasms made her knees buckle. Connor said he didn't have sex with Janelle nor did he want her, and Evie did believe him. She wouldn't have had sex with him if she didn't. He thought she was beautiful. For a brief moment, she did feel beautiful in his arms.

Then she ruined it.

She sighed, thinking about what had happened after. What was she thinking, asking him where he lived and implying she wanted to stay over? Because that's what she had done, right? Guys didn't like it when you were too obvious. With her previous dates and boyfriends, she should have known. When she was dating Richard, she never even hinted that she wanted to sleep over at his place until after a month of going out. She had obviously come on too strong with Connor. When he brought her home but didn't even ask to stay, she just shrugged and said goodbye, even though hurt slashed through her like a knife. She was a better actress than she thought.

But what were the rules in this case? Should you invite yourself over a month after having dressing room sex or before then? She shook her head. She wished there were some kind of dating handbook called "What To Expect When You Boink A Lycan You've Been Crushing On for Months."

She hadn't even seen him at all today, though she knew he was around. She also never got around to apologizing to Janelle, and maybe the pop diva had forgotten her demands. Last she heard, Steven had scheduled a separate rehearsal with Janelle today and asked that the chorus work on the new dance routine for Act Two in the afternoon.

After a grueling morning session and a quick lunch break, it was time for the dance rehearsal. "Evie, good, you're here," Nicole called when she entered the dance studio. "Let's begin."

Evie pushed all thoughts of Connor aside and listened as Nicole went through the revised routine. It took all her concentration, and she was glad for the distraction.

The afternoon passed by and the choreography rehearsal was brutal, but it seemed they finally nailed it. Sweat poured down Evie's face, and the back of her shirt was soaked. She grabbed her towel and dried off, then finished an entire bottle of water. Her stomach grumbled angrily. *Wow, I must have burned some serious calories.* She had just scarfed down a hamburger, fries, and a shake at lunch, and she was hungry again.

"We're gonna hit the showers and call it day," Nicole said. "Then, happy hour at Paddy's around the corner? They've got two for one beers until six."

The thought of alcohol made her nauseated for some reason. *Strange.* Usually a post-rehearsal beer was what she needed to relax. "I'm pretty tired; I haven't had a workout like this in months. Or should I say *torture*." She laughed. "Maybe another time? I think I'll need a hot bath after today."

Nicole chuckled. "All right, next time then." With a wave, the other woman walked away.

Food, her stomach seemed to say. "Ugh." She let out a frustrated sigh. "Fine." She walked to the catering table, which was still laden with bagels, sandwiches, pop, and some healthy snacks like veggie sticks and fruit. She really should go for the veggies, but everything else smelled delicious, especially the basket of homemade chocolate chip cookies that were still warm. Her mind made up, she grabbed a plate and piled it with cookies and sandwiches.

"Hmmmm ..." Finally, her stomach quieted down. She had a sandwich, a can of pop, and was biting into a chocolate chip cookie when she heard a voice behind her.

"I like a woman with a healthy appetite."

The other half of the cookie fell from her mouth and onto the plate. She swallowed and then turned around. "Oh, Aiden, I didn't see you there." Her eyes dropped to the half-eaten cookie. "Sorry," she mumbled.

"Hey." He touched her arm. "No need to say sorry. I should apologize. It's rude to watch someone else eat and then comment on it."

She shrugged. "It's okay. I was just filling up after a long cardio workout."

"You know," Aiden began. "If you like desserts and sweets, there's this restaurant on the Lower East Side that only does desserts. Maybe you'd want to go out with me sometime?"

Evie put down the plate and then turned to him. "Aiden, I'm very flattered."

"But?"

"But ... it's just ..." Inappropriate? She and Connor did the nasty on top of a dressing table in this very theater less than twenty-four hours ago. Who was she to say what was inappropriate and what wasn't?

"There's someone else," Aiden finished.

She bit her lip. "Yes."

He gave her a weak smile. "No worries, I understand."

"Thank you, Aiden," she said. "You really are a great guy."

"You're not going to say 'friend' are you?" He chuckled. "What do you kids call it? 'Friend-zoned?'"

She laughed. "Right. Well, don't worry about it, old man, these young whippersnappers don't got nothin' on you. You're still a catch."

Aiden threw his head back. "I'll remember that," he said.

"Well, I should go check on a couple of things. I'll see you around." He gave her a nod and then walked away.

Evie watched him walk away, then let out a sigh of relief. She really was flattered by the attention, but it was better to just be honest and not string him along. Aiden was a wonderful guy, but she just didn't feel anything for him.

The lights from the stage dimmed, and she knew the crew was shutting down for the day. That meant she would only have a couple of minutes to shower. She was pretty sure no one else on the subway would appreciate how she smelled right now.

She grabbed her bag from the dressing room and raced to the showers, praying the crew hadn't locked up yet. Thankfully it was open, and the lights were still on. She quickly stripped and wrapped a towel around herself, then walked into the shower area. She chose the first stall and pushed the curtain aside.

"Evie."

A thrill ran up her spine at the sound of a rough, low voice. "Connor?" She turned around. He was standing there, his bright green eyes boring into her. Warmth crept up her neck. "What are you ..."

His eyes burned with desire, and she felt breathless. He moved forward, and she had no choice but to step back.

Connor was so big he made the already cramped stall seem even smaller. His coffee scent tickled her nostrils, and memories of last night came back, making her wet. *Oh God.* He continued moving forward until her back hit the tiles.

"Connor." Her eyes dropped to the floor.

"You turned him down."

"Huh?" Her head snapped up.

"Aiden."

She shrugged. "Yeah, I did. So what?"

Hands braced on either side of her. "Evie, can we ..." He stopped short, and his eyes widened.

She wasn't sure what had come over her, but she had dropped the towel, letting it fall to the floor. Connor let out a pained grunt and then swooped down, claiming her mouth in a kiss. His lips were unexpectedly soft, though. A surprising contrast to the rough hairs of his beard.

Hands, warm and large, cupped her bare breasts. The calloused pads of his fingers teased her nipples into hard buds, and she moaned into his mouth. Were they really going to do this here?

She moaned in protest when he moved his mouth away from hers. *What was he ... oh no.* Connor knelt down in front of her and spread her legs.

"Connor ... you shouldn't ... I should ... shower first ..." She felt embarrassed. Connor shouldn't go down there, not when she'd been working out all day.

"You smell delicious," he said with a groan. Shock shot through her system when she felt his wet, rough tongue lick a stripe up her slick nether lips. "And you taste delicious."

"Nnnghhh!" she cried out when he spread her apart with his fingers and pressed his face between her legs. She dug her fingers into his hair and scraped her nails along his scalp. It was sweet torture—the sweeping of his tongue and the press of his lips against her pussy. He slid into her, teasing her, and she clenched around him, making him move faster into her. He fucked her with his tongue expertly, pushing her just close enough to the edge without sending her over.

Fuck, she was going to come any moment. He must have sensed it. He hooked one of her thighs over his shoulders and pushed into her even deeper.

"Connor!" Her voice echoed through the shower room, but she didn't care who heard. Her body convulsed as pleasure tore through her. He didn't stop but kept going, his tongue lashing at her, and she shivered as a smaller orgasm followed.

Her breath came in ragged pants, and her heart finally began to slow down. How long had she been standing there, leaning against the shower door with Connor between her thighs? He stood up and then kissed her again. She could taste herself on his lips and it was dirty, hot and it turned her on even more. Her pussy gushed with wetness, thinking about having him inside her, and she reached down to tug at his pants, her hands brushing against the bulge there. God, she wanted him—needed him—badly. And—

A soft vibration from his pants made her stop and withdraw her hands. Connor let out a soft curse as he ran his hands down his face, then reached into his pocket.

"What do you want?" he said gruffly into the phone. He cursed. "Fine. I'll be there."

Evie quickly grabbed the discarded towel and held it to her chest, like a security blanket. "What's wrong?"

"Quinn," he said. "Says I gotta go to the office now. They got some information from Booth."

"Oh." She tried not to sound deflated, but she wasn't that good of an actress.

"Evie," he began, "shit. I ... fuck." He cursed softly. "I keep fucking things up. I'm sorry."

"It's all right," she replied and took his hand. "Let's go."

"Go?"

"To the office."

"You're coming with me?"

"Of course, I am," she said, squaring her shoulders. "C'mon, Quinn's waiting."

12

*E*vie quickly got dressed, and they went on their way. Connor flagged down the first cab they saw and gave the driver the address of Lone Wolf Security.

The ride was agonizingly slow, but, then again, it was rush hour in Manhattan. Evie was at the other end of the backseat, far away from Connor. He seemed agitated, and it was hard for her to breathe next to him. Plus, she was still thinking about his head between her thighs and his magical tongue.

She stifled a groan. He already gave her an orgasm today, shouldn't that be enough? She wished they hadn't been interrupted by that phone call. The image of them fucking against the wall of the shower filled her mind, and she bit her lip.

The cab jerked to a stop, and Connor pushed the door open, then yanked her along. His strides were much bigger than hers, and she struggled to keep up with him. They took the ancient elevator up to their floor. Connor's movements were tense and minimal, and he wasted no time going up to the door of their office.

"What do you know?" he said before they even stepped foot

inside Killian's office. His brothers, Selena, and Meredith were already inside.

"Hello to you, too," Meredith greeted. Her whiskey-colored eyes turned to Evie. "Oh, what are you …" Her nose twitched, then her lips curled into a knowing smile. "Never mind."

"Connor, sit down," Killian said, motioning to the couch in the corner.

"I'd rather stand. Now, what did Booth tell you? Did he talk?"

"He was a tough nut to crack," Meredith said. "But he's never met my husband. Daric has ways of making people talk."

"And? Did he give up the ringleader?"

Meredith shook her head.

"Then why the hell did you call me here?" Connor groused.

"Because he gave us something else. Or told us that he knew other information," Killian said. "But not about the big boss; it's about you."

Connor's shoulders tensed and his jaw ticked. They waited for a few seconds, but he said nothing.

Killian let out a sigh. "He says he knows about your family. How you can find them. Maybe—"

"No," Connor said in a terse voice. "I need to find him. Their boss."

"Connor," Meredith began, "this is real information. Maybe you can find out where—"

"No! I said I didn't want to know. End of discussion."

Meredith visibly flinched but backed down. Killian and Quinn looked at each other.

"Look, why don't you think about it?" Killian said.

Connor turned and then jerked the door open. He strode out, slamming the door behind him. While the air inside the office had considerably lightened, the tension was still obvious there.

"Let's go talk to him," Killian said, nodding at Quinn. The two of them walked out and the women were left inside.

"Well, I guess I better get home," Evie said and made a motion to open the door. It slammed quickly as Meredith's hand slapped on the wood.

"I don't think so," Meredith said, though her tone was light-hearted.

Slowly, Evie pivoted and faced Meredith. The Lycan's arms were crossed over her very pregnant belly, and she had a sparkle in her eye.

"So, what are you doing here, Evie?" she asked.

"Um ... Connor is working at the theater, and, when Quinn called him, I was ... next to him so I said I'd come with him."

Meredith raised a blond brow. "Next to him ... or under him?"

Evie's face turned all shades of red, and she blew out a breath. "How did you know?"

"Sheesh, you guys are as subtle as a stampede of buffalo, walking in here, smelling like sex. Did we interrupt anything?"

Evie slapped her hand on her forehead. Lycan senses, right. Did Killian and Quinn know, too?

Selena shot to her feet. "Evie! Oh my God!" She giggled. "Really? Since when?"

Evie walked back to the couch and sank down on the cushions. "Er, it's complicated ... but, uh, since yesterday?"

Meredith gave Selena a smug smile, and the redhead rolled her eyes, then pulled a ten-dollar bill from her purse and handed it to the other woman. "You better have not been using your husband's magic or I want my money back."

"I didn't, I swear. Scout's honor."

"I've heard that one before." Selena turned back to Evie. "Wait, what do you mean it's complicated?"

When Evie's face fell, Selena's nostrils flared. "What did he do?" She pushed her sleeves back and glared toward the door. "I swear, if he hurt you ..."

Evie sighed, not really wanting to talk about it. But the moment she opened her mouth, it was like stepping on a tube of toothpaste. It all went gushing out, and there was no way to take it back.

"What?" Meredith said in an incredulous voice. "He just sent you home?"

"Well, he brought me home and made sure I was okay ...," She shrugged. "I was coming on too strong, right? I shouldn't have asked him about staying at his place."

Meredith plopped down on the couch next to her, leaned back, and slapped the back of her hand on her forehead. "Ugh, my brother is such a social retard. Please be patient with him?"

Evie didn't know what to say. "Um ... I'll try."

Meredith sat up. "I have an idea. I'll talk to him."

"No!" Evie protested, but Meredith was already on her feet. She tried to tug Meredith back on the couch, but the Lycan was too strong. She was out the door in a flash.

Evie groaned, and Selena sat down beside her. "So, finally got over that dry spell, huh?" she said, clapping her hands.

"Selena, only you would applaud my sex life."

"What? I can't celebrate your trip to Bone Town?" Selena asked. "C'mon, tell me all the details. How was it? How many times did you orgasm? How big—"

Evie grabbed one of the throw pillows and hit her best friend playfully in the face.

"Why don't you want to know?" Quinn asked. Connor said nothing but crossed his arms over his chest.

"This information about your family could be valuable," Killian reasoned. "Maybe they'll know more about the man who took you."

"We'll find another way." Connor remained still. He didn't give a shit about his birth family. As far as he was concerned, Archie was his family. Killian, Quinn, and Meredith were his family. He didn't need to know anything else, except the identity of the man who had forced him to become a monster.

"Why don't you really want to know about them?" Quinn asked. "Are you afraid?"

"Fuck you, Quinn," he said, uncrossing his arms. He stepped forward, pulling up to his full height, so he towered over his brother.

"Fuck you too, Connor," Quinn said, not backing down. "Don't you get tired of this tough guy bullshit?"

"Connor, Quinn," Killian warned. "Stand—"

"I need to talk to you," Meredith said as she walked into the reception area.

Connor turned to his sister. "What?" He had never lost his temper with Meredith, but, tonight, he had come close today. It was something he never wanted to happen again.

"Evie. What did you do to her?"

All right, he was confused now. He thought Meredith was going to rip him a new one for cutting her off back in Killian's office. "I didn't do anything to her."

Quinn snickered, and even Killian rolled his eyes.

"We all know what you did," Meredith said, tapping a finger on her nose. "We must have interrupted you guys."

"No wonder you sounded more uptight than usual when you answered your phone," Quinn said with a laugh.

"Fuck you, I—"

"Connor, for once, shut up and listen to me," Meredith said. Connor closed his mouth. "I'm not talking about the sex. That's all good, and we're all adults here. But you sent her packing afterward?"

"What?" Quinn and Killian said at the same time.

Meredith shot her brothers a knowing look. "I know, right?"

"I didn't—" Oh fuck. That's exactly what he had done. Three pairs of eyes looked at him, waiting for an explanation, but he didn't know what to say. "It wasn't safe."

"I'm sure you had your own fucked-up reasons why you sent her away."

"I took her home. Made sure she was safe."

"Uh huh. That's something you do with a friend, not a lover," Meredith said with an exasperated sigh, then looked at her brothers. "Guys? A little help?"

"Connor," Killian began. "I know you've never had a relationship, but, if you care for a girl—and I assume you do with Evie—you should do things with her after the sex."

"What? Like cuddling and shit?"

Quinn laughed. "Yeah, cuddling and shit. Chicks dig that kind of thing. You only ever kick a girl out of bed if you're a selfish bastard, like I was before I met Selena."

"But we weren't in a bed," Connor pointed out. "We were—never mind." Quinn was right. He messed things up. That's why Evie had been acting all weird when he took her home last night. "I was doing it for her own good. I can't trust myself to be alone with her. Not with my wolf. You know I've never had the best control."

"Wait, what are you talking about?" Meredith asked with narrowed eyes.

"I ... you know it's always been a problem for me, shifting back. But it's been getting worse."

"Since when?" Meredith asked.

"Since Archie died." He swallowed the lump in his throat. He couldn't tell them what he was planning. They were already involved too much. "Look, it's not important. I obviously made a mistake with Evie—Oww! What the fuck, Meredith?" His sister had hit him in the arm, and, with her Lycan strength, it actually hurt. He rubbed the spot and gave Meredith a dirty look. "What the hell was that for?"

"For being a fucking hypocrite!" she retorted.

"What?"

"You nearly killed Daric when you found out he was having sex with me, and now you're banging Evie and you haven't even taken her out on a date? What would her brother say?"

"You need to romance her," Quinn added. "Make her feel special."

"What in our entire history together makes you think I'm the type to do flowers and dinners and shit?" he asked Quinn.

Meredith put her hands on her hips and gave him a challenging glare. "Connor, if you think she doesn't deserve any of that, then tell us now and we'll tell her to turn around and never look back."

Shit. "Aww, fuck." He couldn't deny it. Evie deserved to be treated like she was the most important thing in the world. He had desperately wanted to protect her by staying away, but he just couldn't stop himself. The battle raging inside him was too great, and he could only deal with one thing at a time.

He wanted her bad and had just taken what he wanted. In any case, it was too late now. He'd already hurt her and needed to make it up to her first. He could figure it out later. "What do I need to do?"

"Well, first, you go and ask her out. On a real date."

"How the fuck do I know what to do on a real date?"

"Just go in there and ask her; I'll take care of the rest," Meredith urged. "Then you can romance the shit outta our girl!"

"Our girl?" he asked, a sinking, suspicious feeling suddenly creeping up on him.

"I mean your girl. Evie. You know what I mean!"

"How exactly do I do that?" he asked. Aside from fighting, he didn't know much else. The few women he'd been with had always come onto him and wanted nothing more than a quick fuck. But he couldn't treat Evie like he had those other women.

"Just be yourself," Meredith said. When Quinn snickered, she sent him a warning glare. "I mean just follow your instincts. You're a good person, Connor."

"Be a gentleman on the streets but a wolf in the sheets," Quinn finished with a wink.

"Maybe you should start over and do things the right way. Treat her like a lady," Killian insisted. "Take her to a nice meal, bring her home, but let her lead and decide what happens after."

"Fine." He lumbered back to Killian's office and yanked open the door. Evie and Selena were on the couch, talking softly. They both jerked their heads toward him when he entered.

"I should go see if Quinn is okay," Selena said, standing up. As she walked past Connor, she gave him a silent, warning glare.

"Is everything all right?" Evie asked. "Did David Booth—"

"We're going out," he stated, then kicked himself mentally when Evie frowned at him. "I mean, you and me."

"What?" she asked, her brows furrowing. "Out where?"

"I don't know. I mean, Meredith's arranging it."

She stood and walked to him. "Meredith's arranging what?"

He swallowed as he looked down at her face. *Why the fuck was this so hard?* "Our date."

Evie's eyes bulged. "Excuse me?"

"I'm taking you out. On a date."

"Now? But I can't. I'm not dressed, and I should really take a shower and put on some makeup ..."

"Look, do you want to or not?" That sounded harsher than he wanted it to come out. "I mean, do you want to?"

"I guess, but ..." She gestured to her outfit.

Connor scrutinized her. After their encounter in the shower, she put on a green dress with seahorses all over it. It was a tad too short for his comfort and showed off way too much skin, but he thought it was cute. Part of him hoped she chose it to match his eyes, which made something in him burst with pride. Plus, even now, he could still smell himself all over her, and it was turning him on. Shit, he needed to control himself. He was going to make this up to Evie and do it the right way, even if all he wanted to do was push that little dress up her luscious body and feast on her again.

"You look fine. I mean, you look beautiful. Look," he ran his fingers through his hair. "If you don't want to go on a date, it's fine—"

"Yes!" she squeaked. "I mean, yes, I do want to go on a date. With you."

The tightness in his middle loosened. "Good. Now, let's go."

13

Meredith arranged for a last-minute table for them at Muccino's Italian Restaurant, which was just around the corner from the Lone Wolf office They walked there together, and Connor held her hand for the quick, five-minute stroll.

As soon as they got there, they were escorted to a booth in the corner of the restaurant. Evie scooted into the middle of the seat and Connor followed. Even though the booth could seat about six people, Connor's size made it seem crowded.

Evie bit her lip. What was going on? Connor had asked her out on a date. Well, technically, he told her they were going out on a date. She stifled a laugh. It was awkward but nonetheless sweet. He even opened the door for her going into the restaurant. It wasn't that she couldn't imagine Connor as a gentleman, but she was still confused what this whole thing was about.

"Would you like some wine? Appetizers?" the eager young waiter asked.

"No wine, just some sparkling water, please," she said. "But do you have any of that artichoke dip?" She looked at Connor. "If you don't mind."

"Get the lady whatever she wants," Connor told the waiter. "Plus, we'll have whatever specials you're making for the night. And I'll have your beer on tap."

The waiter nodded. "All right, sir. I'll get you started then."

And, so, they were alone. Despite the din of the restaurant, the silence between them was deafening. She still wasn't sure what this was about. Well, at least she got a good meal out of it because she was starving.

Mercifully, their waiter came back with their drinks. She took a sip of her water. Unable to bear the silence any longer, she decided to ask him some basic stuff—first date things you usually ask someone. "So ... you like working at Lone Wolf? With your brothers?"

"Yeah, I suppose." He shrugged. "Quinn's a pain in my ass sometimes, but I like being around all of them. It's like old times."

"Old times?"

"Yeah, before Archie—" He stopped short.

"I'm sorry," she said, looking down at her lap. "I didn't mean to bring it up."

"It's fine," he said in a gruff voice.

Okay, so maybe that wasn't such a good idea. Another topic, maybe? "Um, so how do you like New York?"

"I don't," he answered, his voice brittle like glass. "Too noisy. Too cramped. Smells terrible in the summer."

She gave a weak laugh. "True, but the vibe here ... it's so different." When Connor scowled, she fell silent again. Maybe this wasn't going to work. What were they supposed to talk about? Wasn't all this weirdness supposed to go away once they had sex? They were doing this all backward.

Thankfully, the waiter arrived with the appetizers, and Evie busied herself practically demolishing the plate of artichoke dip and bread. She was nervous, for some reason, and eating gave her something to do. "Uh, sorry, did you want some?" She pushed the plate to him.

"No, go ahead; I'll wait for our food."

Oh God, she had turned him off with her monster appetite. She shrunk back. She was still hungry but thought it best to wait and put her hands on her lap.

Connor frowned. "Now what's wrong?"

"Nothing."

He let out an impatient sigh. "If you're hungry, just eat. I don't give a f—care if you finish off your plate."

"I shouldn't," she said. "I have about ten pounds to lose and—"

"Says who?"

Her head snapped up at him. "Huh?"

"Who says you need to lose ten pounds?"

"Well, no one, but—"

"Then eat up," he pushed the plate back to her. "You've already gotten too skinny."

She laughed. "What do you mean too skinny? You don't like my body?"

"No," he said quickly. "I like your body any way it is. But do you like *you*?"

Aside from the fact that he said he liked her (well, her body anyway) his question made her stop. Did she? She always thought she needed to lose twenty pounds so she could finally get a starring role. All the other actresses on stage were thin and in shape. "I ..."

Before she could answer, their waiter arrived and put down two hot plates of delicious Italian food in front of them. She moaned as the scent made her stomach gurgle. Turning to Connor, she saw he was looking at her with a different kind of hunger on his face.

They ate in silence, though it wasn't as awkward as it had

been. Connor watched her with hawk-like eyes, and she made sure to eat to her heart's content. He had also moved closer to her, their thighs pressing together in a delicious manner that had nothing to do with food. It was sensation overload—the scrumptious feast and Connor's nearness—and it made her insides go haywire. And his coffee scent ... grrr ... how could a man smell so insanely good to her? It was driving her crazy, and all she wanted to do was jump him right then and there.

The meal wound down, and they finished off a plate of tiramisu and panna cotta. Evie tried to take out her wallet, but Connor insisted on paying, handing the waiter a wad of bills.

"I'll take you home now."

Evie felt irritation rise in her. She was confused, which only made her frustrated, which then turned into anger. What the hell was this about? He takes her out and then sends her away again? At least the last time she got some orgasms. The only thing she got now was about three thousand calories worth of food that'll be hell to get rid of. With an impatient grumble, she quickly slid out of the booth and dropped her napkin on the table.

"Evie, what the—where are you going?" he called as she stormed away from the table.

"Home," she replied, without giving him a second glance. She barely made it out the door when he caught up to her and stepped in her path.

"What did I do?"

"Nothing."

"Shit," he cursed. "I'm not good with women, but even I know that when you girls say nothing, it's always something. How did I fuck up?"

She sighed. "Look, maybe it's too soon for this, but why don't you want to sleep with me?" He blinked at her, confused. "I mean, sleep with me. Invite me to your place to spend the night?" He stood there, dumbfounded. "Never mind. Forget I asked." She sidestepped him and walked out into the street. It wasn't too late yet, and she could still take the subway home.

"Evie, wait," Connor called. He caught up with her as she was making her way to the station. "Wait." He grabbed her gently by the arm.

"What?"

His jaw was tense. "It's not that I don't want to take you home, but ..." He dropped his hands to the side and let out a frustrated grunt. "I can't."

"I told you, it's fine," she said, trying not to sound disappointed.

"Evie ... I ... I can't. I don't know if you would want to anyway."

"What?" she asked. "What do you mean?"

He stepped back. "Well, first of all, what happened in the dressing room shouldn't have happened."

"Oh." The bottom of her stomach dropped. He was regretting having sex with her.

His eyes widened. "No, don't think that way," he said, as if reading her mind. "I mean, you deserve more. More than me. More than a fucked up Lycan with a wolf he can't control. A Lycan who has no future."

Something in his words pricked at her. "What are you saying, Connor?"

His expression changed as if he had said too much. "Nothing. Absolutely nothing."

"Connor," she said in a calm voice. She put her hand on his arm when he tried to turn away. "Please, tell me what's going on."

A low growl tore from his throat. "I ...You've spent time with Lycans, right?"

She nodded. "All my life."

"You know that Lycans have animals inside of us, as part of us."

"Yes."

"Mine is different. It's not a part of me. I mean, it is, but it's separate."

"I don't understand. But," she moved closer. "I want to."

Connor let out another growl. "The wolf ... it always wants to take over. And sometimes I let it. I can usually get control back, but lately, since Archie ... when I let him die and failed to protect my family, it's been unmanageable. Each time I shift, it takes me longer and longer to come back."

Evie gasped. That wasn't how it worked. The human side was always supposed to be in control. If they weren't, well ... "How long?"

"It used to be hours ... now, sometimes it's an entire day." His hands clenched into fists at his sides. "And, sometimes, I'll wake up in the middle of the night and I'm naked, lying in the middle of the living room with no idea what happened. The couch and the curtains will be ripped up ..." He shook his head. "I'm losing control, Evie. Even in my sleep. I'm no good for you—"

"Stop," she cried, putting her hands on his chest. "Don't say that."

"It's true," he replied, gently prying her hands away. "I could lose control at any moment. There is no future with me, can't you see? Do you know what happens to Lycans who can't control their wolves?"

She jerked her head back, and her spine went stiff. "No. You can't mean that ..."

"That's the way it is," he said. "Grant Anderson will put me down if I ever become a threat to his clan or to humans. He won't risk exposing our secret."

"No," she protested. Her hands moved up to the sides of his face. "No, no. You can't mean that."

"It's what needs to happen." His lips thinned. "But not before I get my revenge."

"Against the man who put you in that place?"

He nodded. "Fuck Lycan law. I'm going to find him and then kill him. I'll let the feral wolf inside me loose one last time and—"

Desperation had built up in her chest, and Evie did the only thing she could think of to stop him. She pulled him down for a kiss, crushing his lips to hers. He seemed taken aback at first but responded quickly. He took charge, slowing down the desperation and turning it into a slow caress. Arms wound around her, pressing her close so she could feel every hard plane of his body.

"Evie," he whispered against her mouth. His eyes were closed, and he touched his forehead to hers.

"You won't hurt me." She truly believed those words. She didn't know how, but she knew. "And if you suddenly shift, I'll know. I'll run the moment anything goes wrong." He hesitated, but she sealed her mouth to his again. "I'll be safe with you. I'm always safe with you."

"Okay," he finally said. "Will you stay with me tonight?"

"Yes."

---

*E*vie wasn't sure what to expect when Connor brought her home. For one thing, 'home' was the W Hotel on the Upper West Side. It was a luxurious place for sure, but, for a moment, she was confused.

"Connor, where are we?" she asked when they entered the elevator. "Are you taking me to a hotel?"

He nodded, and Evie noted the look on his face. At first, she thought it was sadness, but seeing the way the muscles in his jaw twitched and the way he kept rubbing his hands on his pants, it was something completely unfamiliar. *Was Connor nervous?*

She followed him out of the elevator and down the hall to the last room on the left. He took out a keycard and opened the door, then let her in first.

The room—or rather, from the size of it, the suite—was sumptuous. It was modern and sleek, and, as she stepped out into the plush living room, she noticed it was decked out with the latest gadgets. Turning to the large window, she let out a little gasp when she saw the amazing view of Central Park.

"Wow," she said. "It's great ... but I don't understand."

"I live here," he said, shoving his hands into his pockets as he approached her.

"You live here?" she echoed.

He nodded. "I can't stay in one place. It's too suspicious, and my wolf won't let me. It always wants to be on the move in this city. And, like I said, it's always destroying things. It's easier to just let the management deal with it than having to change furniture or explain to the neighbors." He shrugged. "It's another reason I couldn't bring you here. I didn't want you to see how fucked up I really am."

"Connor ..." She moved closer. "You're not. You're doing the best you can. And what you said back at the restaurant ... it's not true."

He looked up at her, his green eyes burning bright. "About what?"

"That you failed your family," she said. "They're still here. You're all together again, and you've kept them together and safe. I know what you do for Killian and Quinn, how you've saved them on lots of occasions." When he opened his mouth to protest, she put her finger on his lips. "I've read those reports about your ops and missions for Creed. And I bet you've also helped protect Meredith. She's special to you, right?"

He nodded, and his Adam's apple bobbed when he swallowed. "She was so young when she came to us—much younger than any one of us—and we could tell she wasn't treated right. I swore, when she came to us, that I would always take care of her and protect her."

"But who takes care of you, Connor?" She really did wonder. This big, burly, giant of a man might think he was everyone's protector, but someone had to take care of him, too, right?

He didn't answer but, instead, leaned down to kiss her. His mouth was warm, sweet, and gentle, yet sent swirls of delight through her. She felt light as a feather, and she realized only moments later that he had lifted her into his arms.

Connor carried her into another room—the bathroom she realized—though this room was just as luxurious as the other room. There was a large jacuzzi in the corner and an enclosed shower in the opposite corner. He placed her on her feet and began to unbutton the front of her dress. When the fabric fell to the tile floor, she stepped out and reached behind her to take off her bra. Then, she stepped out of her panties. Meanwhile, he grabbed the bottom of his shirt and stripped it off, then made quick work of his pants and underwear, shucking them off in one motion.

God, he was magnificent. She realized this was the first time she was seeing him fully naked. Her mouth went dry as her eyes traced along the muscled planes of his broad shoulders, admiring the tattoos on his arms. A light sprinkling of hair dusted his well-formed pecs, and she couldn't help but look lower to the perfect set of eight-pack abs and the deep V of his hips. She lingered on the wolf's head tattoo on his rib cage, her heart aching when she remembered what he had told her. No, she would not let that happen, wouldn't let it get to that. Connor had spent the last few years protecting those he loved, and she would be damned if she let him throw his life away.

He sucked in a breath, and she could feel the heat of his gaze as he looked at her. She lifted her head up, and their eyes locked. Picking her up again, he took her to the shower and closed the stall behind them. He reached behind her and turned on the rainfall showerhead, stepping in front of her to test the water before adjusting it and pulling her under the stream.

The water was the perfect temperature—not too cold but hot enough to soothe her aching muscles. She moaned when two large hands grabbed her breasts from behind. Connor had some bath soap on his palms, and he kneaded the soft flesh, lathering her up. His fingers teased her nipples, and she felt his cock, fully hard, pressing up against her ass. One hand moved lower, between her thighs and down to her slickness. He probed her, moving his forefinger up and down her slit before slipping inside her.

"Oh ..." She rubbed her ass on his cock. It was his turn to moan. His hips thrust forward, the ridge of his cock planting between her ass cheeks, moving in time with his fingers. Soon, she felt the pressure building inside her, and she couldn't stop it. Pleasure crashed over her, and she was gasping as the warm water continued to rain down on them.

He slowed down, withdrawing his fingers from her. She whimpered in protest, but he turned her around and gave her a rough kiss before pulling back. "Let's get to the bed."

She didn't argue when he lifted her up again, then walked to the bed, grabbing a towel as they left the bathroom. He planted her on the edge of the bed and wrapped the towel around her, gently drying and buffing her body. She scooted back, watching as he quickly dried himself before tossing the towel aside.

Connor moved over her, sliding his body against hers.

Feeling his skin on hers made her shiver. He captured her mouth in another searing kiss as he got between her legs.

The tip of his cock nudged at her slick folds. She was still wet from her earlier orgasm, so he slipped into her with little resistance. She pushed her hips up, trying to get as much of him inside her. God, she'd never been filled like this.

"Connor," she gasped when he gave a small, experimental thrust.

"I don't wanna hurt you," he said. "Can't get too rough."

"You don't have to be rough," she whispered. "But you don't have to hold back with me. Make me feel good, please."

"Evie ... so beautiful ..." he murmured against her skin. He moved his hand under her ass, scooping her up and bringing her hips higher. As he thrust inside her, he hit her just right, and she let out a small cry, her nails raking down his back as a shudder of pleasure shot through her.

"Fuck ..." He gasped. "So tight ... wet ... perfect." She couldn't help but blush at his words. He made another low, guttural noise, and one hand moved to the front, skimming over the skin of her pussy where they were joined.

She let out a whine as his thumb brushed her clit—the pleasure almost too much—even as his hips pummeled into her, his cock dragging along her inside passage.

"Come for me, Evie," he commanded, and her body had no choice but to obey. His fingers continued to stroke her clit, and she screamed as he pushed her over the edge. Her back arched, her arms swung backward so her hands could grip at the soft, silky sheets.

He let her recover, slowing down his thrusts until he stopped completely. When she opened her eyes, he was gazing down at her, his eyes like twin orbs of green fire.

"Connor, I—" Before she knew what was happening, he had flipped them over, so she was on top, straddling him. His hands traced up her waist to her breasts, cupping them and brushing the nipples with his thumbs. She suddenly felt self-conscious, but, when she saw his face, the look he gave her made her heart melt and she forgot about her insecurities. It was like she was the only woman in the world, and she had never felt so beautiful.

She moved her hand to his cheeks, cupping his face and gently tracing the scar over his eye. He flinched and tried to turn away, but she held him still.

"No, don't turn away."

"It's ugly," he said with disdain.

"No, it's not." Evie leaned down and kissed the scar over his eye, continuing lower over his cheek to his jaw, stopping only to give him a soft peck on the lips. She touched her mouth to the pulse on his neck, to his shoulders, all the way to his pecs. When she was done, she straightened her back, planted her knees on either side of him, and began to move.

"Evie ... Evie ..." He moaned her name like a reverent prayer as she rode him. From this angle, he seemed to fill her up even more, and she ground against him, seeking the friction that made her body shiver and shake. She leaned back, moving her pelvis back and forth, feeling the drag of his cock in her. She squeezed tight, which made him gasp and grab for her hips. His hands cupped her buttocks and lifted her up, then slammed her down on him.

It was her turn to moan and throw her head back as he fucked into her. His thick cock surged inside her. His fingers found her clit again, and she cried out another orgasm.

"Fuck, Evie ... I ..."

She could feel him, knew he was almost there, and she wanted nothing more than to make him come, to hear him grunt and moan his orgasm, knowing she did it. She moved her hips faster, squeezing him tight until he clutched at her hips hard. His fingers would leave bruises later, but she didn't care. The feel of his cock twitching and jerking as he filled her with his cum was all that mattered. His face twisted as the orgasm hit him, and she could feel the wetness inside her, flowing out and painting her thighs.

She collapsed on top of him, breathing heavily. His chest was damp with sweat, but it didn't matter as she was slick with perspiration, too.

Connor rolled them over, his softening cock slipping out of her. He turned her over, so her back was pressed to his chest, and he cuddled her, his arm wrapping around her and pulling her close. She lay still for a long time, listening to the sound of his breath. When it became steady and even, she closed her eyes and drifted to sleep.

14

Connor watched from off stage as Janelle floundered around like a fish out of water. At least she wasn't 'singing.' He gave an annoyed snort. Why anyone would choose that talentless woman over Evie, he didn't know. Evie had explained something about social media followers and ticket sales, but he still didn't understand. Wasn't this professional theater? Shouldn't they be getting the best singer, actress, and dancer (i.e., Evie) for the job?

Plus, there was the fact that he wanted to wring Janelle's neck for the way she treated Evie. He had to be civil to the girl, at the very least, but he didn't even try to be nice. He also made it a point to never be alone with her, not even for a second. A couple of days ago, she tried to pull some trick where she was changing into her costume and 'accidentally' dropped her towel. He quickly turned around and marched out of her dressing room.

This entire job was torture, and he couldn't wait for it to finish. Right now, he'd rather be facing South American thugs or insurgents in war-torn countries than having to spend another minute around that crazy pop star, her adoring fans, and the frenzied press camping outside the theater. Why anyone would want or need such attention was beyond him. Who the hell wanted this kind of life? Being hounded by photographers and autograph-seekers all the damned time?

Of course, there was one advantage to working here. His eyes locked on Evie, who was standing by the stage, talking to a couple of her castmates. He looked appreciatively down the line of her body, admiring the curves and dips. Her ass looked particularly biteable in her yoga pants, and he had to adjust his crotch to make sure no one saw how turned on he was.

Connor couldn't remember feeling as content as he had in the last week. He also couldn't remember sleeping as soundly as he did when Evie was in bed next to him. After that first night together, he wouldn't let her sleep anywhere but in his bed (though, truthfully, they spent more time not sleeping in it).

As if she read his mind, Evie turned in his direction. Their eyes locked, and her skin got that pretty blush she always got when she caught him looking at her. She bit her lip, and he let out a small groan.

"Connor, Connor. Connor!" Janelle stamped her feet, and Connor snapped his head back.

"What?" He could barely contain his annoyance.

"I'm ready to go back to my dressing room," she said. Her eyes followed his gaze, and, when they landed on Evie, her eyes turned into narrow slits. "Let's go," she huffed and flipped her hair.

"Fine," he said through gritted teeth as he followed her.

The rest of the day's rehearsal progressed much too slow for Connor, and all he wanted to do was get the fuck out and take Evie home. Tomorrow was Saturday, which meant they were both off. He was looking forward to an entire weekend of staying in bed. Hmmm, maybe a nice dinner at the Mexican place near the hotel, too. Evie sure had an appetite, and he was more than happy to make sure she was properly fed before going back to bed. She needed her energy, after all.

The ringing in the middle of the night startled him, and, for a moment, he thought the nightmares were coming back after not having them for a while. Instead of grasping for the digital watch under his pillow, he reached across the bed. Evie. He breathed a sigh of relief as he felt her soft body next to him. But what was that ringing?

He sat up and looked at his phone. Not his. Glancing over at Evie's bedside, he saw her phone glowing.

"Evie," he whispered, shaking her gently on the shoulders. "Evie, your phone's ringing."

"Hmmm?" She muttered in a sleepy voice, brushing her hair off her face. She sat up slowly, glancing around and then grabbing her phone. "Hello? Arthur?"

Arthur? Connor felt ugly jealousy rising in him. Who the fuck was this other man calling Evie in the middle of the night?

"Slow down ..." Evie said. "What ..." She paused. "Tell me again." Reaching for the bedside table, she switched the light on.

Connor watched as Evie listened to the caller and slowly grew pale. Something was wrong, he could feel it.

"I'm on my way," she said in a shaky voice. "I'll take the first flight I can."

"Evie?" Before she could explain, she jumped out of bed and ran to the bathroom, slamming the door behind her.

What the heck was going on? Connor rolled off the bed and lumbered to the door. "Evie?" he called, knocking on the door.

He opened the door and saw her scrambling for her discarded jeans before slipping into them. "Evie?"

She looked up at him, tears threatening to spill from her eyes. "It's my brother. I mean, he called. My dad ..." She choked up, then went very still, then sank down on the toilet. "He had a heart attack and ..." A cry tore from her throat.

Connor crossed the bathroom in two strides and gathered her to him. "I'm sorry." She let out a sob and buried her face in his chest.

"I ... I have to go and make sure ... airport ..." she said between hiccups.

A fierce, protective feeling washed over him. No way was he letting her go to the airport by herself. "Evie, I'll take care of this okay? Don't you worry." He rubbed a soothing hand over her back. "Just relax. Everything will be okay."

15

The entire trip back home was a blur to Evie. She wasn't even sure how it all happened. First, it was that call all adult children dread getting in the middle of the night, then, all of a sudden, she was sitting in the private jet next to Connor on their way to Kansas City.

She was getting ready to leave the hotel and make her way to the airport, but Connor said he'd take care of it. She thought he meant he'd drive her there, not hire a private plane to take her all the way home. The jet must have cost a fortune, but she was too weak to protest. Connor later assured her that he only borrowed the plane from Sebastian, who was happy to lend it to them.

They landed on the private strip just outside Kansas City, and there was already a black SUV waiting for them. Connor opened the door for her, helped her into the passenger seat, and then slipped into the driver's side. She mentioned the name of the hospital to him, and he drove her directly there.

"Charlie King," she said to the nurse at the reception area, who directed her to the cardiothoracic ICU on the fifth floor.

They ran to the elevators in the lobby and made their way to the ICU, where another nurse pointed them to her father's room.

"Arthur!" she called to her younger half-brother. Arthur King was sitting on the bench outside the room, his face in his hands. He looked up and, when he saw his sister, got to his feet.

"Evie!"

Evie threw herself at Arthur. Long, gangly arms wrapped around her and, when she finally let go, she looked up at him. "You've grown again," she said, her smile tight.

He gave a short laugh. "Yeah, puberty's coming at me with a vengeance," he said, his voice low. "Mom's livid. She had to buy new clothes twice this year."

"Where *is* Stephanie?" she asked, looking around for her stepmom.

"Talking with the doctor. Dad's almost out of the treatment room and ..." Arthur's brown eyes, so much like her own, narrowed and looked behind her. "Who's he?" he asked, his shoulders straightening and chest puffing out.

Evie had nearly forgotten about Connor. She turned back and looked at him. He was watching them with a curious look on his face. "This is—"

"Connor," he said, stepping forward and offering his hand to Arthur. The younger man took it and returned the handshake. "Good grip."

"I'm Arthur. Who are you exactly?"

"Arthur," Evie admonished. "He's my ... friend."

"Friend, huh?" Arthur said, eyeing Connor suspiciously. "I've never seen you around here before."

"I'm a friend from New York," he answered.

"And you came all the way here? What for?"

Connor looked at Evie. "Your sister needs a friend right now."

Before she could say anything else, a man in a white coat came out of the room, along with her stepmother.

"Evie, you're here!" Stephanie King cried as she wrapped her arms around her stepdaughter. "Thank God! I wasn't expecting you here so soon." Her blond hair was disheveled, and there were bags under her eyes. Though Stephanie was usually dressed professionally because she worked as an insurance agent in Kansas City, today she was looking more casual in sweatpants and a T-shirt. Evie imagined she probably threw on the first thing she could when ...

"Can we see him?" she asked the doctor, not wanting to picture her father in pain.

The man in the white coat shook his head. "Not yet, I'm afraid."

"Is he going to be okay?"

"I can't be one hundred percent certain, but the prognosis is good. We were able to open up the blocked artery without surgery and, with the proper care, your father should be able to make a full recovery."

Evie felt her knees go weak as relief swept through her. "That's great news."

"He's not quite out of the woods yet, but we'll see. In the meantime, I suggest you all get some rest." The doctor looked at Stephanie and Arthur. "I know you two have been here for a couple of hours. You can't do much more for him, but you can come back this afternoon if you want. We'll call you if anything changes."

After thanking the doctor, Evie turned to Stephanie. "You guys should get some rest. I can stay here and wait if you want."

"Nonsense," Stephanie said. "We'll all go home and get freshened up and rest."

"Even Connor?" Arthur asked.

"Who?"

Evie realized she had forgotten all about Connor. "Oh yeah. Um, Stephanie, this is my friend, Connor. Connor, my stepmom, Stephanie King."

Stephanie peered up at Connor. Wearing his tight white t-shirt, jeans, and boots, and with tattoos up and down his arms, he must have looked intimidating to her stepmom. "Oh, my ... I mean, nice to meet you, Connor. What brings you to Kansas?"

Evie groaned. "I'll ... explain later. Let's go home."

Connor offered to drive them all back to their home, but Arthur had taken the car over. So, they decided that Arthur would drive himself and Stephanie, and Evie and Connor could follow them back.

The hospital was only a couple of miles from the King family home. As they walked up to the ranch-style home in the suburb just outside Kansas City, Connor couldn't help but feel out of place. This was the American dream. The perfect suburban home, complete with the picket fence and perfectly manicured lawn.

"Should I put your friend in the guest room?" Stephanie asked. "You both are staying the weekend, right?"

Evie went red. "Uh ..."

"I can stay at a hotel," Connor offered. "I didn't pack a bag or anything."

"Nonsense. You must stay here. Er," she looked around, "I don't think we have anything we can lend you. Even with Arthur's growth spurt, I'm afraid his sweatpants won't fit you."

"That's fine, I can pick up some clothes later," Connor said.

"Then maybe you'd like to freshen up a bit?"

"Thank you, Mrs. King," Connor said.

"Down the hall, to your right," Stephanie replied. "And, please, call me Stephanie."

"Thank you, Stephanie." He nodded at Evie and headed to the bedroom. He didn't need to freshen up, but he realized that was probably the signal that Stephanie wanted to be alone with her stepdaughter.

As he walked to the bedroom, he couldn't help but look at the photos lining the hallway. There were lots of them, and he recognized a much younger looking Evie, along with Arthur, Stephanie, and a dark-haired man with a bright smile who must be Evie's father. In one picture, he had his arm around her and their heads were leaning together. He could easily see the resemblance between father and daughter.

"Oh my God," Evie said from behind him. "Those were my awkward years. Please stop looking."

He smiled. "You were cute," he said, pointing to one of her school photos.

She giggled. "Right. Pimply, chubby teen. Anyway." She moved closer to him. "Um, sorry about ... the whole guest bedroom thing. Um, my parents are pretty conservative. Catholics, you know? And with Arthur here, they probably wouldn't let us stay in the same room anyway unless we were married." Her cheeks turned pink.

"It's all right." He had to admit, it stung a bit when Evie introduced him as a friend, but he didn't hold it against her. She had more important things to worry about than his hurt feelings. "How are you feeling?"

"I'm ... not really sure." She shook her head. "I'm still processing."

"He'll be okay," he assured her. He wanted so badly to hold her, to comfort her, but he wanted to be careful around her in her parents' home.

"You should—" The sound of the doorbell interrupted her.

"Stephanie and Arthur are trying to get some rest, so I should go get that."

He watched her retreating back and headed to the guest bedroom. He found it easily and used the facilities to wash up. As he was drying his hands, his keen ears picked up raised voices outside. His senses went into overdrive, and he bolted for the front door.

More loud voices, one of them Evie's. He would have ripped the door open if Arthur wasn't already there, peering out the front window.

"What's wrong?" Connor asked.

The younger man turned around, his face drawn into a deep scowl. "Richard. Evie's stupid ex-boyfriend."

The hairs on the back of his neck bristled. Hands curled into fists at his sides. "Is she okay?"

"She's not happy to see him, that's for sure." Arthur turned around. "Are you going to hurt her like that asshole did?"

Smart kid. "I'll try not to." That was the best he could promise for now.

Arthur stepped aside. "Go get rid of that bastard then."

He cracked his knuckles, getting ready for a fight if needed. Pushing the surge of jealousy down deep, he opened the door.

"Evie, please, listen—"

"You said you only wanted to know about my dad's condition," Evie said, cutting him off. "I don't want to talk about us!"

"I do, but, please, you need to—" He reached for Evie's arm, gripping her tight.

"Get your hands off her," Connor growled.

The blond man in a dark suit stopped and looked at him. "Who the fuck are you?"

"I said get your hands off her, or I'll make you."

Richard's face twisted into fury. He straightened up, pulling his jacket to smooth it out. "Look, bro, this isn't any of your business."

"If you touch her, it is," Connor said, his voice chilly.

"Is this your new boyfriend, Evie?" Richard said with a huff. "My, you've really outdone yourself."

Connor stepped forward, but Evie quickly stepped up, grabbing his arm. "Connor, please, it's okay." She turned to Richard. "He was just leaving."

"Fine," Richard sneered. "Don't come crawling back to me when he dumps your fat ass and you--"

Richard never finished his sentence because Evie's fist collided with his face. He staggered backwards, fell on the porch, then let out an indignant scream.

Evie's face quickly morphed from angry to surprise as she looked down and saw the blood flowing from her ex-boyfriend's nose.

"You bitch!" he cried, clutching his face as he struggled to get up. "I'm going to sue you!"

Connor chuckled. "Really, asshole? You're gonna tell the cops and the court some girl knocked you flat on your ass?"

Richard let out another indignant screech and then turned around to lumber back to his car.

"I can't believe I did that," Evie said, her face pale. "Did I ..."

"He deserved it," Connor spat. "For what he said. For everything he did to you."

"Maybe it was too much, but I couldn't help it. I'm just so done..." Her voice shook.

Before Connor could reach out to comfort her, the front door flew open.

"Jesus, Evie! You got that bastard good!" Arthur let out a hooting laugh, then looked at Evie with pride in his eyes. "The look on his stupid face ..."

Connor was disappointed he didn't get the satisfaction of decking Richard himself, but he was glad Evie stood up for herself in front of her younger brother. The young man should learn that women aren't helpless nor do they always need a man to defend them.

"Watch your mouth, young man," Evie warned. "Stephanie will wash it out with soap if she hears you cussing like that."

"I'm sixteen," Arthur moaned. "I've said waaaay worse than that." He turned to Connor. "Did you teach her that?"

Connor shook his head. "Your sister did that all on her own, I'm afraid. So, don't cross her."

"Arthur," Evie began. "Can you give us a moment?"

"But—"

"Please? We'll come right in. I just need to speak to Connor alone."

"Fine." He sulked, then walked into the house.

Evie let out a breath as she rubbed her knuckles. Connor grabbed her hand and then looked at it closely. "Not too bad, but we should get some ice on it." He stared at her face, then tipped up her chin. "What's the matter?"

"Um ... yeah, so that was Richard."

"Dick?" He teased, using Selena's favorite nickname.

She giggled. "Yeah. So, as you can see, I'm not the best judge of character when it comes to boyfriends."

"What's the matter?" He knew there was something else bothering her.

"I just ..." She turned away from him. "I hate that you saw him."

Connor tamped down the jealousy building inside of him. It was unnerving to see the man. From what Connor could piece together, Richard and Evie had been in a long-term relationship. There were some things they shared that made him want to tear the other man to pieces. But that was the past, and

Connor knew Evie had to go through all that to make it here. Evie accepted him and his past, so he could accept hers. "It doesn't matter," he said, drawing her to him. She relaxed against his back, and he wound his arms around her waist. "He was part of your past, but what matters is today. Now."

16

Evie was bouncing on her heels when they walked into the hospital. It was Sunday morning, and the doctor had said her father was up and could now see more visitors. Stephanie had driven to the hospital the night before and stayed there, while she, Arthur, and Connor stayed at the house.

She turned to Connor, who gave her a warm, comforting smile. While she respected her parents' rules in their home, she was frustrated about not being able to sleep with him. She snuck into the guest room when she was sure Arthur was asleep, but Connor made her march right back to her room. He said that while they were staying under her parents' roof, they would obey their rules. Plus, he didn't want to be a bad influence on Arthur.

Not that the last one was a problem. During dinner, Connor had told them some stories about his work for Creed Security and her younger brother was entranced. He practically had hero worship written all over his face when he looked at Connor. He even asked him for tips on how to build his body and learn to fight. While she didn't want Connor to have to relive the memories from before, she was surprised by his patience with her brother and how willing he was to give him some tips and encouragement.

"Dad," she called when they walked into the room. Charlie King was sitting up in the hospital bed with various wires sneaking under his gown. His thinning hair was mussed up, and he looked pale and tired. But he had a wide smile when his eyes landed on Evie and Arthur.

"Evie! Arthur!" He opened his arms and gathered his children in them. Both of them eagerly returned his hugs. "C'mon, now, princess," he said to Evie, brushing the tears from her cheeks. "No need for that. I'm as strong as an ox, you know."

"Uh-huh," she replied, trying to force a smile on her face. "Stubborn as one, too. Didn't your doctor say you should start eating healthier food?"

Charlie chuckled.

"I'm just glad you're okay," she said, giving him another fierce hug. She hadn't seen her dad in weeks, not since she had gone back for his birthday.

"Who's this?" Charlie's eyes narrowed, and he tipped his chin up.

"Oh," Evie turned to Connor, "this is Connor, Dad. Connor, this is my father, Charles King."

"Nice to meet you, sir," he said, extending his hand. Charles took his hand and shook it, but his eyes narrowed suspiciously at the other man. "And, Connor, you know my daughter how?"

"We work together, sir," Connor supplied. "At Lone Wolf."

A brief flash of recognition sparked in the older man's eyes. While Charlie and Evie knew about Lycans, Stephanie and Arthur had no idea. "Of course. She's told me about her job there."

"Connor brought Evie here on a private jet," Arthur interjected.

"It was the company jet," Connor added. "With the good work Evie's been doing, the boss was happy to help her out."

"Glad to hear," Charlie said with a nod. "Evie's always been a hard worker."

There was a knock on the door, and they all turned toward the sound.

"Excuse me," a nurse said as she poked her head in. She looked at Evie. "Ms. King, someone out here would like to visit your father. I told her it's family only, but she insisted."

"Who is it?"

"She says she's your mother. Amelia White."

The blood rushed out of Evie's face, and her throat went dry. She looked at her father and Stephanie.

"It's fine," her stepmom said, holding Charlie's hand. "If it's okay with you, dear."

"Of course," Charlie said with a nod.

The nurse disappeared, and then, a second later, the door opened. An older woman dressed casually in jeans, a t-shirt, and boots strode inside. Her long brown hair was swept back in a ponytail. Amelia White looked young for age, certainly not old enough to have a daughter in her mid-twenties.

"Charlie," she said in a worried voice. "I came as soon as I heard. I—Evie." Blue eyes gazed at her warmly, but then narrowed as they landed on Connor.

"Hello, Mom," Evie replied in a tight voice. "I'm going to get coffee. Does anyone want anything? No? Okay then." She quickly pivoted and walked to the door, yanking it open.

Evie wasn't quite sure what she was going to say to her mother. It had been years since she'd seen Amelia White. Graduation, maybe? She'd never even been to one of her shows. She and her clan lived far away, in a remote area southeast of Kansas City. Bitterness built up inside her, and she swallowed it down like she always did.

"Evie." She turned and saw Connor walking toward her. "Are you all right?"

She shrugged. "I'm fine." Connor crossed his arms over his chest and gave her a knowing look. She sighed. "I'm just ... I don't know, okay?"

"Your mother. She's an Alpha."

She nodded. "Her aunt was Alpha to the Kansas Clan, and, since she didn't have kids, the leadership was passed down to her."

"Evie!"

Evie's head turned instinctively at the sound of her name. Amelia White was walking toward them, her face worried.

She quickly turned and began to walk away, intending to put as much space between her and Amelia as possible.

"Evie, please don't go." Amelia caught up with Evie before she could go any farther. She then looked at Connor.

"Lupa," Connor said, using the traditional honorific for female Alphas. "Apologies for not showing you respect right away." He lifted his shirt to show Amelia the wolf's head tattoo, symbolizing his status of Lone Wolf. "I ask for safe passage while I pass through your territory."

"You brought a Lone Wolf here?" Amelia said in an annoyed voice.

"Technically, being a Lone Wolf means he can freely roam around, as long as he stays neutral," Evie pointed out. "Now, what do you want?"

"I need to talk to you. Alone."

Connor cocked his head at her, and she nodded. "I'll go and find that coffee for you," he said before walking away.

"A Lone Wolf?" She laughed, then looked at Evie. "What have you gotten yourself into?"

Irritation built up in her. "What did you want to tell me? Say it, then you can go back to your clan."

"Evie, baby," Amelia pleaded. "I know you're mad at me for leaving ..."

"I don't want to hear this." Evie threw up her hands. "I know how it went. I was there. You and Dad divorced, and you gave him custody. Then you went back to live happily ever after with your clan. The End."

"It's not like that!" Amelia said. "There was more to it. I loved your father, and I love you."

"But you chose them over me." Evie put her hands over her mouth. She was shocked by her own outburst, but it was so hard to control the emotions churning inside her, especially after the last twenty-four hours.

"I had no choice, baby," she said. "The clan was tearing itself apart. I had to step in."

"Then why didn't you take me?" Evie asked, her voice breaking at the unshed tears.

"Because they would have used you against me," Amelia said. "I did it to protect you. Not all Lycan clans are like New York or San Francisco or those other big cities. There was a power vacuum when your great-aunt died. My enemies would have hurt you to get to me."

A cold wave washed over Evie. She'd always been shielded from clan life, but, after working for Lone Wolf, she'd come to know the cruelty of some Lycans. "Why tell me this now?"

"It took me a long time to build up my power," Amelia explained. "And things have only been stable for a few years. Please believe me; I would have taken you if I could. Leaving you was the hardest decision I've ever had to make."

It was difficult to believe Amelia. After all these years resenting her mother, she couldn't expect Evie to change her heart just like that.

"I'm sorry, Evie," Amelia said, tears in her eyes. "Will you forgive me?"

Evie took a deep breath. For years, she'd denied this part of her, erasing it from her very being. It was easy enough; she didn't even look like Amelia, except maybe for the hair color. "It's going to take a while, but I ... I'll try."

"I accept that," Amelia said. "Your father tells me you've been living in New York and that you'll be on Broadway soon."

"You and dad talk?"

"Of course we do," she replied, a fond smile on her lips. "Mostly about you. He tells me everything. I'm sorry I haven't been able to see more of you these years. But I'm going to try, if you let me."

A strange weight Evie never knew was on her shoulders lifted. "I ... I'd like that."

"Good. Would you like some coffee? Maybe we can talk for a bit. I can't stay very long, but I want you to tell me about what's been happening with you."

She gave her mom a tight smile. "Sure, that would be nice."

"And you can tell me about your Lone Wolf."

"He's not my—"

"Uh-huh," Amelia raised a brow at her. "You may not think he's yours, but he's certainly staked his claim on you." Before Evie could say anything, Amelia hooked her arm through hers. "Let's go find some decent coffee around here."

---

*E*ven though Evie wanted to stay at least another day, Charlie wouldn't hear of it.

"You're finally living your dream, princess," Charlie said. "You're going to be onstage next month! You can't miss any rehearsals now. No buts, young lady!"

Evie made them promise that they'd call her if anything at

all happened, and told them she would be video chatting with them every day.

"Ready?" Connor asked as they pulled out of the hospital parking lot.

"Let's go," she said.

They gave a final wave to Arthur and drove them back to the air strip.

The flight back home was quick, and Evie joked that he had spoiled her and she could never fly commercial again. They landed late in the evening, and he drove them back to Manhattan in his truck. As Evie watched the scenery of the city go by, she couldn't help but think about how different it was from Kansas. And how Kansas City seemed so different this time around. Had anything changed? Had she? Whenever she left home and her family, there was this heavy feeling inside her, like lead building up in her chest. But now that she was back in New York, she felt ... lighter. Like that weight inside her heart had lifted. She was home. Perhaps that was it. New York was now her home.

"We're here," Connor announced.

She still couldn't believe he went with her to Kansas. That he held her and comforted her, befriended her brother, and maybe even charmed her parents in his own way. "Let's go home."

17

The next few days were routine at the theater, though Connor could definitely tell things were at the boiling point in the production. Even as an observer, he could feel the tension hanging in the air like a thick fog. The director was pulling his hair out at Janelle's antics, the cast was annoyed at their star's demanding ways, and even Aiden James was frustrated at trying to keep things in order with the press and securing the theater. Someone had sent another threatening note to Janelle, this time, telling her that they would kidnap her as soon as the curtains closed on opening night. The diminutive diva was hysterical, and she even posted a video to her fans telling them how frightened she was. Connor had a good laugh (in his head, of course) when Evie showed him the video the other night, especially when she was crying and her makeup stayed perfectly intact.

Connor was not one to make light of a threatening situation, especially on a job. But, ever since he came here, there was just something not right. He could feel it. Rather, he couldn't feel anything. It had been bothering him for days now, and he finally pinpointed it. His instinct was not screaming at him, telling him there was real danger. He tended to trust his gut, and this strange feeling was gnawing at him.

"All right, let's take a break! Again." Steven threw his hands up.

"I'm just so tired," Janelle said in a breathless voice.

"Maybe if you didn't stay out partying all night, you'd have more energy," Steven muttered.

"What was that?" Janelle asked.

"Oh, nothing. Go on to your dressing room and have a coconut water or something," Steven replied.

"Let's go, Connor," Janelle said as she passed by. "I think I need to change my outfit, too. I'm going to post another Instagram later today, and I can't be wearing the same thing!" She batted her eyes at him. "Maybe you can help me pick something out."

Connor didn't reply but began to walk to the dressing room with Janelle at his heels. He was getting tired of this shit. It was an easy job, but he didn't want easy. He was starting to get restless, and he needed action. He needed to get on with his revenge, too.

Thoughts of the red-haired man flooded his brain, but, somehow, the rage he felt inside wasn't as strong anymore. And when was the last time the feral wolf had burned inside him, trying to claw out and control their body? It had been days at least. Sometimes he thought he could feel it, just under his skin, but he must have been imagining things. The feral wolf only made its presence known when it wanted *something*.

"Connor," Janelle said, catching up with him. "Wait!"

Connor was in front of the dressing room, his hand about to open the door. "Yes?"

"No! I mean, you shouldn't have to open the door for me." Janelle gave a nervous laugh. "Here, let me!" She flung his hand away, jerked open the door, then pushed him aside to get through.

His keen senses picked up some noise from inside the room, and his gut twisted. A split second later, a dark blur leaped up from the side, knocking into Janelle.

"Connor!" she cried. Something metallic glinted in the attacker's hand, and Janelle screamed again.

Connor roared and lunged forward, grabbing the first thing he could. The attacker was dressed in all black, complete with a ski mask that obscured his face. Connor pulled him off Janelle, slammed him against the wall, and knocked the knife to the ground.

"Connor!" Janelle screamed from the floor. "Help me up!"

He turned for a second, and the attacker took the opening to get to his feet in one smooth motion, then sprung toward the door. Connor let out an angry growl and sprinted for the exit. He ran after the man, who was headed for the stage.

Most of his opponents thought that, because of his size, he'd be slow and lumbering. True, he was efficient with his movements, but he was in no way slow. His Lycan speed and senses allowed him to move quickly and avoid obstacles and people along the way.

The attacker reached the stage and jumped off toward the house seats. He hurdled over them, scrambling and climbing expertly. But Connor was quick and caught up with him. He grabbed him by the neck, pulled him back, then slammed him to the ground.

The man's head knocked back on the carpeted floor with a soft thud. Connor wrapped his hand around the guy's collar and hauled him up, then pulled the ridiculous ski mask off.

"Who the fuck are you? Who sent you?"

The man's eyes went wide. No, he wasn't a man. He was young and boyish looking, probably no more than nineteen or twenty. Sweat, anxiety, and fear dripped from every pore in his body.

"I wasn't going to hurt her, I swear!" The young man said, his Adam's apple bobbing. "Please sir, it's not what you think!"

"You one of her fans?" Connor asked. "You get your jollies scaring celebrities?!"

"N-n-no! I swear man, it's not that! I'm not trying to hurt her!"

Connor wrapped one hand around his skinny neck. "Then what are you doing?"

"I just wanted to make some cash! That guy said all I had to do was jump out of the dressing room, make the girl scream, and run away!"

"What man? Who?"

"I-I-I—" The boy shook his head. "I don't know! A dude in a suit! He was bald and short."

Connor felt the veins in his neck bulging. His instincts were screaming now, and he dropped the boy to his feet. His hand wrapped around a skinny arm, and he hauled the boy down the aisle and up to the stage. He scanned the room and found who he was looking for.

"You," he said, walking up to the producer, Andrew MacAllister. He released the boy's arm. "What's your name?"

"J-j-Jimmy," he muttered, his eyes shifting to the floor.

"Is this him? Look at him, asshole," Connor commanded, and Jimmy's head snapped up. "Is this the man who hired you?"

Jimmy's eyes went wide. "Y-y-yes!"

MacAllister's face turned various shades of purple and red. "What's the meaning of this? Who is this kid?"

Connor could hear the other man's heartbeat speed up and his sweat glands go into overdrive. "You're lying. Did you hire this kid to do your dirty work? Are you some sick bastard?"

"I don't know what you're talking about!"

Connor's patience was running thin, so he let go of Jimmy and lunged for MacAllister instead. His wrapped his hands around the man's suit jacket and lifted him off his feet. "Stop lying. Tell the truth. Now, asshole."

"All right, all right!" MacAllister choked. Connor dropped him, and he landed on the floor of the stage with a satisfying thud. "I did it! All right? I hired him to scare Janelle."

"What else did you do?"

MacAllister cowered under Connor. "I ... I also hired some guy to break the lights that first day and a-a-also to send Janelle that package and those notes."

"Why the fuck would you do that?" Connor roared.

"For publicity!" MacAllister screamed. "You stupid goon. You know nothing about business, do you? Broadway shows are losing money year after year. All these idiots, all they want is to stare at their little screens like zombies! No one wants to pay for quality entertainment anymore." MacAllister got to his feet and brushed himself off. "I did it to save your jobs. All your jobs!"

A crowd had formed behind him. Everyone was there, including the director, the composers, Evie, and even Aiden James.

"You did it to make your company money," Jane Collins huffed. "You didn't have faith in the art or in this cast and crew who put their blood, sweat, and tears into this production!"

"Grow up, Jane," MacAllister said. "That's not what people pay for these days."

"Fuck you and fuck Atlantis Artists," Annie said, slamming her script to the floor. "I'm going to talk to my lawyer."

"And we'll be talking to ours," Aiden James added.

Connor looked at MacAllister in disgust. "I hope you get what you deserve." He walked away from the stage.

Really, he wasn't sure why he was angry. He'd be paid for this job, so that wasn't it. Maybe it was because Evie had almost been hurt that first day. It didn't matter. He hated liars and schemers. At least when he dealt with dictators, insurgents, and thieves, they didn't try to stab you in back.

"Connor! Connor!" Evie called. He stopped and turned. "Are you okay?"

"Yeah, I'm good." He ran his palm down his face. Shit. Evie. If this production shut down, what would happen to her career?

"Connor, wait a second!" Aiden James was running toward them. "Sebastian's on his way. He wants to be debriefed, then we're going to talk with the production company. Don't go yet, okay?"

He nodded. "Fine."

Sebastian Creed was not very happy to be pulled away from important matters to deal with the shit that went down at the theater.

"I assure you, Mr. Creed," the severe-looking lawyer said. "Andrew MacAllister was acting independently, and my client, Atlantic Artists, had no knowledge of his or Ms. Edwards' actions." She sat across from Sebastian, Aiden, Connor, and Creed Security's legal counsel, Anthony Carelli, in the theater's small meeting room.

"My client was not involved in this," another lawyer in a gray suit said. "Ms. Edwards was a victim, too."

Connor snorted. "She didn't look very surprised when that guy jumped out at her."

"In any case," Atlantis' lawyer continued, "we'd be happy to release Creed Security from their contract and pay the full amount promised for the entire month."

That seemed to satisfy Sebastian, and, after ironing out a few more details, they concluded the meeting.

"Fucking show business," Sebastian muttered. "Fucking lawyers. Give me a terrorist with an AK-47 any day."

"At least it's all done," Aiden said. "I'm sure Connor will be happy to be going back to Lone Wolf."

"Sure," Connor said with a shrug. Without another word, he left Sebastian and Aiden and went in search of Evie. Guilt had spread into his chest. Would the show go on? He saw more men in suits waiting outside the meeting room. There were whispers that the insurance guys and the president of the production company would be meeting, too. Fuck. What would happen to the show now?

Evie was standing by the stage, her face a mask of worry. An ache in his chest spread as he watched her wistful expression. "Evie," he called softly.

"Oh, Connor," she said, turning around. "Is everything okay?"

"I'm fine. What about you? What about the production?"

"Screw this production," she said, fists curling at her sides. "I mean, not Jane or Annie or Steven or the cast, but this whole thing is bullshit." Her face scrunched up in anger. "I can't believe they would do that! Those assholes!"

"But your show ..."

"I'm quitting. I mean, we don't know what will happen anyway. The insurance providers might pull out, or Atlantis might even cancel the show." She shrugged. "But I don't want to be part of it. Not like this. A show has to have integrity." She looked up at him. "Let's go home. I can't be here anymore."

Connor let out a sigh of relief. "Me neither."

---

*C*onnor glanced down at Evie as she slept soundly. Her face was calm as an angel and even more beautiful. After picking up her things from the dressing room, they left the theater, not even stopping to say goodbye to anyone. Despite her words, he could tell her heart was breaking. He was no critic or art lover, but, being around the crew and the cast these past weeks, he knew all of them had put their hearts and souls into the show. They all wanted it to be good and successful, and it was crushing that a few bad apples had ruined it for them.

He rolled off the bed. Now that he didn't have to be in the theater, he could go back to his old life. He should be happy or, at least, be glad he could go back to his normal routine.

Revenge. The Facility. The red-haired giant. He had been too distracted all this time. *Not that he minded*, he thought with a glance back to Evie. Still, there was no further movement on that front. There were no more usable names on Archie's list and, according to Killian, David Booth had refused to give up his boss. But there was still information he was willing to give.

He snorted. His family? Did that really matter now? Did he want to know? All these years, he tried to remember what life was like before The Facility, but he couldn't recall a damn thing. So, he decided he must not have a family. Maybe he was bred in The Facility. Because if he had been born to some family, wouldn't they have fought for him? How could they not have done everything to find him and bring him home? It was what he would do for his siblings. What he would do for Evie. What he would do for his own children.

A rumble in his chest jolted him out of his thoughts. He wasn't sure where they were coming from, but he scoffed at the idea. Him? Children? He had a fucked-up life, why would he subject children to it? Still ... he glanced at Evie again, and an ache bloomed in his chest.

Without knowing why, he reached for his phone.

"Hello?" the voice on the other end said. "What is it?"

"Killian," he began, "I want to talk to Booth."

18

"So, boy," David Booth said as he sat across from Connor in the New York clan's basement facility. "Ready to know more?"

"I'd rather you tell me about him," Connor said through gritted teeth.

"Sheeet," Booth cursed. "Like I told your friends, I don't know anything."

Connor leaned back and narrowed his eyes. "You don't know where he is, do you?"

Booth remained as cool as a cucumber. "You'll never know, will you?"

"Tell me where he is!" Connor slammed his fists on the table. "You bastard, tell me or ..."

"Or what?" Booth mocked. "What could you possibly do to me in here?" He leaned in and whispered, "They got you by the short and curlies, right? Can't do anything to me. Lycan law and all."

"You'd rather be in Lycan prison?"

"I'd rather be alive, boy," Booth replied quickly. "Now, do you want to know what I know?"

Connor sat back, the metal legs screeching in protest as he dropped his weight on the chair. "I suppose you want something in return."

"I want leniency if the truth comes out."

"But you won't tell us what really happened in The Facility?"

"I ain't no rat," he spat.

Connor looked at the one-way mirror covering one wall. Grant and Killian told him he could make a deal in exchange for good intel, as long as he didn't promise Booth he'd be free. "Fine. What do you know?"

Booth smiled. "Shenandoah. West Virginia. That's where they said they got you."

"'They said'?" Connor let out a bitter laugh. "You're not even sure?"

"Go check it out, boy," Booth said. "Check out the Shenandoah Clan. And, if I'm wrong, then do what you want." He looked at the mirror. "You can't possibly make my life worse."

Connor stood up, kicking the table as he walked to the door. It slid open automatically, and he made his way to the room next door, the one behind the mirror.

"Shenandoah Clan?" Killian asked. "Have you heard of them, Alpha?"

Grant shook his head. "Cady Vrost will know more; we can ask her and get any records we can from the High Council. But can you trust his information? What if you walk into a trap?"

"Something's off," Connor said, tapping his finger on his chin.

"I know," Killian said. "He's hiding something. Why not give up the ringleader and get an even better bargain? He's going to end up at the Lycan Siberian Prison anyway, whether it's for trespassing or being part of The Facility. He could only get a better deal if he helps us."

Connor thought for a moment. "Alpha, your security's pretty tight here, right? You can trust all your people?"

"With my life," Grant replied.

"What about the Lycan Siberian Prison Facility? The High Council?"

Grant's jaw tensed. "I can't be certain. They're not under my control."

"If he snitched and the ringleader got wind of it, then they could get him at the prison," Connor finished.

"He's scared," Grant added. "Could the ringleader have something on Booth? Something he's hanging over his head to control him?"

"Maybe Booth's protecting someone else," Killian said. "Could be the ringleader's threatening to hurt someone Booth cares about if he snitches."

"I think Booth's hoping we'll either find the ringleader without it getting back to him that he ratted or we won't be able to use the info at all and the ringleader stays free," Grant deduced. "Either way, Booth and whoever he's protecting, if anyone, stays alive."

"Motherfucker," Connor cursed.

"So, can we trust his information about Shenandoah?" Killian asked.

"Only one way to find out," Grant said.

"No, absolutely not."

"Please, Connor?"

"No," he said firmly. "You are not going with me."

"But you can't go alone," Evie whined.

They were standing in front of his truck, arguing. He had been loading up the back with his duffel bag and supplies when

Evie came down to the garage, her packed bag in hand. Last night, he told Evie what he could about what they found out from Booth. Then, he told her about the trip. She said she understood, kissed him, made love to him, and then they both fell asleep. He woke up and began to prepare for the trip, hoping to give her a last kiss before he left. He didn't think she'd assume she was coming, too, but here she was.

"It might be dangerous," he reasoned. "We don't know what to expect. According to Cady Vrost, the clan is isolated and secretive. They live out in the sticks in the Shenandoah Valley in West Virginia, and we barely know anything about them. They haven't updated their records in years." Cady Vrost had told them the last known Alpha was Clifford Forrest. He didn't have a designated Beta, Lupa, or even heirs.

"Or they could be your clan," she pointed out. "And they'll welcome you with open arms."

Grant and Killian agreed it would be better if they didn't let anyone know about their suspicions, since they weren't one hundred percent sure it wasn't a trap. They didn't want to raise any alarms and come in full force, lest they rile up the clan and risk war. So, they thought it was better for Connor to go alone. Quinn would be monitoring the situation the entire time though, as he rigged Connor's truck with a dashcam and put a tracking and listening device on his phone.

"Please, Connor, I don't want to be without you," she said. "I can't stay in your hotel room, watching TV and eating room service all day. I'll go bonkers!" Evie was on the verge of tears, and something inside Connor was ripping him up. "Fine," he relented. "But you stay close to me and follow what I say, okay?"

Evie squealed in delight and kissed him on the cheek. "Road trip!" She tossed her bag in the back and ran to the passenger side seat.

Connor growled. He really shouldn't be taking her, but he

had a hard time saying no. Besides, it was a long trip and he didn't want to be without her either. Six hours non-stop to West Virginia from New York, which was why he was leaving at the butt crack of dawn. He hoped he wasn't going to regret his decision.

19

*E*vie watched the scenery turn from the city streets of Manhattan to the highways of Pennsylvania and Maryland to the Blue Ridge Mountains of Virginia. She had lived in the flat plains of Kansas her whole life and then moved to the urban jungles of Manhattan, so this was way different from anything she'd seen before. Everything was big and green and majestic. They were also going up the mountain roads, and she could hear her ears pop as they climbed higher and higher. Along the way, she saw all kinds of wildlife, even a family of black bears by the side of the road. She wanted to stop and take pictures, but knew Connor was on edge and moody.

She pouted and slunk deeper into the seat. A couple of hours ago, he'd snapped at her and she snapped right back at him. Over what, she couldn't remember. But she was sore and tired and hungry, and he was being a grumpy wolf. She snuck a look at him. He was staring at the road, eyes forward, and she couldn't help but watch his handsome profile. Her eyes traced down his aquiline nose, firm lips, strong jaw. Her eyes moved lower to his shoulders, down his tattooed forearms as the muscles flexed while he shifted gears. She bit her lip. Was there anything he did that wasn't sexy?

Connor slowed the truck down and pulled it to a small gas station. He cut the engine and faced her. "I'm sorry," he said quietly.

Evie unbuckled her seatbelt and scooted closer to him, cuddling up to his side. "It's okay. I know you're nervous."

"Nervous?"

"We could be meeting your clan, right? And maybe ... your family?"

"Sure," he said. "I should go pump some gas. According to the GPS, this might be the last station until we get to Winter's Creek." He kissed her on the forehead and slipped out of the truck.

Evie bit her lip, wondering what Winter's Creek, West Virginia would be like. It was a town deep in the Shenandoah Valley, and, apparently, where the clan was located. It was isolated, and Evie couldn't find a lot of information on Google about it. From the few photos she saw online, it seemed like a typical township with a little Main Street, but most houses were on acreages or farms, spread out and far and few between. According to the GPS, they were almost there, maybe thirty more minutes on the backcountry roads.

Connor had explained the plan. He would go to Clifford Forrest's house and ask him if he knew anything about The Facility. As a Lone Wolf, it would be easy for him to just come to town without having to announce his arrival. Quinn was also tracking their movements and would be listening in on audio the entire time.

Did Connor even want to know if he had family left? Evie was sure the Alpha would know. Maybe if he saw Connor, he'd recognize him.

"Ready?" Connor asked when he jumped back into the driver's seat.

"Ready," she said, placing her hand over his.

Connor started the engine and put the truck into gear. They sped down the one-lane highway and eventually veered off onto small country roads. It was breathtaking out here, especially now that they were in the middle of spring. Everything was so green and smelled so fresh.

The robotic GPS voice led them down Main Street. It was quaint, with small shops, houses, and cafes lining the street. They turned right and drove past identical little bungalows. Eventually, it turned into a country road again and there were fewer and fewer houses.

The air around them changed as they got farther and deeper away from the town. Evie felt a shiver run down her spine. Were they getting closer to the clan?

Finally, they saw a small post box with *8 Garden Lane* painted on it. That was the address the Lycan High Council had on file for Clifford Forrest.

Connor maneuvered the truck onto the dirt road. Evie squinted and saw a house in the distance. As they drove closer, she realized how big it was. It was a classic, two story country-style home with all white paneling and a wraparound porch, plus a balcony. It looked old but well-maintained. Parked outside was a couple of vehicles, including a black Dodge Ram that was quite similar to Connor's.

Connor parked right next to the other truck, and, for some reason, Evie felt goose bumps rise on her arms. *Silly*, she thought. Black Dodge Rams were common, especially in these parts. Why would she have such a reaction to what was obviously a coincidence?

"Stay here," Connor said. "I'll have audio on, and Quinn will

All for Connor 179

be listening." He switched on the small earpiece in his palm and put it in his ear.

"All right," she said.

Connor gave her a nod and then slid out of the driver's seat. As she watched him walk up the porch steps, a small, niggling feeling scratched at her brain. "Stay here?" she huffed out loud to no one in particular. "No way."

She opened the passenger side door and hopped out, then strode in the direction of the house. Connor was already at the front door, but he wasn't moving. She slipped in beside him and put her hand into his.

"Dammnit, Evie," he cussed. "I told you to stay in the truck!"

"I'm not letting you do this alone," she protested.

"It could be dangerous," he said. "I can't protect you if I don't know what to expect."

"You're worried about nothing!"

"How do you know?"

She slammed her foot on the floor like a child. "I just do!"

Noise from inside made both of them whip their heads toward the door. Soft voices and heavy footsteps were approaching.

"Shit," Connor cursed. He tried to turn, but Evie gripped his hand hard to prevent him from leaving.

"Don't go," she said. "Stay and see what happens." Her heart was pounding in her chest, but she wanted to know, too.

The lock turned, and Evie went still, though her heart continued to hammer in her chest. She gripped Connor's hand and watched his face closely. The wooden door swung open.

"Who the fuck—"

Connor tensed visibly and then went very still. Evie looked at the figure standing in the open doorway, and she had to do a double take just to be sure she wasn't seeing things. She started from the bottom, scrutinizing the man's well-worn work boots up his faded jeans to the tight white t-shirt molded around a broad chest. His shoulders were wide, and tattoos curled up his neck and down the bulging muscles of his arms. She gasped as she went higher to the ruddy beard and the familiar face with green eyes.

Only the man standing toe-to-toe with Connor wasn't just familiar to her, he was an exact mirror image. Same height, same face, same nose, same high cheekbones, same square jaw under the thick beard. And a Lycan, of course, she could tell, just like she could when she first met Connor. There was only one thing different: the other man was missing her Connor's scar.

Both men stood there, not budging. Evie herself couldn't breathe or move. Was this really happening?

Finally, mirror-Connor turned his head and braced his arm on the doorframe. "Momma," he called, his voice rough. "I think you should come out here!"

"What is it, Jackson?" a feminine voice answered from somewhere inside the house. "I have my chicken on the stove, and you know I can't just leave that." Soft footsteps approach them, and a small, older woman with reddish blonde hair ducked underneath the mirror-Connor's arm. "Now what's so important that—" She let out a gasp, and her eyes went wide as saucers when she looked up at Connor. She didn't move for what seemed like forever. The wooden spoon in her hand dropped to the floor, the clattering sound breaking the silence.

"C-C-Connor?" she said, her voice breaking. "Is that ..." She reached out slowly as if she were afraid he was going to disappear into thin air if she touched him. When her hand landed on his cheek, she let out a cry and launched herself into his arms. "Connor, it really is you!"

Connor's face was still inscrutable, but he wound his arms

around the tiny woman clinging to him. He swallowed, then relaxed.

The woman was full-out sobbing, her body trembling as she wept and bawled. Evie looked over at mirror-Connor—his face was pale, and his expression was that of complete and utter shock.

"Momma, c'mon now. Let him breathe," he finally said and gently pulled the woman off Connor.

She gasped and stepped back, her eyes shining with more tears. "I can't believe ... you found us. You came back. But how?"

A muscle in Connor's jaw ticked. "I don't know. I mean ..."

"It's a long story," Evie interjected.

Familiar green eyes stared at her. "Oh my, I'm so sorry. I'm just so ..." She wiped her hands on her apron. "I'm Lily. Lily Forrest." She nodded to mirror-Connor. "And this, as you can probably guess, is my son, Jackson Forrest. He's Alpha of our clan."

"I'm Evie King," she said, extending her hand. "Alpha," she said with a reverent nod.

"I think you should come in," Jackson said. "You're both welcome in our home."

"Thank you, Alpha." She looked up at Connor. "May we follow you in a minute? I need to talk to Connor."

Lily looked worried for a moment, but Jackson tugged at her arm. "All right, we'll be inside. Oh, my fried chicken! I should check on it! You'll stay for lunch, right?"

Evie nodded, and Lily and Jackson disappeared into the house. She turned to Connor, touching his arm. "Connor?"

His back was stiff and his jaw tense. "I think we should go." He shook his head. "No, Quinn, it's fine," he said, and she realized he was talking into the comm unit in his ear. "I said it's fine, we're driving back now."

"No!" Evie protested. "We're staying."

"No, we're going," Connor said. "Shut up, Quinn...no..." He let out a growl and tossed the earpiece away.

"We're staying," Evie said, planting her hands on her hips.

"We're going."

"No, you stubborn ox," she said. "We're staying. We need to find out more."

"Find out what?" Connor said in a terse voice. "They obviously knew about me. And they let them take me ..." He let out an angry growl and slammed his fist on the wall, causing the white paneling to break under his hand.

"Connor, you don't even know what happened," Evie said, tugging on his arm.

"And I don't wanna or need to know." He was really angry now, and Evie's lungs were choking from the heaviness of the air around her.

"Hey!"

They both stopped and looked toward the door. Jackson was standing there, arms crossed over his chest. The scowl on his face was so much like Connor's. Evie still couldn't believe there were two of them.

Jackson walked out onto the porch, stretching up to his full height. "If you're done destroying my house, asshole, then you should come in. You shouldn't keep a lady waiting, especially your mother."

Connor snorted and turned away. "We're not staying."

Jackson huffed. "Look, stay or not, I don't give a fuck. But you should listen to what she has to say before you make any judgments. You don't know what she's been through."

Evie looked at Connor with pleading eyes. "Connor, c'mon. Let's go in."

"Fine."

Jackson nodded. "I swear, though, if you break her heart, I'm gonna break your face."

They followed Jackson into the house, and he led them to a large, airy kitchen. Lily was standing by the stove, watching over a cast iron pot as the oil bubbled. The smell of delicious frying chicken filled Connor's nostrils. Much like the outside of the house, the kitchen interior was old and worn but clean and well-maintained. Lily obviously kept everything in order and took pride in her kitchen.

"Have a seat." Lily motioned to the chairs around the large table.

"I'll watch the chicken," Jackson said as he urged his mother to sit down as well.

"Would you like some coffee? Tea?" Lily asked.

"We're fine," Evie answered for them.

Connor was still holding his tongue, unable to speak. To say that he was in shock was an understatement. The moment he saw Jackson, everything he knew had flipped upside down. A twin. He was a twin. And Jackson was Alpha, which meant ... Clifford Forrest was their father. Where was he, then?

Evie glanced at him, then turned to Lily. "I know this must be a shock."

"It is ... I never thought I'd see my baby again." She laughed. "Well, not a baby. But you were a baby when they took you. How did you escape?"

All eyes turned to Connor. "A man helped me." They waited for him to explain further, but the pain gnawing at his chest made it difficult to talk.

"Lily," Evie began. "If you don't mind, could you tell us what happened, please? You said someone took Connor?"

Lily nodded. "My husband, your father, was Alpha of our clan. He was a wonderful man, and he did what he could to protect us. The Shenandoah Clan has always preferred to live out here in isolation because our wolves ... well, they tend to be more aggressive and unmanageable. It's easier to let lose without too many humans around." She paused. "You and Jackson were only eight months old. Eight months and twelve days," she said, her eyes wistful. "A group of Lycans came. Lone Wolves. They were asking for help, for shelter. There were storms and flooding, you see. Cliff gave them shelter out in our barn." She nodded to the red structure in the distance. "But ... that same night, they came in. Barged into our home and they went to your room. One of them had both of you in his arms. We thought they were trying to kill you."

Evie gasped and gripped his hand tight. "Then what happened?"

"We fought them, but there were too many. Five against two. Cliff managed to take out the man holding you both, and he dropped Jackson. But one of them, this huge red-haired man with a thick beard, got your father and ..." She sobbed, tears streaming down her cheeks. "I tried ... he tried, but we couldn't and ..."

"Shhh ..." Evie got up from her seat and embraced Lily. "I'm sure you did all you could."

"We tried to look for you," Lily said. "I'm sorry ... I heard what you said outside. That you think we just let them take you. But we couldn't fight them. I'm sorry we failed to protect you ..."

"They tried looking for you," Jackson added. "I know, believe me. They told me everything while I was growing up. But put yourself in her place before you judge. All of a sudden, Mom lost her husband, the clan lost its leader, and she had an infant to take care of." His eyes hardened. "Maybe if you want to blame someone, you should blame me."

"No," Lily cried out. "No, no, Jackson, don't think that. I love you." She looked at Connor. "I love you both. But he's right. I had to step up as Lupa and keep the clan together. I had to be strong for them and for Jackson. We've tried all these years, looking for you. Even hired a detective, and for ten years, he searched for you."

Connor took a deep breath. "You wouldn't have found me," he said in a quiet voice. "No one did. They made sure of that."

"Who?" Lily asked. "Who were those Lone Wolves that took you?"

The tightness in his chest began to loosen, and he somehow found the voice to speak. He told them what he could remember of the early years and, briefly, of the time he spent fighting in The Cage. Lily's face went from shock to horror.

"Jesus," Jackson muttered, rubbing his palms down his face.

"I'm sorry, son," she whispered. "I could never ..."

"I'm not telling you this to make you feel guilty." Why was he telling them, then? He wasn't sure, but it was like something inside him broke and it all came spilling out. "The night I got this," he pointed to the scar down his face, "there was a man in the audience. Even from The Cage, I could feel his eyes on me and that he was different. He was a human. My handlers patched me up, and I spent the night in the infirmary. That man, he broke in, despite the fact he could have been ripped apart by the wolves, and got me outta there. He took me far away from that place and brought me to his home in Portland."

"He freed you," Lily said.

"He gave me a family." He offered a small laugh. "A fucked-up family. Sometimes I want to kill them, but they're mine." And he realized he wouldn't have had it any other way. Archie, Killian, Meredith, even that idiot Quinn were his family; not one he was born into, but one they all made together. He could have left anytime. Archie never forced any of them to stay, but he did. They all did.

"I'm sorry for what you went through," Lily said. "I'm glad

you found your place in the world and people who love you. But, how did you find us?"

"A man led us here. He was my trainer," Connor said. "Someone had told him I was from the Shenandoah Clan. We looked through the High Council records and found your address."

"We tried to find you. We really did," Lily insisted. "But we didn't know the names of those Lone Wolves. Not their real ones anyway."

"Sounds like they did their best to stay under the radar," Evie said.

"Yes," Connor agreed. "I doubt the owners of an illegal cage fighting operation would keep records or register with the High Council."

Lily wiped the tears from her eyes with her apron. "Oh goodness. This has been quite a morning. You'll stay for lunch, right?"

Before Connor could say anything, Evie put her hands on top of his. "Yes, of course. We'll stay."

"Good. Now, I—" The front door slamming open and the sound of footsteps running interrupted her. Lily and Jackson looked at each other. "What in the world—"

"I'm not here!" a voice cried out from the foyer. "If anyone asks, tell them I'm not here! And I didn't set fire to no field!"

Jackson let out an exasperated sigh. "Excuse me," he said, nodding to Evie and Connor. He disappeared into the hallway, then came back moments later. He shoved a small figure into the kitchen by the ear.

"Oww! Pa, what'd you do that for?" The figure—a young boy who was maybe eight or nine years old—rubbed his ears and looked at Jackson indignantly.

"We have guests, Austin," he said.

Austin, who was the spitting image of Jackson except for the platinum blonde hair, turned to the kitchen table. He looked at Evie curiously, but, when his gaze landed on Connor, his face turned pale. "Holy shitballs! You look just like my Pa!"

"Watch your language, Austin!" Lily admonished. "Or do I have to wash out your mouth with soap again?"

"Aww, Grams, c'mon," Austin whined. "It was an accident! You didn't expect me not to piss my pants when I saw him, didja?"

"This little troublemaker," Jackson said, pushing Austin closer to them. "Is my son, Austin Forrest. Say hello to your Uncle Connor and Aunt Evie, Austin."

The young boy staggered forward. He eyed them suspiciously, but then held out his hand. "Nice to meet ya, sir. Ma'am." He gave Evie a sweet smile.

"Aw, he's so cute," Evie said, as he took the boy's hand. Austin shook it vigorously, then jumped into her arms for a hug. "He's ... uh, quite friendly."

Connor scowled when the young boy pressed his face against Evie's chest. It seemed like an innocent move, but Jackson's deep sigh told him otherwise.

"Hey now, Cassanova," Jackson scolded, pulling Austin off Evie. "How about saying hi to your Uncle Connor?"

The boy stepped toward Connor, his eyes growing wide. Connor let out a loud growl, and the young boy squeaked and then turned tail, running out of the kitchen.

"Connor!" Evie admonished. "Why did you do that?"

"Little pervert deserved it," Connor grumbled.

Jackson laughed. "He sure did. Maybe I should call you when I need to discipline him. God knows he needs an ass whooping now and then."

"Let's get ready for lunch, shall we?" Lily said. "You all wash your hands and clean up."

"I'll help you," Evie offered.

The two men went to the sink to wash their hands as Evie and Lily set the table. Jackson called Austin back from upstairs where he was hiding in his room. When everyone was in the kitchen, they all sat down for lunch.

"This is delicious, Lily," Evie said as she bit into some chicken. "The best fried chicken I've ever had. And these biscuits are phenomenal."

"Thank you," Lily said.

"Grams makes the best food," Austin said through a mouthful of mashed potatoes. "If you're my Aunt Evie, are you Uncle Connor's girlfriend? Wife?"

"Austin," Jackson warned.

"Oh, the mouth of babes," Lily laughed, then looked at Evie, a hopeful glint in her eyes. "Well, are you? Because I'd love another grandchild. A girl, maybe?"

Evie blushed furiously.

"Momma," Jackson said with a tight laugh. "Sorry," he said to Evie apologetically. " She's a bit nosy."

"Well, I can hope, can't I?" Lily said. "And she's so pretty too! You'd make such beautiful babies."

"Please forgive my Momma," Jackson said. "She's baby-obsessed right now."

"Hey, I thought I was your favorite grandkid," Austin pouted.

"Aw, you will always be special to me, Austin," Lily soothed, ruffling his hair. "But wouldn't you like a little cousin?"

"No, because babies are stupid," he retorted, his nose wrinkling.

Evie snorted. "I don't think you have to worry about that." She avoided Connor's eyes, but her cheeks turned about ten shades of crimson.

Connor didn't know why, but her words sent a strange pang across his chest. They had both avoided the question of what Evie was to him, even to her parents, but maybe soon they'd have to face it. He didn't know the answer himself; all he knew was Evie was his.

"So, did you drive all the way here from Portland?" Lily asked.

"No, New York," Evie supplied. "Connor and his siblings moved to New York to work for Creed Security. I work as their part-time assistant."

"Is that how you met?" Lily asked.

"Er ..." Evie turned red again. "Kind of."

"Wait ... Creed Security? As in the Creed Dragon?" Jackson asked.

"Holy fu—dge nuggets," Austin exclaimed as a piece of chicken fell from his mouth. "You work for the dragon?"

"You know about him?" Connor asked.

Jackson nodded. "We're not totally isolated out here. The High Council keeps all Alphas up to date with news, and I read up once in a while. There was that big thing with some bad people in Norway, right?"

Connor nodded. "We were there."

"And you saw the dragon?" Austin blurted through a mouthful of mashed potatoes.

"Sure did."

"What was he like? Is he really a hundred stories high? Can he breathe fire and lava?"

"Austin," Lily warned. "Don't talk with your mouth full. And stop pestering Uncle Connor with questions."

"It's no bother," Connor said, taking a swig of his iced tea. "I've only seen him once. We were fighting the mages, and then I saw something gold flying above us. He must have been a hundred feet tall and his wingspan maybe twice that."

"And then what happened?" Austin asked, completely transfixed.

Connor continued the story of the battle in Norway, and

Austin was even more impressed (and a little less scared) by his Uncle.

"That's so cool," Austin said. "One day, I'm gonna be Alpha and I'm gonna fight battles like that! And maybe I can even fight for the Creed Dragon, too!"

"Hopefully that's not for a long time," Lily said with a resigned sigh. "So, Evie, Connor, you're not going to drive all the way back to New York today, are you?"

"We weren't planning on a long trip," Connor said.

"But we could stay the night, couldn't we, Connor?" Evie asked with a hopeful look.

"We didn't make reservations for a hotel."

"Nonsense," Lily said. "You'll stay here. We've got six bedrooms and only three of them occupied."

"We'll stay," Evie declared. "What?" She looked at Connor. "I don't have a job to go back to, and your brothers owe you a vacation."

The two women and Austin looked at him as if daring him to say no. He grumbled, then looked at Jackson. "If it's okay with the Alpha."

His twin chuckled. "Even if I wanted to say no, I'm outnumbered. You're welcome to stay."

"It's settled," Evie said, clapping her hands. "Thank you for your hospitality, Alpha, Lupa. We would love to stay."

20

News of Connor's return had spread to the members of the Shenandoah Clan. Evie was surprised when they all turned up the next day. Yes, the entire clan showed up on their doorstep. And to welcome their lost son, they all decided an impromptu barbecue was in order.

Evie watched the men set up tables and chairs as she helped the women prepare the sides. She was surprised because she thought most clans were small, but the Shenandoah clan, along with its human members, had to have been at least a hundred strong.

"How do you manage so many Lycans?" Evie asked Jackson. "New York is the biggest clan on record, and there are only about two hundred fifty Lycans registered."

"We like to keep to ourselves," Jackson said. "We do the bare minimum with the High Council. Enough to keep 'em happy and away from us. Most of the Lycans around here, they couldn't live in the cities or in big communities with humans. Their wolves are too difficult. Probably because we've been living in isolation for too long. We would cause too much trouble if we lived among a large human population." He nodded to the wide, rolling hills of the valley. "But, here, they have lots of space to roam. They can even work on the farm. Hard work helps keep them steady and distracted, plus they can shift safely if they need to."

Evie bit her lip. Jackson's words stuck in her mind. Maybe that's why Connor hated New York so much. It was in his DNA to hate the crowds and the smell and the feeling of being cooped up.

"So, are you Connor's mate?" Jackson asked out of the blue.

"I ..." What was she to him? "I'm not sure."

"Well, shit. He better make you his or someone else might want to snatch you up." He gave her a wink and a flirtatious smile, which made her chuckle. It was strange how the two men looked so much alike, yet so completely different. On Jackson, that smile seemed to fit, yet, if Connor attempted to flirt like that, it would only be awkward. Awkward and completely adorable.

"I'm joking," Jackson said. "But it must be nice. To have someone to care for."

"What about Austin's mom?" Evie saw Jackson's face fall for a second before he put up a cool mask. "I'm sorry, that wasn't an appropriate question."

"No, it's fine." He shrugged. "We're not together anymore. She took off when he was a baby. Said she couldn't hack being a mom." He straightened his shoulders. "Well, I gotta go take Dolly to the store and grab some meat. We've got to feed a hundred hungry people, so I'm gonna load 'er up with ribs and burgers."

"Dolly?"

He jerked his thumb to the Black Dodge Ram, which he had driven to the backyard to bring the tables over. "My truck."

"You named your truck Dolly?" Evie asked with a giggled. "After Dolly Parton?"

"Yeah. What's so funny?"
"I'll tell you later."

One night at the Shenandoah Clan farm turned into a few days. Evie and Connor called his siblings back in New York to tell them the news. Needless to say, they were happy to let him have a few days off.

"Oh my God!" Meredith exclaimed over video chat as she waved to Lily and Jackson. They were outside on the back porch, crowded around Evie's phone. "Twins? This is so cool!"

"Two of you?" Quinn said, his face filling the screen as he yanked the phone from Meredith. "There's two of your ugly mugs in this world? Tragedy!"

Normally, Quinn's insults would have rankled him, but this time he let out a chuckle. "Wait 'till you see this. Austin, c'mere!" he called. "Come say hi to your Uncle Quinn and Aunt Meredith."

Austin trudged forward and peered at the screen. "Hi."

"Shut the front door!" Meredith squealed. "He's like a mini-you! So adorable! I wanna squeeze him and kiss his little cheeks!"

Connor gave her a wry smile. "We'll see about that." Austin definitely deserved the label troublemaker. The little shit couldn't seem to not get himself in trouble. Just yesterday, his principal called Jackson in for another meeting about his son's behavior. Something about trying to set the football field on fire. Austin wasn't even old enough to be in the high school where said football field was located.

"You're multiplying! Someone call the CDC!" Quinn said from off camera. "Ow, Selena, quit it!"

"We'll have to come visit," Meredith said. "Maybe Daric and

I can pop in sometime."

"We'll be back in a few days," Connor said.

"Take your time, get to know your family," Meredith said. "We'll take care of things here."

"I appreciate it," Connor said. He said goodbye to them, then hung up.

"Nice family," Jackson said.

"Most of the time," he replied.

"I'll get dinner started," Lily said. "Pot roast and mashed potatoes tonight." She waved goodbye to them and disappeared into the house.

"I'm going to go and help Lily with dinner," Evie said. "Want to come with me, Austin?"

"Sure, Aunt Evie." The boy took Evie's hand, and they walked back into the house.

Connor turned to Jackson. With the barbecue the other day and with Jackson being busy around the farm, Connor hadn't had time alone with his twin until now. "Did you want to show me some more of the farm?"

"Sure, let's go."

Jackson led him off the porch and to the back of the house. They began to stroll across the field, past the small fishing pond and the barn. Jackson explained it was a working farm, and they kept horses, livestock, chickens, and even some alpacas (for their high-quality wool). They also grew vegetables, hay, and grain. The farm was completely self-sustaining and off the grid, using a combination of solar and wind energy for power. Most everyone in the clan pitched in, whether it was working with the livestock, harvesting grains and eggs, spinning wool, or selling produce at the market.

"We're not rich," Jackson explained. "But we do all right."

"Cowboy Lycans," Connor commented.

"There are lots of different Lycans all over the world,"

Jackson said. "Why not cowboys?"

"I didn't mean anything by that, it's just that I've never had the chance to see other clans." The silence that followed was deafening. Connor looked at his twin, the similar face still so jarring to him. His eyes, however, filled with an emotion he couldn't quite peg. "Jackson." He placed a hand on the other man's shoulders.

There was more silence until Jackson opened his mouth. "I often wonder what it would have been like."

"What?"

"If it were me."

Connor knew exactly what he was saying. "No. Don't think that."

"But it could have been."

"Jackson, listen to me." He tugged at his brother so they were face to face. "Yes, it could have been you. But it wasn't. And now that's all and done. And we're all here. I wouldn't have it any other way."

"You could have been Alpha."

"But I'm not." He ran his hands through his hair. "I could never do this. Take care of everyone. Of Lily and Austin. And run this farm. And I don't want to. I'm not here to take it away from you."

"Then why are you here?"

The question, as well as the look in Jackson's eyes, jolted him. Like he knew what he was hiding. "Fine. I'll tell you." Jackson was his brother. His twin. He could trust him. So, he told him the rest of the story and the stuff he had left out. Told him about the red-haired man.

When he finished his story, Jackson kicked a rock and let out a curse. "Shit. Well, we'll do what we can to help you. I'm sure Momma still has the records from the detective. In fact, I'm pretty sure he still lives in town. We can talk to him tomorrow."

"Thank you," Connor said. "That means a lot." He didn't have much hope at this point. It sounded like the Lone Wolves who took him had covered their tracks well. Heck, even Archie couldn't track them down. But he would take what he could get.

Jackson flashed him a smile. "So, I do have one more thing I wanted to show you. Something you'll really thank me for."

"What?"

"You'll see." Jackson led him back to the house and then around to the front where their trucks were parked. He opened Dolly's tailgate and pointed to the pile of canvas on the bed.

"What's this?"

"It's a truck bed tent and a mattress." He sighed when Connor glanced around, a blank look on his face. "Seriously? It's for you and Evie. It's supposed to be a clear night tonight and not too chilly." He sighed. "I know staying in the house isn't ideal, especially with two Lycans who have super hearing."

"Oh." Now he understood. Though Lily had put them in the same room, finding time for frisky fun was difficult. There were always people coming and going, plus, with his mother under the same roof, it was too weird. The last time they had had sex was ... he smiled to himself and glanced at Jackson's truck. Better keep that to himself.

"Feels weird having sex in the same house as your mom, right?"

"You screw girls on that thing?"

"Huh? Hell no. Well, not in the camping tent, but that Dolly's seen plenty of action." Jackson chuckled. "Go ahead and use it tonight. Put it on your Jolene—it still creeps me out that you named her that—then drive her out to the middle of the property. I'll tell you the best spot for stargazing ... among other things. You and your blue balls can thank me later. "

"Thanks, Jackson," Connor said with a chuckle.

"No prob, brother."

21

*E*vie wasn't quite sure what to expect when Connor said they were going "camping." When she was a kid, she went with her dad all the time. They would go to one of the campgrounds a couple of hours away from their house, spend the whole weekend hiking, fishing, cooking by the campfire, and sleeping in the little tent they pitched. Tonight, however, after dinner, Connor said goodnight to Lily, Jackson, and Austin, then led her out to the truck.

"Where are we going?" she asked.

"You'll see."

They drove further into the property, past the livestock pens and the solar panels, and deeper into the valley. As they turned down one of the dark, dusty roads, Connor pointed out the window.

Evie gasped. The sky was full of stars. They seemed to twinkle and sparkle, filling the sky with a dazzling display. Out here, away from the light pollution of the city, they seemed more brilliant. "Oh, a falling star!" she exclaimed, pointing to the faint streak as it painted the heavens.

"What did you wish for?" Connor asked as he cut the engine.

"I can't tell you that or it won't come true," she said, then flashed him a smile. "But maybe it's already come true."

Connor eased out of the truck, and, as was his newly formed habit, walked around to her side, opened the door, and helped her out. It was a little chilly, so she wrapped her arms around herself to stay warm as Connor began to unload the truck. She gazed up at the night sky as she thought about the past few days.

Being out here with Connor and spending time with his family had been one of the best experiences of her life. Coming here with him had been the right decision. She'd also never seen Connor so relaxed and at ease. And why wouldn't he be? He was reunited with his family, and this place obviously affected him in a positive way. He seemed content and maybe even ... happy?

But, then again, there was a strange pit forming in her stomach. This place seemed so right for him. She remembered his words about hating New York, and, seeing how he was here, she understood now. But that didn't mean she didn't feel a bit resentful that he abhorred New York. A part of her missed it. The vibrant energy, the life, the hustle and bustle. She missed the art and the coffee shops and the noise and the streets.

And then there was the fact that she had had her dream in the palm of her hands and it just disappeared. No, she didn't regret leaving the toxic environment that had grown around the show. That part she could do without. But, now, she wished she was back there, scrambling up the subway steps to rush to an audition or even being at the open mic at the Stage Bound Bar, singing in front of an audience.

A loud crash caught her attention, and she looked around.

Connor had set up some lamps around the truck for light, and she saw the tangled mess of tent poles and canvas by his feet.

"Sorry," he said. "This looked much easier in the pictures."

She laughed and walked over to him. "Where does it go?"

He nodded to the truck bed. There was a mattress made up with some thick blankets. "Over there."

"Hmmm ..." She walked over to the tailgate and hoisted herself up, then scrambled over the to the mattress. "Maybe we don't need a tent."

Connor's eyes glowed in the dim light, and, in a flash, he leaped onto the truck bed and was beside her. He caught her mouth in a fiery kiss, his warm lips a contrast to her cool ones. She moaned as he pushed her down on the mattress, pressing his large body over hers. His kisses sang in her veins, quickly heating her up.

He pulled away from her and tossed his shirt over his head as she fumbled with the buttons on her blouse. She opened the fabric, baring her lace-covered breasts to his hot gaze. He leaned down and pulled the cups off, then bent his head to suckle on her nipples. She jerked forward as his wet mouth made contact.

His large hand crept between them, slipping under her leggings and panties. Fingers teased at her damp slit, moving up and down, brushing against her clit. She bucked up against him, but he continued his slow torture with his mouth and fingers.

"Connor," she pleaded. "I'm begging you ..."

"You don't have to beg, Evie," he said in a rough voice. "You never have to beg with me." His fingers plunged into her core, and she grabbed at his arms. He moved his fingers in and out of her, his thumb stroking her clit. She came in an instant, the orgasm nearly tearing her apart. Connor whispered soothing words into her ear, encouraging her, telling her she was beautiful. She shuddered as the pleasure slowed and eddied.

"I need you inside me," she said. "Now."

He sucked in a breath and withdrew his hand from her leggings. She shucked them off, along with her panties. Connor kneeled over her, unbuckled his belt, and pulled down his pants and underwear. In the moonlight, she could see that his cock was already hard, thick, and heavy with wanting and she licked her lips, thinking of him inside her.

He covered her, spreading her legs apart and getting between them. Evie held her breath as she felt the tip nudge at her.

She cried out his name as he suddenly pushed himself inside her in one stroke as if he couldn't wait. She couldn't either. They could do slow later; right now, she needed him. He began to move, fast and rough, and she wrapped her legs around him.

Evie threw her head back and gazed up at the stars as Connor made love to her with deep, quick strokes that had her panting. As she felt the orgasm build up inside her, the stars blurred in her vision. Hot tears formed in her eyes, but she didn't even realize she was crying until they fell down her cheeks. Tears of joy, of sadness. All for Connor. This broken, wonderful man she loved.

"Evie," he called as his body stiffened. She felt the explosion in her, spreading fast like a hurricane. Tearing into her and leaving her breathless.

He collapsed on top of her and kissed her neck. He shifted to his side, taking her along with him as he pulled her to him "Cold?" he asked.

She snuggled into his chest. "Not anymore."

Heartbeats passed and they lay there, contented. Connor pulled the blankets over them and drew her closer, wrapping his arms around her as he fell asleep.

Evie stared up at the stars again, as another one fell from the sky. What should she wish for? For Connor to love her back, as much as she did him. But that would be selfish, wouldn't it? Instead, she wished for Connor's happiness, whatever and wherever, that may be.

The next morning, they packed up their meager little campsite and headed back to the house. As they exited the truck, Jackson and Lily were waiting on the front porch, having their morning coffee. Evie blushed as Lily flashed her a knowing look and Jackson gave Connor a thumbs' up sign and huge grin.

"How was stargazing?" Jackson asked.

"Beautiful," Connor said, though he was looking at Evie.

"It was—" A ringing in her pocket cut her off. "Sorry." She looked down at her phone and saw the name. Annie Fox. *Huh?* "Sorry, I have to take this."

"Go on, dear," Lily said. "We'll sit out here and have some coffee."

She nodded at them and then slid the button on her phone to take the call. "Annie?" she said as she entered the house.

"Evie!" Annie's breathless voice crackled through the speaker. "I've been trying to reach you all night!"

"I didn't have reception, sorry. What's up."

"Evie, I have some news. Great news. Phenomenal news."

"What is it?"

"*Love and Regrets* is back on."

"What?"

"Yeah! I can't believe it either. But our lawyer tore Atlantis Artists a new one for the whole stalker debacle. They didn't want any bad publicity, so they're going on with the show. Without Janelle."

"I'm so happy for you, Annie. And for Jane, too."

"Thanks! But, Evie, I'm calling you because we want you back."

"Oh, I'd love to," she said. "I'm sure I could help out whoever you found to fill in for Janelle."

"You silly girl," Annie laughed. "We want you back. In the starring role."

Evie's heart thundered in her chest, and she suddenly felt faint. "S-s-say that again?"

"We want you to play Colleen. In the show. Can you come back to the theater tonight?"

"I ... I'm not in New York. I'm in West Virginia."

"Seriously? What are you doing there, girl?"

She laughed. "Long story."

"We can wait for you until tomorrow, but that's about it. We've already lost days of rehearsals, and we want to go into previews as scheduled. So ... will you do it?"

"I ..." She bit her lip. "Can I get back to you ... I just need a minute to process."

Annie sighed. "Fine. But you need to make up your mind, like, yesterday."

"I just have to make some arrangements," she said. "I'll send you a text message as soon as I know I can be in New York tonight."

"All right girl. I have my phone in my hands, so just let me know quickly."

"Thanks." When the phone line went dead, Evie sank down on the nearest surface she could reach, which was the steps leading upstairs.

This was her chance. She would not only be on Broadway, but she'd be in the lead role. She could go back to New York and live her dream. But a glance at the door made her stop. Connor. He hated the city; he was happy here. Even now, she could hear his throaty chuckle. It was a real laugh, one she'd never heard before. She crept up to the door and pressed her ear against it.

"I'm serious, Connor," she heard Jackson say. "Stay here, pledge to the clan, and you can have half of this. It's your birthright, you know. I could even name you Beta. I haven't really needed one, but the clan's grown so much."

"Ha, Beta?" Connor joked. "Like I'd be second to your sorry ass ..."

Evie's heart leaped to her throat. Connor staying here would be the best thing for him. It would make him happy and help keep his wolf steady. He wouldn't have to be put down if he stayed here. Taking a deep breath, she opened the door and stepped onto the porch.

"Evie? What's wrong?" Connor asked as he stood up from this chair.

"Nothing," she said. "I mean, it's all good."

"Who was that on the phone?"

"It was Annie. From the production." She quickly explained what had happened.

"My dear, that's great news!" Lily said, embracing her. "It's your dream, right? To be on stage."

"Yes," she said with a tight smile. "It is."

"Congratulations." Connor drew her into a tight hug. "You'll be great."

Her heart dropped to her stomach. Connor was telling her to go. "Thank you. But it means I have to be at the theater in the morning."

"Oh." Connor dropped his arms to his sides. "If we leave in an hour we can make it back to New York by mid-afternoon."

"What?" she said with a tense laugh. "Connor, don't be silly. I can't force you to leave now." She shook her head. "You've hardly had any alone time with your mother or Jackson. Plus, you told me last night that you're going to talk to that detective."

She turned her face away from them. "I'll go pack, and then I can catch a flight or a train or something. Let me go and check now." Before they could see the tears building in her eyes, she tore back into the house, jogging up the steps two at a time.

When she reached the guest bedroom, she grabbed her duffel bag and started flinging her things into it. She only paused to send Annie a quick text message, telling her she'd be in the theater first thing tomorrow.

A knock on the door made her stop. "Evie?"

"Come in," she said.

Lily walked into the room, a worried look on her face. "Evie, honey, are you okay?"

She wiped the tears from her eyes and took a deep breath before she faced the older woman. "Yes, I'm fine. Just ... uh, nerves, you know?"

Lily smiled at her sadly. "Is that really it?"

"Uh-huh."

"Are you sure?" She walked closer to her and then touched her cheek with a gentle hand.

The emotions were too much, and something inside her broke. Evie's face crumpled, and Lily drew her into a hug as she cried softly.

"There, there dear ..."

"Please don't tell Connor," she sobbed. "Don't tell him."

"Don't tell him what?"

"That ... that I'm selfish, and I want him to come with me so bad."

Lily pulled away from her. "What do you mean, dear?"

"Promise me, Lily." Evie wiped the tears from her face. "He needs to stay here. I've never seen him so happy. And ..." She took a deep breath. "If he goes back to New York, he'll die."

Lily's expression turned to that of fear. "Tell me everything. From the beginning."

Both women sat down on the bed, and Evie began to explain to Lily what Connor had told her about why he chose to say in New York. "Can't you see? He's steady here. With you and Jackson and Austin. With the clan. He should pledge to your clan—he'll find purpose. And, if he fixes his wolf, Grant Anderson won't have to put him down."

"Evie, I ..." Lily looked conflicted.

"You know it's the right thing to do," Evie reasoned. "So, will you convince him to stay here? He has to stay here, you know it."

Lily nodded sadly. "I'll do what I can."

She pulled the older woman into a fierce hug. "Thank you."

"Evie?" Connor walked into the room, and the two women pulled away from each other.

"Connor," she said with a bright smile. "I think I found a flight that'll get me to New York by tonight."

He gave her a tight nod. "All right. If this is what you want."

"It is. It's my dream," she said. "I'm finally going to be on stage." The words sounded hollow, even to her own ears.

---

*C*onnor offered to drive Evie to the nearest airport, which was about an hour away from Winter's Creek. As she waved goodbye to Lily, Jackson, and Austin, her heart felt like it was being crushed under a heavy weight. She didn't even want to know what saying goodbye to Connor would be like.

The hour sped by quickly, even during the silent ride. Connor's face was inscrutable the whole time. As he pulled to the curb and was about to slide out the door, she stopped him with a hand on his arm.

"Hey, it's okay. You don't have to do that."

He jerked away without a word, and the weight pressing on

her heart grew tenfold. His movements were tense as he crossed to her side and opened the door. She slid out, and he reached into the backseat, took out her duffle bag, and handed it to her.

"You have a safe flight," he said, his voice terse.

"I ... I will," she said with a nod. "Connor—"

She stopped when he pulled her into his arms and planted his mouth firmly on hers. It took all her energy not to cry. She focused on the kissing, infusing it with all her emotions and love, hoping he'd understand. So many times she wanted to scream it at him during the ride over, to tell him to please love her back and ask to come to New York. But she couldn't. Not when this was his one chance to be happy and to live.

"Good luck. Or break a leg," he said.

"Thank you." She gave him a two-fingered salute, slung her duffel bag over her shoulder, and turned around. As soon as she stepped into the air conditioned airport, she ran for the bathroom, barely making it into a stall before she lost her lunch.

22

"For God's sake, Connor, calm the fuck down," Jackson roared.

"I am calm!" Connor growled, waving the hammer. He held it high and then slammed it down on the wooden post. "It's this fucking post. That. Won't. Stay. Up!" He punctuated each word with a strike, and the post was now buried halfway into the ground.

"Well, that's no help at all," Jesse, one of the Lycans working on the farm with them, said.

Connor bared his teeth and then pointed the hammer at Jesse's face. "I swear to God—"

"Connor," Jackson bellowed, then strode over to them, stepping between him and Jesse. "Stop it. Take a break. You're of no use to me now."

"I was helping."

"No, you're not. You're fucking it up, and you're scaring the horses!"

"Fuck you!" He threw the hammer to the ground and started walking away.

"Connor!" Jackson called. "Connor!" His brother grabbed

him by the shoulder. Connor shrugged him away, but that didn't stop Jackson. He put his hand on Connor's shoulder again and forced him to turn around.

"The only reason you're not flat on the ground is because I don't want to set a bad example for your son," Connor jerked his head toward Austin, who was standing under the shade of a big oak tree with Lily. "Now, let go of me."

"Connor, what the fuck is going on with you?" Jackson asked. "Ever since Evie left—"

"Shut up! I don't wanna hear it!"

Connor was being torn into pieces inside. The feral wolf was there, he could feel it. Looking around, he saw the horses, all of them skittish and neighing nervously. They could feel it, too. What he wouldn't give to just be able to let it out so he wouldn't have to feel like this anymore.

Evie. She had been his light, his world. And she just left. The pain ripping through him intensified as he remembered that day at the airport. How he wanted to take her back and lock her up in his truck and drive away. But he couldn't. She was about to go and do great things. To live her dream. He couldn't take that away from her. He loved her too much to stop her. It was costing him his control and his sanity, but he would never do that to her.

He thought about leaving, and then asking her to come back to West Virginia, but what would Evie say? What would she do? He couldn't ask her to give all that up. Not for him and his worthless soul.

"Connor."

"What?" he hollered, then bit his tongue when he realized it was Lily. "What is it, Momma?"

"That's the first time you called me that," she said.

"It is?"

She nodded. "Now tell me what's wrong."

"Nothing," he groused.

"I may have only known you for a little over a week, but I'm still your mother. I know when one of my children is hurting. Now," she took his hands into hers. "What's wrong? Why is your wolf acting up like this?"

"It's always like this. I'm broken. My wolf is broken."

"That's what Evie told me," Lily said.

"She did?" *Of course Evie knew that*, he thought bitterly. She sensed it and got the hell away from him.

"Yes. Which is why she wanted you to stay here."

Blood roared in his ears. "What?"

"She made me promise not to tell you. But I can't watch you tear yourself apart anymore," Lily said in a choked voice. "She wanted you to stay because she thought it was the best for you."

"That's stupid."

"She said that you'd never been so happy. She wanted that for you."

"She didn't want me to go with her to New York," Connor said bitterly.

"Because she didn't want you to be put down," Lily said, her voice shaking with anger. "Connor, she told me everything. That you wanted the Alpha of New York to put you down once you got this revenge business done. Is it true?"

He didn't answer, but his silence said it all.

"Goddamnit, Connor, you're better than that. Stronger than that. You're my son, and I'm not going to lose you again. Evie loves you so much. She was dying inside, leaving you here, but she did it because she wanted you alive and happy."

"Momma ..." He didn't know. How could he know? Evie did that? For him?

"Are you happy here, Connor?"

It was the easiest and hardest question to answer at the

same time. "I'm happy with her." It was Evie all along, he knew it. Being with her was what soothed him and his wolf.

"Do you love her?"

He didn't miss a beat. "Of course I do."

"Then what the hell are you waiting for?" Lily asked, hands on her hips. Tears shone in her eyes, but her smile was wide. "You go and be with your girl."

Connor drove back to New York like a madman. He promised Lily he'd visit as soon as he could with Evie. She joked that they better come back with a grandchild on the way or she'd have Jackson rescind his invitation. Jackson clapped him on the back and wished him good luck. "Though really, with that handsome face, who would need it?" his brother told him. Even Austin said he was rooting for them to get back together, even if it meant having gross baby cousins.

The drive took him less than five hours as his foot barely left the pedal. Tonight was the first preview of *Love and Regrets*. He begged Quinn to scalp him a ticket online; he didn't care what it cost. He was planning to go back to the hotel and freshen up first, but when he hit Manhattan traffic he let out a curse. He was stuck, and there was no time for a shower.

By the time he pulled up to the front of the Nina Haas theater, the show would have been nearing the end. He parked his truck and cut the engine, then hopped out.

"Hey, buddy, you can't park there!" The Meter Maid screamed at him as he bounded for the front door. "I'm gonna have you towed!"

"Do it; I don't care," he shouted as he tore into the lobby of the theater. He reached for the door, but an usher quickly stepped in front of him

"Sir, I can't let you in there!"

Connor was ready to fight whoever got in his way. He was ready to roar at the usher when he stopped short. She was an older lady—sweet-faced, with white hair, reminding him of a kindly old grandma. "I have a ticket. I need to get in."

"The show's almost over, sir," Sweet Grandma said. "Even if I could let you in, you wouldn't be seeing much. Maybe you can buy another ticket for tomorrow?"

"Please," he begged. "I need to see her."

"Connor?"

He turned around. The writers, Jane Collins and Annie Fox, were standing behind him.

"You're Connor, right? Evie's Connor?"

He nodded. "Yes. Can I go in, please?"

Annie and Jane looked at each other. Annie spoke first. "C'mon, I'll do you one better," she said with a chuckle. "Oh, you crazy kids."

Annie took his arm and then tugged him to the right side of the lobby. She knocked softly, and the door opened. They walked into a dark tunnel, lit only with floor lights, and they followed it to the end. When they emerged, they were in the backstage area.

There was a flurry of activity all around them. People were running around, bringing props here and there and helping the actors get into costumes and wigs right before they went on stage. Annie brought Connor to the wings where he had a good view of the stage.

His breath caught the moment he saw Evie. She was in the middle of the stage, singing the final number. He thought his heart was going to burst the moment her voice soared over the stage and sounded in his ears. He had never heard anything so beautiful in his entire life.

There was a hush, not just in the audience but backstage,

too. Everyone stopped what they were doing as she went through the song, hitting every note perfectly and overwhelming their senses with the pure emotion she displayed.

When she was done, there was a long pause, then applause broke out. It was thundering, the claps and cheers coming from the audience. He saw Selena and Quinn jump to their feet in the front row.

The orchestra began to play, and the cast gathered onstage for the curtain call. The crowd cheered the loudest for Evie, of course, when she took her solo bow. The music wound down and, when the curtain dropped, the cast erupted into shouts and cheers.

Everyone was gathering around Evie, congratulating her. She was smiling, nodding, and thanking the people surrounding her. Connor was content to watch her from the wings, to let her have her moment in the sun. He'd surprise her in the dressing room, maybe.

Just as he was stepping back, Evie's head whipped in his direction. His heart collided with his ribcage as toffee brown eyes crashed into his gaze. She stopped what she was doing and dropped her arms to her sides.

Connor spent most of the drive thinking what he'd do when he finally saw her again. What he would say and do. He played it in his mind. He wanted it go perfectly, so he played out the different scenarios of how he'd say sorry for letting her go.

But he didn't expect what happened next.

Evie walked toward him, ignoring her castmates. She swung her hips in a seductive manner as she strode in his direction. As she got closer, she reached out her arms. He grabbed her by the waist as she swung herself up and wrapped her legs around his waist. Sliding his hand around her neck, he pulled her closer until their lips met. Around them, people cheered, though they might as well have been invisible. The taste, smell, and feel of her were threatening to overwhelm his senses. He never wanted it to end.

"Connor, you're here," she said when they finally pulled apart.

"Of course I am," he said.

"But ... Lily ... Jackson ... I don't understand. You were happy there."

"I was happy with you," he said. "Evie, I love you."

A sharp cry tore from her throat. "Connor ... I love you, too!" She jumped back in his arms, and he staggered back. Thankfully, he regained his balance before they toppled over.

"You silly woman," he said, laughing against her mouth. "Why would you think I'd be content without you?"

"I didn't want you to be put down," she said. Tears formed in her eyes. "I ..."

"Shh ..." He kissed her again. "I won't be. I have too much to live for now."

23

"Connor?"

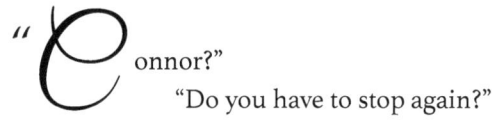

"Do you have to stop again?"

Evie's face turned a shade of green. "Yes, please."

Connor pulled over to the side of the road. The truck barely stopped before she pushed the door open and ran out to the bushes. He grabbed the packet of wet wipes and slid out of his seat, then walked over to Evie.

The previews for *Love and Regrets* had gone phenomenally well. The critics loved it, and tickets were sold out for weeks. Everyone loved the music, the story, and, of course, the show's star. The show ran six days a week, with matinees on Wednesdays and Saturdays. Though she was exhausted, Connor could tell Evie was ecstatic. She loved being in the show, and, now that everything ran like clockwork, she didn't have to be in the theater all day. That meant they spent every moment she wasn't onstage together. He had never truly felt this happy.

After two weeks, Evie insisted on visiting the Shenandoah farm and his family again. She had Mondays off and didn't have to be in the theater until 4 pm on Tuesday, so as soon as she took her bow on Sunday night, they raced off to West Virginia.

Traffic coming out of Manhattan was light, and they slept at a motel somewhere in Pennsylvania around midnight. Connor didn't want or need to stop thanks to his shifter side, but Evie had started feeling sick halfway through the trip. They got up bright and early and were now on their way back to the valley.

A worried feeling niggled at him. Evie had seemed healthy enough during the past two weeks. She certainly ate enough. She chalked it up to all the calories she burned dancing and singing for two hours, eight times a week. He wondered if she was tiring herself out and it was catching up with her.

"Thanks," Evie said weakly as she reached for the wet tissue. She wiped it across her mouth and took a deep breath.

"Are you okay? Should we maybe stop at a restaurant or a motel and you can lie down?"

Evie shook her head. "No, I want to go. Lily's expecting us. I texted her last night that we were going to be delayed, but I haven't heard back. Maybe the reception's spotty again. I don't want her to be worried."

Another strange feeling scratched at him. It wasn't like his mother not to text. She called and messaged them every day. Jackson was trying to get things in order at the farm, and they were scheduled to come to New York to watch the show next month.

"All right, let's go."

They got back on the road, driving deep into the Blue Ridge Mountains. Soon, they were pulling up to the house. It was early still. The sun was peeking behind the hill, bathing the house and green hills in a warm light.

Connor pulled up to the front and cut the engine. As he opened the door, he stopped and then closed it.

"Connor?"

A chill ran over his skin. He looked at the front porch. Empty. No Momma sitting on the rocking chair reading the paper. No Jackson drinking his coffee. In fact, the house was eerily still. There was something not right.

"Stay here," he said.

"What's wrong?" Evie asked, her tone panicked. "Connor, tell me."

He looked at her. "Please, Evie, just this once do as I say." He grabbed her hand and squeezed it. "When I get out, come over and sit here. Turn on the engine, lock the door, and if you hear so much as a mouse squeak, you step on the gas and get out of here, okay?"

"What? No!" she protested. "Connor, what's going on?"

"I don't know, but I'm going to find out."

Before she could protest further, he slipped out of the truck. He heard the click of the lock behind him, and, feeling assured, he made his way to the house. He bounded up the front porch steps and walked to the door. It was open, which rang more alarm bells in his head.

"Momma?" he called as he pushed the door in and carefully walked inside. "Jackson? Austin?"

"Out here." It was Lily. "On the back porch."

The sound of her voice did not make that feeling go away. There was still something that wasn't right. Quiet as a mouse, he walked through the kitchen and slowly opened the door that led to the back.

"Glad you could join us, boy."

Connor hadn't heard the voice in years, but he'd know it anywhere. He took one step out and turned to the right.

The red-haired man stood at the end of the porch, leaning casually against one of the posts. Two Lycans, both large and mean-looking, flanked him. As far as Connor could tell, the man looked almost the same as he did all those years ago. Same scraggly hair and beard, though now streaked with gray. However, he wasn't as tall as Connor remembered him. Maybe it was because he'd grown himself. He guessed they were probably the same height now.

But that didn't matter because on the other end of the porch was Lily, Jackson, and Austin. They were all sitting down, tied up with ropes, and surrounded by six large men—no, Lycans. Definitely Lycans. Lily and Austin wore frightened looks, while Jackson was naked and had healing cuts and bruises on his face.

"Bastard. Let them go. This isn't their fight."

"Oh yeah? Well, you made it their fight." He clucked his tongue as he walked closer, his boots stomping on the wooden floor. "Why couldn't you have stayed away, Connor? You could have kept them safe. And, now, they're going to die, too."

"Fuck you!" He stepped forward.

"Don't move an inch." The red-haired man shook his head, then nodded to Connor's family. One of the men took out a gun and pointed it at Lily's head. "What do you think? Momma first, then your twin, and then the brat? Or should I take out the kid first and watch you all scream."

"No!" Connor curled his hands into fists. "What do you want?"

"What do I want?" he asked with a sneer. "I wanted to be left alone and in peace. When that old man took you, our backer got spooked. See, Baeles didn't know about the fighting ring. We were trainin' you to be part of the Lone Wolf army, but The Cage was a little side gig to make us extra cash. When he found out you had escaped and that we were doing those fights, he shut us down and made sure I was under this thumb. Of course, that bastard rose to power in the Lycan High Council, while his friend, the mage, gathered his own forces and magic." He scoffed. "And me? I was left to pick up the pieces. To punish me for letting you go and ruining our fighting ring, Baeles made me deal with the shit and cleanup. Who do you think kept tabs on Boyd and Booth to keep their traps shut? Threatening their families to make sure they stayed quiet?"

So that was why Booth wouldn't talk. "How did you find me?"

"The day you showed up at Boyd's trailer and took care of him, one of my guys was there. I should've thanked you for taking care of that. I was really looking forward to you getting Booth, too." His eyes glinted with hate. "But then you took him, brought him to New York. Didn't know you got friends in high places now."

"Booth didn't give you up."

The red-haired man laughed. "You think I'm stupid, boy? I knew you'd come sniffing around here soon enough. This is where I took you from, after all, from your sweet Mama's arms. I swear, I can still hear her crying for you. I can still taste your Daddy's blood—"

"Enough!" Connor roared. "What do you want?"

"I want you dead," he said. "You and your family. You're the last witness. That traitor Baeles is gonna talk soon. He's gonna rat me out. But once I take care of all of you, no one will find any evidence of The Facility or The Cage."

"Let's end this now," Connor said. "You and me."

"Ha! You think you can take me?"

"I know I can."

"This isn't The Cage, boy. There won't be no fight." He turned to his men. "Take the kid and bring him here."

Lily let out a piercing scream.

---

*E*vie waited in the driver's seat as long as she could. She felt antsy and uncomfortable. She wanted to throw up again. *What the heck was going on?*

There was no noise from the house. It was strange that it was so quiet this early in the morning. Usually, by this time, Jackson and Lily were up and about. Austin should already be on his way to school.

A dreaded feeling formed in her chest. She thought about Connor's words, about driving out of here if there was any sign of trouble.

"Screw that!" Connor was in danger, she could feel it. She opened the door and slipped out of the truck. *What to do, though?* Connor had walked into the house and hadn't come out. Going in there would be horror movie-level stupid, so she thought she'd swing around to the back.

As quietly as she could, she walked around the house, sticking close to the wall. The sound of voices made her freeze, and she scrunched up against the side of the house. Taking a deep, calming breath, she swung her head around the corner to take a peek.

She could see a tall, bearded, red-haired man standing on the back porch. Her heart slammed into her ribcage, beating a thundering rhythm as she realized who it was. *The ringleader.* The man who took Connor from his family. He was talking, but she couldn't quite hear what he was saying. She shut her eyes, trying to concentrate on his voice.

"I want you dead," he said. "You and your family. You're the last witness ..."

Shit! Connor was in trouble. That bastard probably had Jackson, Lily, and Austin, too. But what could she do? She wasn't a Lycan or a witch. She wasn't even trained to fight. She couldn't just go in there. But she couldn't watch and do nothing, either.

Wait.

She couldn't rescue them, but she could call for help. She grabbed her phone from the pocket of her jeans and dialed Meredith's number.

"Hello?" the sleepy voice on the other end said.

"Meredith, it's Evie," she whispered. "Connor's in trouble. The man—the ringleader—he's here, and he's got them."

"Wha—oh fucknuts! Where are you?"

"We're in Shenandoah. At the farm. Can you come right away? Daric can bring you, right?"

"Hold on ..." There was whispering in the background and Evie could hear a masculine voice talking. Daric, probably. "Shit, you're right!" Meredith said to her husband. "Evie," Meredith began. "Daric can't transport us because he's never been there or seen the place. But, we're gonna go to Quinn's now so he can show us satellite photos. We'll bring the cavalry if we have to. Please hold on."

"Please hurry! I don't know what to do! I think ... it's bad. He's threatening to kill them all. He brought other Lycans here, too. I'm not sure how many."

"Just a couple of minutes. Distract them or something."

"Distract them? I can't do that!" she said in a hysterical voice.

"Evie ...." Meredith let out a breath. "Daric made me promise not to tell you, but you're Connor's True Mate."

"I'm what?"

"Surely you've realized it by now? Connor smells really good to you? Tell me you haven't been eating a lot and maybe throwing up?"

Evie's hand went to her stomach, but she stayed silent.

"Ding ding ding! Congratulations, you've won the True Mate bingo," Meredith said in a wry voice. "If he hasn't been wrapping up his willy while you do the horizontal mambo, then you know you're riding the baby train! And guess what, honey? You're invincible. Nothing can harm you. Not bullets, not poison, not animal bites. Your basically Superman. Er, Supergirl? Anyway, you know what I mean. Now, I just need two minutes! We're already at Quinn's loft, and we're hauling him out of bed to track your phone. Go and save your man, okay? Quinn! Selena! Cover your bits, we're coming in!" The line went dead.

Evie stood there, the information sinking in. She was pregnant? Shit, she knew Lycans didn't always reproduce easily, which was why she never worried about protection. Damn Connor and his super True Mate sperm. Or did she have super True Mate eggs? Uterus?

A scream tore through the air, jolting her out of her inner monologue. It sounded like Lily.

"Don't kill him! He's just a boy!"

"Shut up, bitch!"

Fuck! "Austin," she whispered. She had to go in there. One minute, forty-five seconds. That's all Meredith needed now.

"Don't!" she shouted, running around to the back porch. "Don't hurt him."

The red-haired man turned in her direction. "Well, what do we have here? Did you bring your bitch, boy?"

"Evie!" Connor growled. "I told you to stay put in the truck!"

"Get her!"

One of his goons strode to her and grabbed her by the arm, yanking her up to the porch. She saw Jackson and Lily to one side, Connor by the back door, and Austin kneeling in the center. Another Lycan had a gun in his hand and was pointing it at Austin.

"Austin!" she cried as she wrenched herself away from the goon and stumbled toward the young boy. She wrapped her arms around him protectively.

"I'm brave," he said in a small voice, then let out a sniffle. "I'm brave like my grandpa. Like Grams, and Dad and Uncle Connor."

"That's right," she said, running her hand down his back. "You're a brave boy, and I won't let anything happen to you."

"You let them go now," Connor yelled. "Or I swear to God ..."

"You'll what?" The red-haired man laughed. He strode forward, grabbed the gun from his henchman, and pointed the barrel at Evie and Austin. "Say goodbye."

"No!"

The sound of the gunshot sounded so loud to Evie's ears. Pain ripped through her shoulder, and her grip on Austin loosened. The bullet tore straight through her and left a streak of blood flowing down her arm. She slumped over Austin and heard him calling her name.

When her ears stopped ringing, she could make out loud growls, ripping clothes and paws landing with a loud thud. More footsteps. Voices. Screams. She blinked and sat up.

"Aunt Evie," Austin cried as she sat up. "You're not dead!"

"No, I'm not." A quick glance at her shoulder told her there was no more wound or flowing blood. She looked at Austin, tears staining his cheeks and eyes wide with terror. At his age, Lycan healing abilities wouldn't have kicked in yet. She had to get him to safety. She picked him up and put him on his feet, then moved him toward the back door.

There was a loud snarl behind her, and she could feel the wolf's hot, moist breath right at her ear. With a final shove, she pushed Austin through the door and shut it just as the gigantic Lycan with red fur pounced on her.

Claws slashed at her back, ripping her skin through her shirt. The pain this time was unbearable; she thought she'd pass out. She staggered back. "Motherfucker!" she cried. Meredith said she was invincible but never told her it would hurt like the dickens. It was a good thing she could already feel the wound sealing up.

The red wolf made another lunge at her, and she braced herself. But he never came. A large, light gray blur knocked him down.

"Connor!"

The two wolves tangled on the porch, breaking through the banisters, and landing with a loud crash on the ground below. Evie scrambled forward to get a better view of what was happening around her.

There were Lycans everywhere in full-wolf form, fighting and ripping at each other. She saw a white wolf cornered by two large ones, and a black wolf running to the rescue. A brown wolf fought alongside two gray ones. A flash of blond hair to the left caught her attention, and she saw Daric as he waved his hand, sending one of the wolves crashing against a tree.

Evie ran to where the two wolves had fallen earlier and looked below. They were now circling each other slowly and carefully. She gasped. Connor's feral-looking wolf was massive, probably the largest she'd ever seen. It was eight feet tall on its hind legs with light gray, mottled fur and giant paws with razor-sharp claws. Its large maw opened up, baring fangs that could rip into bone, as saliva foamed at its lips. The wolf had the same scar down its eye and cheek as Connor.

Fear gripped her heart. This was it. *Please,* she thought. *Fight Connor.* She wanted him to win so he could put his demons aside. This was what he needed. What his wolf needed.

The red wolf gnashed its teeth at Connor, goading it. But Connor didn't take the bait. *Good.* "Give up!" she screamed. "You've already lost!" The red wolf looked around itself, seeing the other Lycans quickly being defeated by Connor's family. It let out a fierce growl and looked up at her, its dark eyes filled with fury. While it was distracted, the gray wolf lunged at the red one, tackling it to the ground. They rolled around, but Connor's wolf ended up on top. The feral wolf opened its jaws and went straight for the throat.

Evie turned around and fell to her knees. She buried her face in her hands as tears of relief sprang from her eyes. She could hear the ripping of flesh and crunching of bones, a cry, and a sickening gurgle. Then silence.

She wasn't sure how long she had been sitting there with her hands over her eyes, slumped down on her shins. Heavy footsteps came close to her and, slowly, she put her hands down, but kept her eyes on the floor. Two large feet came into view, and she looked up.

"Connor," she said with a relieved sigh. He was naked, and there were streaks of blood on his forehead and chest, but he looked like he had wiped off most of the carnage. She reached up to him, and he bent down and pulled her into his arms. He wrapped her in a fierce hug before setting her down.

"I thought I lost you ... what's going on?" He had a confused look on his face as he examined her bloody, ripped clothes. "Are you ..."

She nodded. "Yes. I'm pregnant. With your baby."

His face went white, and, for a moment, she felt dread. But when his mouth curled into a smile, her heart nearly burst. "I love you so much," he whispered into her ear as he put her in another crushing hug.

"I love you, too." She pulled away and looked up at him. "But how did you get back? I thought you said you couldn't just shift back right away?"

"When I saw you hurt, I lost it," he said. "The feral wolf ripped out of me, and I wanted nothing more than to kill the ringleader. But, when I shifted this time, it was different. I could actually see what was happening. I wasn't blacked out. The wolf shared our body. It didn't push me down. For the first time, I was in control."

"So, how does it feel?"

"How does what feel?'

"Revenge."

Connor shrugged. "It's not like I thought."

"How so?"

"I've imagined it lots of times, you know. What it would be like. I thought I'd feel satisfied. Or even happy."

"But now?"

"I just feel relieved," he confessed. "That you and my family won't be in danger anymore. And I'm glad because I know I have so much to live for now."

"You do," she said, placing his hand over her belly. "So much."

"Hey lovebirds!" Meredith called as she bounded over to them. "Oh. My. Freakin'. God. Another baby on the way!" She was smiling, but tears were also forming in her eyes. "I'm so happy for you guys!" She hugged both Evie and Connor. Behind her, Daric walked up to them.

"You knew, didn't you?" Connor asked the warlock.

"Yes," Daric said with a nod. "I'd seen Evie in my visions for a while now. Both her and Selena and even Luna. You were all destined to find your mates. I'm sorry I couldn't tell you. But the journey has been worth it, I hope?"

Connor looked down at Evie, his hand still on her stomach. "Definitely worth it."

EPILOGUE

Six months later...

"Connor, seriously, I'm fine," Evie grumbled as they walked down Broadway and crossed 79th Street. "Do you want to carry me? Is that it?"

"I just want to make sure you're not tired," he growled.

"Magical baby, remember? I'm feeling fine. Better than fine. I'm not even tired, and I'm not even doing eight shows a week. The only reason I quit the show a month ago was that I couldn't fit into the costume when I popped."

"You'll tell me if you want to go back to the hotel, right?" he said, placing a hand over her bulging belly.

"I will, now stop hovering! I want to get to the ice cream place sometime today."

The continued to walk down the street, making their way to the trendy new ice cream shop that had just opened up in the neighborhood. It was a beautiful fall day in New York. There was a crisp chill in the air and, frankly, Evie was so glad for the cooler weather. Autumn was the best time of the year, and it also meant

All for Connor

she was close to her due date. Of course, while she was enjoying being pregnant, Connor was nearly tearing his hair out with worry. He never left her side, unless he had to go overseas for an op, and even then he tried not to be gone for too long. He was always asking her what she needed, never even letting her lift a finger. It was sweet at first, but it was starting to get on her nerves.

Still, she was happy. A part of her was a little sad at having to leave *Love and Regrets* in the middle of its successful run. The cast, crew, and fans (she still couldn't believe she *had* fans) were sad, too, but they all understood. Steven, Jane, and Annie said she'd be welcome to come back anytime, especially since they were expecting the show to run for a long time. Being in the show had been exhilarating, but she figured there would be time enough to go back to work. For now, she'd enjoy the time alone with Connor and then being a mother. Besides, there were tons of other things she wanted to do. Maybe writing her own show? She had lots of idle time now, and ideas were constantly popping in her head. She even bought a keyboard so she could start writing down some music. Connor said he believed in her and that she could do anything she wanted if she put her mind to it.

"Hey, are you sure this is the way?" Evie frowned when she realized Connor had led them off the main drag. They were in the middle of a residential area, lined with beautiful, turn-of-the-century brownstone buildings.

"This is a shortcut," he said curtly, tugging her down the street. "Oh, look at that."

"Huh?" She followed his gaze to one of the houses, which had a big red "For Sale" sign out front. She looked up. The ornate and elegant brownstone was three stories high with large bay windows. The stoop steps led up to the door. "Oh, wow. Nice."

Connor walked up to the steps and cocked his head. "Let's go."

"Huh?" Her brows wrinkled. "Connor, we can't go in. That's someone's house!"

"If it's for sale, then don't they expect people to go in and take a look?"

She laughed. "That's not how it works."

"C'mon." He jogged up the steps and opened the door. "See? It's not locked."

"Connor!" she called when he disappeared into the brownstone. Oh shit, they were going to get arrested for trespassing.

She followed him inside, and, as soon as she stepped through the door, she gasped. It must have been fully renovated because it still had that smell of fresh paint and cement. The main foyer was done entirely in white, including the sconces and the moldings, which were probably original. On the right was a set of steps that led to the upstairs.

Where was Connor?

"In here," he called as if reading her mind.

Evie walked over the shiny hardwood floors and through the entryway on the left. Connor was standing by the large window, his back to her. This room was huge and airy with high ceilings. It was fully furnished, though, with a large, L-shaped couch, coffee table, a plant in the corner, and a 60-inch flat screen TV on one wall. There was even enough space for a baby grand piano in the corner.

"We shouldn't be in here," she said wryly when she approached him. "What are we—" Connor turned around, and she gasped. In his hand was a velvet box and nestled inside was a sparkly diamond ring. "Oh ..."

"Evie ... I'm not the best with words, but let me try. I thought I was broken and lost, and all I wanted was revenge. My wolf was broken, too. But since I've met you, you've turned my world upside down. In a good way, I mean. You've given me something to live for. So ... will you marry me?"

She still couldn't believe what she was seeing. She looked up at him. "Yes, of course, I'll marry you."

Connor took the ring from the box, and she could have sworn his hand shook a little as he slid it onto her finger.

"I love you," he said as he wrapped his arms around her and pulled her close.

"I love you, too."

He bent down for a kiss. By now, he must have kissed her a thousand times, but, still, each one felt just as thrilling as the first. She moaned into his mouth, and she felt his hands move lower to cup her ass. Something hard poked at her hip. *Oh wow. Here? Really ... well ...* She slid her palms over the bulge in the front of his pants and began to unzip the fly.

"Evie, er ... sorry, I couldn't help it, but no ..." he said.

"Huh?" *Oh right.* "Sorry. The owners won't be happy if they catch us doing the nasty on their couch."

"It's not that ... you see ..."

"Surprise!"

Huh?

Evie turned around. Standing in the doorway was everyone. Seriously, *everyone*. Meredith was in the middle, lifting a big "SOLD" sign, and beside her was Daric, holding their son in his arms. Killian was there, one arm slung around Luna and a baby carrier in the other. Quinn and Selena were smiling at them, and, behind them, was Jackson, Lily, and Austin. But there were more people coming through the doorway, too.

"Oh, my ... dad? Stephanie? Arthur? Mom!" She gasped. Even her family was here? "What are you all doing here?"

"Well, we couldn't miss this, could we?" Amelia said as she embraced her.

"Yeah, we couldn't miss you finally making an honest woman of my daughter," Charlie said wryly at Connor.

"Sorry sir," Connor said, rubbing the back of his head with his palm. "I was waiting for the right time."

"The right time was before you got her pregnant," Charlie grumbled.

"Oh, come now," Stephanie said. "She was destined to have this baby." About a month ago, Evie told her stepmom and brother about Connor and Amelia being a Lycan. It seemed only right, since not only was Amelia trying to be part of their lives, but soon, they were going to be related to even more Lycans. They were shocked, of course, but they had come to accept it. Arthur, of course, thought it was pretty cool.

"Sorry, were we a little late?" Meredith said as she came forward. She shook the sign. "I had to hide this, so we didn't ruin the surprise."

"I don't understand …"

"Connor bought the house."

"The house?"

"This house, silly."

"What?" Her jaw practically dropped to the floor. "This … house?" She looked at Connor, and he nodded. "You bought …"

"Yes," he said with a nod.

Tears rushed to her eyes. Evie had never asked Connor about renting an apartment or even moving out of the W Hotel. She figured they could sort it out when the time came. She understood the feral wolf's restless nature and that it couldn't stay in one place. "But this house … what if you want to move? What if the wolf—"

"I won't," he said. "And I think the wolf wants to settle. It wants to be with you. With our pup."

"Oh, Connor …" She looked around her at her family and

his. The ones they were born into, the ones they chose. They were all there, looking at them, many with tears in their eyes.

"Do you like the house?" he asked in a hopeful tone.

"Like it? Of course, I do! I love it, Connor."

"Good," he said. "Let me show it to you while everyone gets the food ready. A couple more people are coming to our housewarming slash engagement party."

He led her up the stairs, carefully placing his hand on the small of her back. They went room by room, exploring their new home. Connor seemed proud, showing off every nook and cranny of the brownstone and telling her about the renovations. It was massive: three floors, five bedrooms. Connor said he wanted to fill it with as many of their pups as possible and, if they ran out of room, he could buy the place next door, too.

"How long ago did you buy this?"

"About three months ago."

"Three months?" she asked in a surprised voice. "You've been planning it for that long?"

He nodded. "With the baby coming, we couldn't keep living in hotels. So I asked around. Meredith helped, too. There's a small garden out back. We can put in a swing and a sandbox. It's on the subway line to the theater district. That means you don't have to be far from work."

"I don't know what to say …"

"Say that you love me and you'll be mine."

"I love you," she whispered and placed his hand over her belly. "And yes, I'll be yours. And you'll be mine."

A small kick in her belly surprised them both. They looked at each other. As she saw the the bottomless peace and satisfaction in his eyes, a warm glow flowed through her.

EXTENDED EPILOGUE

Five years later...

"Here you go, buddy," Connor said as he popped the top of a cold beer can and handed it to Dante Muccino. Even though it was a long holiday weekend, the chef was still on food duty.

"Thanks, dude," Dante replied, taking a sip.

Two familiar squeals of delight made him turn his head. Lizzie and her brother, Anthony, were running down the lawn, followed by their parents. He waved to Quinn and Selena, who was carrying their newest addition, baby Jacob, in his carrier.

"Oops, watch it, Connor," Dante chuckled. "Don't get your precious package too close to the grill."

He looked down at his "package." Two-month-old Charlene Tala Forrest was sleeping soundly in her baby carrier, her chubby cheeks resting on his chest. He had gotten a little too close to the heat and Charley stirred a bit. "Oops," he said, moving back half a step. "Thanks."

"No prob." The chef smiled at him, his mismatched blue and green eyes briefly glancing down at Charley. His expression seemed ... wistful? He wondered what was going through the other Lycan's head. Dante Muccino's career had exploded in the last five years, and he was the hottest chef in the country. Connor didn't spend a lot of time with him socially, but he seemed to enjoy his celebrity status. But, despite the fact that he hobnobbed with stars, Connor knew him to be a great guy. He was also one of the last single Lycans in their circle. He wondered if the chef was still enjoying his bachelorhood.

Looking down at Charley, he couldn't imagine trading her or his life for anything. Had it been five years? Time really did go by when you were having fun. And that was his life with Evie. Five years, two kids, and a whole barrel of fun. He was content. No, he was more than content.

The nightmares sometimes still haunted him, but he knew that Evie would always be there, soothing him and telling him that things were all right. Slowly, he also made peace with his demons and his wolf. The feral wolf was still unmanageable some days, but he no longer had trouble getting his body back. It was there when he needed it, especially on those dangerous missions, but the wolf helped him. After all, he had to come back to his family.

"Daddy! Daddy!" A tugging at his shorts made him look down. Four-year-old Cliff looked up at him, his toffee-brown eyes so much like his mother's. "Everyone's headed to the living room. It's time!"

"I'll finish up here and follow," Dante said. "You go ahead."

He nodded at Dante and picked up Cliff. The little boy let out a whoop of delight as his father put him on his shoulders. He strode into the mansion, and followed the crowd of people heading into the entertainment room.

"Okay, I think I got it set up!" Quinn said as he pointed the remote control toward the TV. Everyone was gathered around, waiting for the show to begin. The screen blinked to life.

"Welcome, everyone to the pre-awards show red carpet countdown," the host on the TV said. "I'm Melanie Arkin, and we're here in London for the Lord Andrew Lloyd Webber Awards where we celebrate the best of the stage world! It's almost time for the show to begin, but we wanted to catch up with some of the theater world's biggest celebrities first." Melanie pointed off camera. "Oh, here's someone everyone should recognize. Two-time Tony Awardee for Best Actress in a Musical, Evie King. She was also the voice of Arya in the Disney movie, *The Last Princess*."

The camera panned to Evie, who was walking the red carpet in a beautiful red gown. As she passed Melanie, the host stopped her and called her name.

"Thanks for stopping by, Evie."

"Oh, I'm always happy to talk to you, Melanie," she said.

"And with you, of course, is your writing partner, Jack Donohue." Jack looked handsome next to her, wearing a custom-fitted black tux. "So, you guys must be nervous! You're up for an award for Best Book of a Musical and Best Musical for your hit show *Changes*."

"Yes, we are pretty nervous," Evie answered. "But whatever happens, we're just happy to be here."

"Everyone was pretty surprised when, at the height of your career and you were playing Colleen in *Love and Regrets*, you quit the show to have your first baby. Tell me, do you regret giving up that show?"

"Melanie, working on *Love and Regrets* was one of the best times in my life. I loved the cast, the writers, the director, the crew. But, no, I don't regret anything. I love being a mom. And having my son was the inspiration I needed to write *Changes*."

"And you just had another baby, right?"

"Yeah." She looked at the camera. "I'd like to say thanks,

Connor, for taking care of the kids while I'm away. I'll be home very soon."

"Awww ... so sweet!"

A soft cry caught Connor's attention, and he realized Charley was stirring. He sat down on the couch, removing the straps of the carrier with practiced ease as he turned her around so she could face the TV. "Look, Charley, there's mommy. Isn't she pretty?" The baby gurgled in agreement.

Music began to play, and, soon, the awards show began. There was excitement in the air as they watched. Everyone was sitting around, chatting, having a good time. There were loud cheers, of course, when they announced Evie and Jack as winners for Best Book. Evie seemed shocked, and she was speechless for about two seconds before Jack nudged her. She thanked everyone in the show and everyone back home.

Finally, it was time for the big award, and a hush fell over the room. The two presenters introduced all of the nominees. Connor smiled as the camera focused on Evie, who was trying to look calm, though he could tell she was nervous.

"And the winner for Best Musical is," the presenter opened the envelope. "*Changes*, music and book by Evie King and Jack Donohue."

The entire room erupted with cheers. Popcorn was tossed in the air and people were jumping up and down. Cliff bounded onto the couch, hopping on the cushions, screaming "Mommy won! Mommy won!"

"Shhhhh!" someone shouted. "Sit down! We want to hear her speech!"

The camera cut to the podium where Jack was standing by himself. "Thank you, thank you, everyone. From the bottom of my heart, both our hearts, thank you!"

Connor frowned. This was Evie's big moment. Why wasn't she up there with Jack?

"So, first of all, Evie relays her most sincere apologies. But we've been gone for a whole week now, and she really misses her kids and her husband, so she's gone home. I mean, she's headed home. But, we wanted to thank ..."

A pair of small hands covered Connor's eyes, and the sweet scent of peaches filled his nostrils. "Evie?" He turned his head, and the hands pulled back. Standing behind the couch was his Evie, all made up and still dressed in her red ball gown. "Evie, your award—"

"I told Daric to come get me as soon as they announced the winner. Whether it was me or not." She waved to the warlock, who gave her a nod, then turned his attention back to his sons. "I couldn't wait another second to come back home to you guys." She grabbed Charley from him, and held her up. "Aww, did you miss Mommy? I missed you too, Charley." Evie put her little head on her shoulder and rubbed her back in a soothing manner.

"Mommy's home!" Cliff cried, jumping into Connor's lap. He scooped up his son, then stood and walked to his wife. "Ahhhh! You're squishing me, Daddy!" he giggled as Connor wrapped him, Evie, and Charley in his arms.

"Aww, squishing just means I love you," he said, giving his son a kiss on the forehead.

"I love you too, daddy."

Connor felt a tug at his heart. Those words were what he lived for. He looked at his daughter. Already, he told Charley he loved her every day, and he couldn't wait for her to say it back. A rumble from his chest made Cliff giggle. "Does your wolf love me, too?"

"Of course it does."

"Good." Cliff laid his head on Connor's chest, then patted it with his little hand. "I love you, too, Princess Tiffany Spankinbottom."

"Princess ... what?"

"Yeah, Uncle Quinn told me that was your wolf's name."

Evie guffawed, and Connor let out a laugh. "He did, did he? Well, did you know Uncle Killian, Aunt Meredith, and I used to call him Mr. Poopie Pants?"

Cliff giggled. "You did?"

"Uh-huh. We were working with your Grandpa Archie, and he was stuck under some bushes, doing surveillance. He had to go, but the bad guys were all around us. He didn't have a choice, and he crapped in his pants." He set Cliff down. "Now, why don't you go tell your cousins and your friends about that story? I'm sure Auntie Selena would love to hear that one, too."

"Yeah!" Cliff zoomed off, running to the group of children playing in the game room next door.

Evie raised a brow at him. "Mr. Poopie Pants? Really?"

"Actually, it was Mr. Shitty Pants, but that didn't seem appropriate for the kids."

Evie laughed. "Right."

There was a loud crash, laughter, and the sound of children screeching, "Mr. Poopie Pants!" from the other room. It was followed by an indignant cry from an annoyed-sounding Quinn.

"CONNOR!"

FROM THE AUTHOR

Lone Wolf Defenders is only my second series, but still, writing "The End" on All for Connor was bittersweet. There's that empty feeling I have in my heart, similar to when I've watched or read the end of the movie or TV or book series. I'd never thought I'd feel it as an author. It was such an amazing journey, following Connor and Evie throughout the series, starting from Tempted by the Wolf (did you notice that little breadcrumb there?) all the way to their own story.

Of course, All for Connor is not the end of my writing career. I still have Dante's story to write (which will be very different, because it'll be more rom-com than suspense). And maybe, if enough nice readers leave me a review on Amazon or Goodreads to tell me they enjoyed the Lone Wolf Defenders, I may extend it to *one more book* featuring a certain Alpha twin. ;) And, by Spring 2018, you can expect everyone to come back and read about the kids in True Mates Generation Two.

Until then, allow me to leave the world of True Mates, just for bit, and take you all to Blackstone Mountain. I'm already excited as I begin this new journey and hope you'll all come and join me. ***The Last Blackstone Dragon*** will be available by end of October and it will actually be a FREE novella. That's right! If you're not too sure about starting a new series, you can try it and see if you like it! You'll get it if you sign up for my mailing list. If you're already on the list, then you'll get in in your inbox.

Anyway, I hope you enjoyed Connor!

All the best,

Alicia

ABOUT THE AUTHOR

Alicia Montgomery has always dreamed of becoming a romance novel writer. She started writing down her stories in now long-forgotten diaries and notebooks, never thinking that her dream would come true. After taking the well-worn path to a stable career, she is now plunging into the world of self-publishing.

Sexy shifters, billionaires, alpha males, and of course, strong, sexy female characters are her favorite to write. Alicia is a wanderer, along with her husband, they travel the world and have lived in various spots all over the world.

Printed in Great Britain
by Amazon